Lilli stared up at Max, her heart beating rapidly.

With a frown, he lowered his head and pressed his lips against hers. She rested her palms on his chest and sank into the kiss, falling for Max a little harder. But just as she slid her hands to his shoulders, he pulled away.

"Not a good idea," he said, his voice low, clipped. "I should go before I do something stupid."

"Like kiss me again?"

He closed his eyes. "I'm not the right guy for you. You need promises. A sure thing. I'm not that guy."

"You could be."

He stepped back. "I need to go." He opened the door and slipped away before she could think of any words to stop him.

She leaned her forehead against the cool door, eyes closed. Did he regret coming here tonight? Kissing her? Did he want more between them, or would he always blame her for a past she couldn't change?

Dear Reader,

I so enjoyed creating the characters in *Orange Blossom Brides*. Lilli and Max had plenty of obstacles before getting their happily-ever-after, but doesn't every journey have a few bumps along the way? That's what makes life so interesting.

The inspiration for this story came when a friend dragged me to a spring fashion show. The room, filled with bright flowers, soft harp music and decorated in a wedding motif, caught my attention. As I sat there, observing the well-dressed guests chatting before the models took the runway, suddenly this story idea came to mind. I love weddings (who doesn't?) so I decided to take the fashion-show theme and make it my own. I invite you to *Tie the Knot—A Montage of Vintage Bridal Fashions through the Decades*. No RSVP needed, just turn the pages and enjoy.

I'd love you to visit me at www.tararandel.com. Stop by and leave a message.

Tara Randel

HARLEQUIN HEARTWARMING

Tara Randel

Orange Blossom Brides

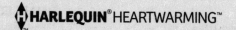

Recycling programs
for this product may
not exist in your area.

ISBN-13: 978-0-373-36638-5

ORANGE BLOSSOM BRIDES

Printed in U.S.A.

HARLEQUIN®
www.Harlequin.com

TARA RANDEL

has enjoyed a lifelong love of books, especially romance with a bit of mystery, so it came as no surprise when she began writing with the dream of becoming published. Family values, mystery and, of course, love and romance are her favorite themes, because she believes love is the greatest gift of all. Tara lives on the West Coast of Florida, where gorgeous sunsets and beautiful weather inspire the creation of heartwarming stories. This is her first book for Harlequin Heartwarming.

To my beautiful daughter, Megan, who always dreamed of being a bride.

CHAPTER ONE

THE EARLY-MORNING SUN warmed Lilli Barclay's shoulders as she stood in front of the Cypress Pointe Historical Society building, arms full of charity event files she'd just received from the secretary. She'd have to finish the job sooner rather than later, but later sounded so much better. Squaring her shoulders, she took a deep breath before speaking into her cell phone.

"Does this have to be done today?" she asked her mother, Celeste, who had taken off to deal with another one of Aunt Marian's legal issues instead of staying here in Florida to co-ordinate her latest fund-raiser. "I have a full schedule at work."

"He's the only groom who hasn't given me an answer. He's perfect, Lilli. The ladies will adore him, and the model will love walking arm in arm with him down the aisle."

"I could just call him. I've already missed more hours from work than I can afford with this fund-raiser."

Lilli had recently found, and hoped to sign

on, a new client for the marketing firm where she worked. A project that would not only be a profitable account, but would land her the coveted promotion she'd been working toward. She loved research and the creative part of marketing, but she really wanted to work directly with the customers as an account executive.

The job entailed finding new customers and maintaining relationships while catering to their advertising needs. To climb up the corporate ladder, she'd worked long hours and made herself available to the point of having no social life. Since her five-year plan had gotten derailed a year ago, she'd started over with a new plan to get her life on track, and this promotion would be the first step in that direction.

She wasn't a shoo-in, especially with two other people in the office actively seeking the same promotion. The first, Nate, had a few more years' experience than Lilli. Definite competition. The other, a woman who had recently been hired, was new to marketing. A long shot. Still, Lilli took nothing for granted.

Filling in as charity coordinator for her mother didn't fit the plan, but her mother had sounded desperate. Lilli hadn't been able to say no. Never had. Only now her mother's request might very well get in the way of this promotion.

"You know I wouldn't ask if it weren't an emergency."

Yes, she knew that. For as long as Lilli could remember, her mother had been involved in some type of charity activity. She'd spend weeks on a project, leaving Lilli to snatch a few hours of quality time here and there, and even then, her mother would be preoccupied. That meant a lot of time alone. But how could she be upset with her mother when the woman did so much good for others? And how could Lilli not help when her mother asked? Since her parents' divorce, it seemed like the only connection they shared.

"So you'll take care of this for me?" her mother asked.

Procrastinating, Lilli opened the thick file in her hand and narrowly avoided spilling the collection of papers. Her gaze stopped on the top line of the official invitation: Tie the Knot—A Montage of Vintage Bridal Fashions Through the Decades, to be held at the prestigious Cypress Pointe Country Club. Bad enough her mother had asked her to fill in as coordinator for this event in her absence, but the country club? How could Lilli ever set foot in that place again?

She scanned the list given to her by the historical society secretary. She loved lists, herself, so she felt a degree of relief that she didn't have to start from scratch. Everything from timetables, committees and local businesses supporting the show to couples serving as models were listed. Each woman would wear a bridal dress, either from her family legacy or donated by a member of the historical society. A clever idea. One of her mother's best.

But a wedding-themed benefit? Lilli cringed. She'd put visions of silk and lace, cake and fondant, and happily ever after out of her mind this past year. Getting dumped at the rehearsal dinner made a girl leery of wedding dreams.

And still, the worst part of her duties lay moments ahead of her: getting an answer from the final volunteer groom on her mother's list. A groom not obligated to marry his paired bride. Wouldn't that be a dream come true for any guy? No commitment and a bunch of fun? The participants were local businesspeople or town elite, except for the last man in question. He had recently set up shop in town. Celeste had yet to pin down a definite yes from the man. Apparently he'd been dodging her calls. So, today, the recruitment duties fell to Lilli.

She closed the file and stuffed it into her purse. She'd go through it later. Right now, she had historical society business to take care of before she could get back to ensuring her promising future at KLC Media Enterprises.

"Yes, I'll take care of it, but I'm going to call his office," she said, decision made.

"That won't do any good."

"Why not?"

"Every time I call, his secretary tells me he's out."

"Maybe that's because he is out. After all, he is a…" Lilli shuffled through the purse again until she found another file. Her stomach dropped when she read his name. "Max Sanders. Private investigator?"

"Yes, dear. I mentioned to you that I'd hired someone to take care of the security system at the historical society office. It's in the information I left behind."

Lilli stared down at the familiar name. It couldn't be, could it? He'd left town years ago. How many Max Sanderses could there be?

"You'll have to go to his office and ask in person."

Oh, boy. Her mother had to know how sticky this would be. Why would she even consider him as a volunteer groom in light of their history? The Max Sanders she'd met twelve years ago would not be happy to see her, let alone agree to anything she asked. She'd be lucky he didn't kick her out of his office right from the get-go.

"You do remember who Max is, don't you, Mom?"

"Of course. So I had him thoroughly vetted."

Ironic, her mother hiring a P.I. to do a background check on a P.I.

"Lilli, please. This is important."

"Why?"

"Because he has a new business here in town. We have to support our own."

"Willie Anderson is single and owns a toy-train store, but you haven't targeted him."

"That's because Willie is thirty-five and still lives with his mother. None of the volunteer brides will walk down the aisle with him."

Okay, that was true.

"And I've met with Max. He's handsome. The women will love him."

Bottom line: if Max's presence would help sell tickets, her mother wouldn't take no for an answer. Coming from a marketing standpoint, Lilli could appreciate that.

Asking Max to participate was just a formality. Everyone in town knew that once Celeste had her mind set on charity matters, you couldn't ignore her. She hounded folks until she wore them down. After so many years "suggesting" they help, it became town tradition to commit first and ask questions later. Since Celeste now served as president of the historical society, she wouldn't back down on this particular event.

Still…benefit or not, facing Max Sanders would not be the highlight of Lilli's day. She grasped at any excuse not to visit him. "His secretary can just as easily put me off there."

"Then I guess you'll have to demand that he see you. Be firm, Lilli. Let them know you mean business."

Lilli blinked. "You expect me to strong-arm him into it somehow?"

"I'm sorry. Sometimes I get so carried away with my charities I forget I have boundaries."

Boy-oh-boy, these historical society women took charity events to a whole new level.

"The historical society ladies and I want to work with Max," her mother continued.

"I'll see what I can do." Lilli had to take care of this so Celeste would stop worrying and Lilli could coordinate the fund-raiser while still giving the necessary attention to her job. Multitasking had just become her middle name. It wouldn't be that bad, right?

"Also, I spoke to Max about providing security the night of the benefit, but we didn't finalize the particulars. If he hesitates about attending, suggest he look at volunteering as undercover work. As a groom, he'll be able to keep an eye on the event with no one the wiser. Between the designer wedding gowns and the Wingate jewelry, I have a lot riding on this night, Lilli. You know if this weren't an emergency, I'd be there. Honestly, I'm depending on you."

Lilli stifled a groan. Could her life get any more complicated? "Max might not want to work with me."

"What happened is in the past. You both moved beyond the incident. I spent enough time with Max to see that he's gotten his life together and is now a respectable member of society. Besides, he's a businessman. He'll do what he must."

Her mother was banking on that. And what Celeste wanted, Celeste always got.

Unlike Lilli.

Lilli's childhood had been far from simple. Her father, a corporate lawyer, and her mother, a stay-at-home mom who mostly flitted about as a society charity queen, rarely saw eye to eye on anything. Their marriage, difficult at best, worked when they weren't in the same room. Lilli spent her vacations with one parent or the other.

She longed for a real family, to have Thanksgiving dinners together instead of going to a different resort every year, alternating parents. She dreamed of her family sitting before the twinkling tree on Christmas morning, opening the presents they'd given each other, of knowing without a shadow of a doubt that her parents loved her because she was their daughter, not a bargaining chip to use against each other.

Prior to her mother's most recent phone call, Lilli had spent twelve months excelling at a job she loved, and living the calm, quiet life she craved after growing up in a home mired in emotional chaos. She'd spent years as the object of her parents' arguments. What should their only child should do? Where should she belong? Their ideas had differed vastly from what Lilli wanted.

Not that they'd asked. And not that they'd put her first in their lives. She'd been an obedient daughter, had tried to give them what they wanted, but failed at every task. So she'd set her mind on being the best student, best employee, best…everything so they'd be proud of her. And still they hadn't been able to work out their problems to keep the family whole.

After her parents' divorce, Lilli had worked hard in high school and college to cover the hurt and disappointment. She might be what some called an overachiever, but going after specific goals kept her mind focused. She'd realized she could only depend upon herself. This promotion would prove her resourcefulness. And it had nothing to do with her parents. Or this fund-raiser.

"I'm counting on you to get this done, Lilli. Give me a call when Max is confirmed."

That one night with Max had been out of character for her. And now, all these years later, she'd pay for it.

"That's assuming he agrees."

"We're on a deadline, Lilli. Confirming Max is your first priority."

Yeah, after getting on with her day job, nailing the promotion, living her life and enduring Max's wrath. "I can't believe you talked me into this," she muttered, even though her mother had hung up.

One phone call and her life tilted out of control. Her resolve to create emotional steadiness in her life went by the wayside. Her world had suddenly turned messy, and she didn't like messy. Except for the year she spent planning her doomed wedding, she'd achieved that long-awaited stability. She dated "safe" men, when she dated at all. At twenty-eight, you'd think she had it all together.

Until her mother called in a panic. That call thrust Lilli back into the craziness of her mother's world and Lilli had an ache in the pit of her stomach to show for it.

With a sigh, she glanced at her watch. Just past 9:00 a.m. With any luck she could get to Max's office, coerce a firm yes from the man without a major degree of difficulty and get back to work with productive time still left in the morning. The research on the organic dog biscuits wouldn't get done by itself. Nor would the itinerary for the town business forum her boss had asked her to put together, plus planning her strategy to land the Danielson account.

Nine in the morning, and she already had a headache.

Three weeks until the benefit.

Could she do this?

MAX SANDERS RUBBED his weary eyes, hoping the letters on the computer screen he'd been staring at would stop swimming. No good. He hit a key to close the file and downed the remainder of his coffee, flinching when the cold mouthful hit his tongue. How long had he been concentrating, anyway? With a grimace he swallowed, then rose from his chair to get a refill.

In his cramped second-story office overlooking Main Street, he slid out from behind the desk, tripped over a stack of unpacked boxes and bumped into the lone wooden straight-back chair reserved for clients before he reached the door. He really needed to take thirty minutes to straighten this place up.

His secretary, Blanche, ran the clerical end of the business. Her desk, a couch and a small coffee station filled the main office just outside his door. Talk about looking like a movie set out of a 1940s B movie. Raymond Chandler's idea of a hard-nosed investigator he was not.

Thankfully, Blanche had filled the pot before she left for an appointment. From the first day she'd come to work for him and tasted his version of coffee, she'd forbidden him to touch the machine ever again. Today he needed caffeine too much to worry about secretarial retribution.

Last night he'd stayed at the veterinarian's office until the early morning hours, waiting for his black Labrador, Jake Riley, to be out of danger. According to Doc Williams, the Lab had tangled with a cane toad and been poisoned. Jake Riley, resilient and stubborn, pulled through with the help of the vet's knowledge of poisonous toads. Max, on the other hand, was tired and out of sorts. Doc had suggested Max leave Jake at the clinic so the staff could keep an eye on him. Later this afternoon the dog could go home.

Max took a sip of the coffee, savoring the warm brew as he enjoyed the unusual quiet. He could handle things himself, even though Blanche would probably beg to differ. After all, he'd made it to twenty-nine without a major mishap—depending on who you talked to—through a stint in the navy and years on the job as a cop in Atlanta. He'd already landed a few cases since he opened his doors. He had his mentor—Cypress Pointe police chief, Bob Gardener, fondly known to the town as the chief—to thank for that.

Max had returned to his desk when he heard the outer door open. He didn't have any appointments scheduled this morning. Blanche usually dealt with clients before they saw him, but in her absence he would have to play host. Hoping for new business, he put on his game face, stopping short when he spotted the gorgeous female who'd just walked in.

This day was looking up.

She hesitated at the door as if she didn't know what to do next until she locked gazes with him. Her eyes, a pretty shade of green, opened wide and the tentative smile playing at her full lips went flat. A flash of a memory teased the back of his mind as she gracefully sauntered the few steps toward him. He couldn't help but check her out. Dressed in a soft blouse that matched her eyes, a skirt and impossibly high heels, she stopped before him, tucking a lock of her tousled, shoulder-length reddish hair behind her ear. He caught a whiff of her rich floral scent—a pretty, unforgettable perfume. Or maybe it was the woman who was unforgettable.

"Max Sanders?" she asked in a soft voice.

"That would be me." He extended his hand, taken off guard by a rush of heat from her soft skin as her fingers slid against his. Interesting. He hadn't expected that. Nor had she, evidenced by the way she quickly let go.

No doubt about it, she'd piqued his interest the minute she'd come through his door. No one in their right mind could ignore the confident sway of her walk, the slim hand with ruby nail polish and the overall pretty package beaming back at him. Something about her...

He watched her with curiosity. Victim of a home invasion while her husband worked out of town and now needed a security system? His quick glance to her left hand indicated no wedding band. Something else, then?

"Did you have an appointment? My secretary must have forgotten to tell me you were coming."

"She didn't know."

Even more interesting. "Can I get you some coffee?"

"No, thanks. I'm in a time crunch but I need to speak with you." The airy tone of a few minutes before disappeared and she became all business. "I'm sorry. I didn't call before arriving because I hoped to catch you in person. It's important."

Good, she needed his services. "In that case, come on back to my office."

He led the way, sweeping a pile of electronics magazines from the chair in front of his desk, motioning for her to take a seat. He rounded his desk before settling back in his leather chair, observing her as she gazed around his office, from the papers piled on his desk, to the boxes in the corner. Finally, her eyes widened a fraction as she read his wall calendar. Then she looked down at the chair he'd pointed to, wrinkling her pert nose as she reached out to brush the wood seat before sitting. He frowned. The office might be cluttered, but it wasn't dirty.

"I usually make office or house calls, so I'm not completely organized yet." He'd ignored Blanche when she'd nagged him about decorating to impress the clients. Man, he hated it when Blanche was right.

He settled in and took another long look at this prospective client. That elusive memory still niggled the edges of his mind. Then it hit him, hard and fast.

"It's you."

Her cheeks flamed. "Yes."

"I can't believe it. It's been twelve years."

"That's about right."

"That's exactly right."

"And it's in the past." She squirmed in her seat. "I was hoping we could look beyond that."

Wishful thinking. His gut burned with memories. "I don't think so."

"It was an...unfortunate night."

"Especially after the police showed up."

"That, too."

A bonfire. Mischief. A pretty girl and a stolen kiss. Great times, until the cops broke up the party. And he'd ended up spending a few nights in juvenile detention because of her.

"You ratted me out."

"It was either that or get in trouble for something I didn't do."

"You could have forgotten my name."

"I could have, but I didn't." Her face colored. "It was all a misunderstanding."

"You were a far cry from a misunderstanding."

"It was a long time ago. I was hoping today we could calmly discuss business."

"Calm isn't at the top of my list right now."

Her eyes closed for a moment, and when she met his gaze again, he saw the reluctant yielding there.

Okay. So she didn't want to walk down memory lane. Neither did he. He'd been angry with her for a long time after that night. What had started out as a flirty game of teasing ended with both of them in trouble, questioned by the police for a few hours before she went home to her family. He'd never found out why she dropped his name so she could go free. He'd asked, but the chief had been closemouthed about the details. All he knew that night? She'd caused him a world of trouble.

Now, all these years later, he was about to find out why. "Now, tell me, Miss… Miss…"

She rolled her eyes. "Barclay."

"Right. You're related to Celeste Barclay? The woman who keeps calling?"

"That would be my mother," she said, her business tone ratcheting up a notch. "I'm here on behalf of the Cypress Pointe Historical Society."

"I've already installed the new security system at the office. Your mother made sure I had it completed before the loaner gowns arrived."

"That's not why I'm here. You haven't returned her follow-up calls."

He inwardly groaned. "For the charity thing, right?"

"Yes. She'd like an answer."

"The chief said your mother wouldn't stop calling until I talked to her."

"Then you know just how persistent she is. That's why she sent me here."

"Not to cause me more trouble?"

"Of course not." She lifted her chin.

"Miss Barclay… It is Miss?" he couldn't help asking. And thinking, why was her marital status important? In light of their history, he shouldn't care, but found that he did. And wanted to kick himself for it.

"Yes."

Even though she owed him, she didn't seem inclined to elaborate. One glance at her set mouth and he decided to bide his time. He picked up a pen and tapped it on a notepad. "Your mother mentioned that she wanted me to volunteer for the benefit. What did she have in mind?"

She looked at the pen in his hand, then back at him. "You already know the Cypress Pointe Historical Society is holding their annual fundraiser in three weeks." She handed him a white invitation. "Tie the Knot charity wedding fashion show. At the Cypress Pointe Country Club. My mother has requested that you act as one of her volunteer grooms for the night. She felt that in your capacity as security for the event, this role as a groom would work out well. She'd be sure to have someone watching over the expensive donations during the event, but not calling attention to your undercover status. She doesn't want to upset the guests. "

He stared at her, trying not to flinch. No way. No possible way. "Are you kidding?"

She tilted her head. "I'm sorry, I was under the impression your answer is a formality."

"I agreed to upgrade security at the historical society office and for the jewelry collection. Nothing else."

"And the night of the benefit? At the club?"

"We hadn't exactly nailed down the details for the night of the event. Your mother and I keep playing phone tag."

"She had to go out of town and she asked me to handle it."

He narrowed his eyes.

"You know the history of the Wingate jewelry?"

"Yes." He nodded at his computer. "I read the file."

"Then you know the collection is worth a lot of money."

Oh, yeah. He'd noticed.

"We can go into the particulars at a later

date, but I need to know that you're on board and you'll have things under control the night of the benefit."

A fresh rush of anger swept over him. "First you show up at my office, now you question the quality of my work?"

Her eyes went wide. "No. Of course not." She ran a hand over her skirt. "I'm sorry. My mother recently put the responsibility of the benefit in my hands and I'm playing catch-up." She tried for a smile. "And it would really help us out if you volunteered."

Hmm… Well, he supposed it would be a good way to keep an eye on things. But still… "Volunteer groom, huh?"

"It is a town tradition, after all."

He snorted. "I don't think I could pass as a groom, volunteer or not. I'm not a settling down kinda guy."

She shifted, giving him the once-over. If he read her right, she silently agreed with him. "You do realize it's just for one night. And afterwards, your P.I. business will get publicity."

"Private security consultant."

She pulled some papers from her bag. "My notes read P.I." She looked at him, confused. "Isn't that the same thing?"

"My major focus is security, but I do some investigating on the side."

He did P.I. work while waiting for the security end of the business to build up, so he could focus on that full time. He'd piled all of his own savings into this venture so he needed these short-term cases to generate revenue. Once he landed one large account, the word would get out and he'd be on his way to making Sanders Security a high-end firm.

"That's all well and good, but I need a commitment from you. The money raised will go toward deserving organizations. Did I mention this year the funds will help the local animal shelter as well as the historical society?"

He groaned. Animal shelter? He'd found Jake there, half-starved and in desperate need of a home. His home. He'd never forget those beautiful pleading eyes staring up at him. Just like the pair staring at him now.

Okay, he had to take time to consider this. Volunteer groom aside, was his pride more important than his empty bank account? More important than proving his services were needed in this town? Right now, he needed to capitalize on being the sole security consultant in town. But would the exposure bring in business, or would his professional image take a hit with the whole cheesy-groom thing? He might not be taken seriously after that.

Considering all that, he studied her. Did she

think she had him? With her composed smile, he couldn't tell.

"I'm sure you wouldn't want to let those poor defenseless animals down. We're only asking for a few hours of your time."

The alluring female had grabbed hold of his attention and wouldn't let go. Just as she had that night twelve years ago. Their gazes clashed, but she gave nothing away. All business, not trying to flatter him or outwardly flirt with him, not trying to use her womanly wiles to get him to say yes. Wait. Why wasn't she flattering or flirting? He didn't want the answer to that particular question.

"The animal shelter?" he asked, dragging out the minutes.

"Yes," she replied, cool victory evident in her voice. He detected a small curve of her lips, ready to smile in triumph the moment he acquiesced. If he acquiesced. "It's a very good organization, I can assure you, since I work with them."

He hadn't gotten a hard-nosed reputation for nothing. And she looked as though she could use a little shaking up, if her buttoned-up-tight persona gave any indication. What had happened to the fun girl he'd met on the beach that night long ago?

Lost in the staccato beat of the tapping pen, Max pretended to mull over her request.

"Must you keep doing that?"

The pen stopped midair.

"Doing what?"

She nodded toward the pen.

"Sorry." The tapping may be bothering her, but her starchy condescension peeved him. Instead of saying yes, so he could get back to work, he decided to go another way. One that would give him long overdue satisfaction. "And you'll be attending? As a bride?"

"Not as a bride." Her eyes widened for a second before that less-than-confident smile slipped back into place. She tucked her hair behind her ear again. Great. Even her earlobes were cute. "As I said, I'm coordinating the event."

"So, you're not going?"

"I didn't say that. It depends if my mother is back in town by then."

He pondered his decision, purposely dragging out the minutes, before saying, "My answer is still no."

"But what about security for the jewelry?"

"That I can do, but not as a groom."

"My mother really wants you to do this. Think of it as a plug for your business. I can certainly do some publicity work for you that won't give away your status during the event."

"The job she hired me to do didn't include groom duty."

"It's just a minor change. You'll hardly be inconvenienced."

"Unlike the night we met?"

She pursed her lips. The regret in her eyes said it all. And for some perverse reason, even though it shouldn't matter now, he needed to know why she'd turned him in.

"It was confusing. Look, I also ended up in the back of a police car," she told him, her voice tight and controlled. "Then sat at the police station for hours with you fuming and not speaking to me."

"Really? You want to complain? Where did you go afterward?"

Her face colored again. "Home."

"Right. I went off to juvenile detention. So I think you need to make that up to me."

Her posture went all stiff. "How do you propose I do that?"

"I propose you accept that I will not be a groom. Not for the benefit. Not ever."

Displeasure crossed her face. "I could ask someone else."

He may have started out making demands

for payback, but now he was just having fun. "You could, and you should. I'm out."

She considered that for a second. He'd expected a snarky reply, but instead she said, "Fine. You're right. You're aren't the groom type."

"And you know that how?"

"By the fact that you're being very disagreeable."

"I'm sure there are lots of disagreeable grooms. Doesn't make me a type."

She frowned then asked, "Do you own a tux?"

"Never needed one."

Her gaze dropped to his faded T-shirt. "Any formal attire?"

She gave him an assessing look, cringing over his less-than-designer jeans and faded T-shirt and boots, his usual stakeout *attire,* which he wore for the job he had scheduled for later this morning. Or maybe the stubble he'd failed to shave. Okay, so maybe he needed a haircut, but he'd been too busy to worry about it. Still, she didn't have to look down that impertinent, freckled nose of hers.

He scrubbed a hand over his chin.

She had a standoffish look about her that rubbed him the wrong way. And the prissy way she perched on the chair, like she didn't want to get her skirt wrinkled? Well, that toasted him, too.

It took a few seconds for him to respond. Poised on the tip of his tongue hovered "none of your business," but how juvenile would that sound? "I have nice clothes. In fact, I just ordered work shirts with Sanders Security stitched on the front."

She smirked at him, clearly thinking she had the upper hand.

"Right. Whatever. Look, I'll be at the historical society offices tomorrow to test the system, and I'll drop off a proposal for the security of the jewelry collection. Nothing more."

Her lips tightened a fraction before she said, "That's your final answer?"

He crossed his arms over his chest. "Yep. Final answer." He didn't owe her more than that. He and Miss Prickly had nothing in common except a night on the beach that had ended before they'd had a chance to get started.

She stood. Something about her, a vulnerability she couldn't disguise, made him think of the carefree girl he'd once met. It also managed to soften the hard edges of his heart.

"Thank you. The historical society appreciates your support." She gathered her things and rushed out of his office, a waft of alluring perfume in her wake.

Max sat there for a moment, trying to ignore the twisting in his gut. Her walking through the door had caught him off guard. To be honest, he hadn't thought about her in years. Even when he'd decided to return to Cypress Pointe, he'd had only a passing notion that he might run into her again. But this way? Because of a charity event?

Working for the historical society meant access to future clients, just by word of mouth alone. Cypress Pointe was a small town, after all. He'd make connections, secure a few more jobs. Positive. But the negative? Working with the new charity coordinator, a woman who happened to be from his past. A past he'd worked hard to overcome, although sometimes it felt as if he'd fallen short.

Sitting back in his chair, he realized that his life had taken a hard right turn when she'd walked into his office. No. Today's visit had only ramped things up. Really, it'd started for him the night at the beach. The anger still simmered, but when he pictured her pretty face, a surprising spark of interest ignited.

No. No way. He had to put her out of his mind. They might be connected by this historical society project, but he didn't have to like it.

CHAPTER TWO

OF ALL THE rotten luck.

Why did the one guy she needed to convince to attend the benefit end up being the guy she met on the beach twelve years ago? One night. One night she goes all crazy and sneaks out of the house, only to end up in police custody.

See, that's what happens when you try to be something you're not. You end up flirting with a cute boy who grows into an even more attractive man. At least now she was smart enough not to end up in a police car at the end of the night.

She hoped so, anyway.

She entered the historical society office, still shaking her head over her meeting with Max.

"How did it go, dear?" Mrs. Rumpold asked before Lilli made it all the way through the door.

"He refused."

"Oh, no. Your mother won't be happy."

Yeah. Lilli already knew that.

"Didn't you use your feminine charms to

convince Max? It's my experience that no man alive can resist a woman if she sends out the right signals."

Okay. First, female charms had nothing to do with it. Max didn't want to be a groom, as he'd so adamantly let her know. Now she had to figure out what to do, because knowing her mother, *his* refusal would definitely upset *her* well-organized life. Even, if she didn't factor in the old anger at how that night had ended, he'd made it clear he would only attend Tie the Knot in a security capacity. She rubbed her temples.

And second, right signals? Lilli regarded the older woman with surprise. She hardly seemed the type of woman with…experiences. Not that Lilli would ask.

"Oh, I know what you're thinking," Mrs. Rumpold said. The historical society secretary had to be seventy if she was a day. "I may be a bit worn around the edges, but there are a few tried-and-true tricks to catch a man's eye." At least five inches shorter than Lilli and two times as wide with a halo of short, curly gray hair, there was clearly more to Mrs. Rumpold than met the eye.

"Mrs. Rumpold, what are you suggesting?"

"Please, call me Mrs. R." The older woman gave a saucy grin, as if she were about to reveal some truly juicy secrets. "And I'm not suggesting anything. I'm saying. First of all, there's the eye wink. Make sure you wear lots of mascara to make a statement. Next, the finger wave." She demonstrated, and Lilli suppressed a groan.

"And the hair flip," Mrs. R. continued. "Shows your fun, flirtatious side." With a flick of the wrist she tossed her silvery curls. Since they were permed tight, not much happened, but Lilli got the idea.

"It works every time," Mrs. R. intoned with sage wisdom.

Lilli held back a smile. Maybe in the nineteen-fifties, but not today. Today if she did that, people would think she had serious problems. And besides, she had no interest in catching a man's eye right now.

"I can't imagine any single men able to resist a lovely young woman such as you."

Yeah, Lilli knew that by the oodles of men lined up at her door. Right now she only concentrated on her job. The promotion. The added headache of the charity event. She had enough on her plate—she didn't need Max Sanders. He'd directed his smoky gaze at her once before, and she'd melted on the spot. Look where that had gotten her. She wouldn't let it happen again.

But for a split second she'd wondered if he

would find her attractive after all these years.
Would he even want to flirt with her again?
No. Not after the way she'd turned him in that
night at the beach. She couldn't change the past
any more than he could, but his reaction when
he'd recognized her said he definitely didn't
want anything to do with her.

"The display wedding dresses will be arriving this weekend." Mrs. R. changed the subject
as she rambled on. Her wrinkled face beamed
with pleasure. "What a stroke of luck that you
know the curator of the vintage collection. I'm
sure you can't wait to see the how they look."

Actually, wedding dresses weren't high on
her priority list at that moment in time. Hard to
get excited when she'd been dumped the night
before her wedding, not to mention that she
wasn't even dating at the moment.

Mrs. R. jabbered on. "They will be exhibited
here all spring and summer. We were so fortunate to get vintage gowns from the private
collection of Renata Ogilvy. What a boost for
the society. Your mother pulled out the stops
this year."

"Yes, she did," Lilli agreed, more overwhelmed than impressed. But then, her mother
often rubbed elbows with high-profile people
like Renata, a retired fashion designer who had

set the New York fashion scene on fire during her heyday.

Even though her mother knew the designer, Lilli had a connection to the curator, Gabrielle, an old friend from college. When her mother first thought up the wedding show, she'd batted around some ideas with Lilli. Since Lilli kept in touch with Gab and knew she worked for Renata, she offered to get in touch. After a few calls, Lilli got the go-ahead to showcase priceless vintage gowns, Renata's own along with other famous designers', from Renata's private collection. She'd thought that would be the end of her involvement with the benefit. Until her mother had left town.

"Oh, before I forget." Mrs. R. thrust a full-to-overflowing accordion folder at Lilli, who barely caught it, glossy photos spilling onto the already messy desk. As she gathered them together, a flurry of lace and satin bridal designs dredged up an interest she refused to acknowledge. "Keep the file so you can give it a look-see. You'll need the pictures when you write up the fashion show fliers and program."

"When I what?"

"Your mother didn't get that far before she left on her emergency, so you'll have to do it. It's all right there on the list." The older woman tapped the paper she'd clipped to the side of the file. "You already do that for your day job, don't you?"

She nodded. Lilli did media research on products and wrote up reports, sometimes put together descriptive brochures or information booklets for clients and worked to find ways to best promote her clients. Besides being involved through her contact with Gab and the designer gowns, she'd done some of the publicity for Tie the Knot at her mother's request, playing up the charity and the chance to view one-of-a-kind wedding gowns and exquisite jewelry.

"There are also ideas for the reception decorations in there. You know, flowers and doodads that make up the whole wedding experience."

"I have to plan a mock reception, too?"

"Oh, yes," Mrs. R. nodded.

Please. Like she wanted to do that all over again.

"Some of the ladies have opinions, but your mother has been cutting ideas out of magazines for months now." Mrs. R. leaned closer to Lilli, her tone conspiratorial. "A word of warning—Marisa Vandermere wanted to fill in as coordinator, but your mother turned her down. She's not happy about that. She'll most likely think she's still in charge, because, well, she's Marisa. Don't let her railroad you. We're on a tight schedule. The benefit is less than three weeks away." Mrs. R. nodded at the file. "Everything you need to complete the fashion show is in the file."

Great. She had to coordinate dresses, write fliers and plan an entire reception in just three weeks while trying to get a promotion at work. Now she had to work with her childhood nemesis, as well?

What have you gotten me into, Mom?

Lilli closed her eyes. She couldn't renege now, not when her mother needed her. Just as Lilli had needed Celeste the night of the rehearsal dinner, doing damage control and canceling the wedding after Lilli fled the scene, demoralized beyond words. Yes, her mother had come through for her when Lilli needed her most. So she'd do the same as stand-in coordinator. Once the entire event ended, she'd go back to focusing entirely on her job.

With a sigh Lilli glanced at her watch. Just past ten. Her boss had given her this morning to deal with historical society business, but he wouldn't be too pleased if she screwed up the Canine Candy presentation for the Natural Puppy account.

"Is there anything else, Mrs. Rumpold?"

"Mr. Sanders will be here tomorrow to test the security system. I'm assuming he told you."

"He did. I can't be here, but he is going to drop off a proposal I'll need to read." She couldn't afford to take more time off. And, she admitted, she didn't want to be around Max unless absolutely necessary.

Coward. Yeah, there was that, too.

Mrs. R.'s face went all dreamy. "I'll make sure he leaves it here."

Lilli blinked, then hid a smile. Someone had a crush.

"And don't forget the event committee meeting. Nine o'clock Saturday morning. At the club."

Of course. The club. She'd stayed far away from that place, hoping distance would dilute the miserable memories of the night Rob had dumped her. Time had anesthetized her heart, but her mind still carried the images as if they'd occurred yesterday.

"I'll be there" she replied glumly, before escaping to work.

AFTER MRS. R. DROPPED the news that she'd be planning the mock reception, Lilli sat in her car, staring at the file. More documents to add to the already overflowing files her mother had provided. She needed to get a huge tote bag to hold all this stuff. Sighing, she dug her mother's files from her purse to place in the passenger seat until she had a chance to get a bigger bag. As she moved them, the top folder flipped open, revealing a newspaper article. Curious, Lilli started to read.

The article—eleven years old, she noted— from the *Cypress Pointe Weekly*, announced Max Sanders's admission into the navy. Her gaze moved over the picture. Tall and lean, with short dark hair and austere features, a very masculine Max Sanders filled out his uniform. His stern expression said, "Don't mess with me."

And she had.

She slapped the file shut.

The guy still got to her, although she couldn't say why. Then or now.

When she'd met him that night at the beach, he'd spelled trouble. The long, shaggy hair and cocky attitude had been the first sign. But when he focused on her, with that lopsided grin and those intense gray eyes, he'd had her. She'd ignored the warning bells clamoring in her head. She'd always been the good girl, the one who'd gotten straight A's and never made her parents miserable. She'd already had her goals set out, knew which college she would attend.

That evening long ago, her parents had gotten into the worst argument ever, and per standard operating procedure, had drawn her into the middle, the convenient pawn in their troubled game. This was the first time divorce had come up in the conversation. As much as she had anticipated a split between them, it had still rocked her world. Disgusted and angry at the situation her parents had put themselves and her in, Lilli hadn't thought twice when her friend Nealy had called to see if she wanted to sneak down to the beach.

She hadn't known what to expect, since she'd never done anything like that before. Then Max walked by and the earth shifted. He stopped to talk to Nealy and the guy she'd come to hang out with. Then he glanced at Lilli. Their eyes met. Her stomach tilted and tipped. A slow smile spread over his lips, and he made his way over. Her inner flirt, which she didn't even know existed, materialized. They bantered and teased. For the first time in her life, Lilli felt powerful and in control.

And when he kissed her? Let's just say she'd experienced a little bit of heaven.

Lilli frowned down at the folder. This time her stomach burned with regret. Never in her wildest imagination had she thought she'd ever run into Max again. And when she did? He still held a grudge.

Against her better judgment, she opened the file to stare down at his photo again.

The young man in the picture had matured from the teen she remembered. The uniform and serious expression threw her off, because she still recalled him as the cocky guy who'd swept her off her feet. After years of hanging around country-club boys, she'd found Max's bad-boy vibe very exciting and had fallen for his charm.

When the group of boys decided to throw firecrackers, which were illegal on the public beach, into the bonfire, her excitement level skyrocketed. Why had she missed out on all this fun? Her parents didn't care about her. Why should she care about them? She had the attention of a cute guy and she'd never felt more alive.

Soon, firecrackers progressed to cherry bombs, with a few bottle rockets thrown into the mix. It wasn't until she sat in the squad car, with the police chief calling her parents, that reality set in. Some wild girl she'd turned out to be.

After that night, especially when she'd been sent away to a new school, she'd had time to think. Her walk on the wild side had been reckless and breathtaking, but not practical. Not for the girl who made lists, planned out her future with exacting care, never expecting anything less than accomplishing it all. So she'd reverted back to dating the type of guys she knew were safe and drama-free.

She may not have seen Max again, but in the very depths of her soul, she never forgot him or the excitement of that night. And always wished she hadn't told the police chief that Max was involved.

She closed the folder and started the car. Already late for work, she needed to get her mind on more serious matters. She drove to the office, thinking about the adult Max.

His choice of office dress was downright appalling, as if he'd thrown the idea of professionalism out the door. But she had gotten a whiff of his tangy cologne, which had affected her more than she cared to admit. And the way he'd needled her? She wanted to…to…scream.

She parked and hurried into the building, more than ready to get back to her desk and finalize her workload. An hour passed, and she should have been focused on the dog food account, but her mind kept going back to Max and their meeting in his office. He'd come across as annoying and rude. A pain in her… shoulder?

A constant poking brought her out of her snit.

"Earth to Lilli."

Lilli shook her head to clear the images of Max superimposed over the graphics on her computer screen. "What?"

She blinked, having forgotten she sat at her work desk or that the intern's current choice of hair color was a deep plum with streaks of pink. The outrageous do framed large hazel eyes and brought out the natural blush on the girl's cheeks. With her wild hair, fun personality and desire to work hard, Jewel had become a welcome addition to the KLC family. Also a good friend.

At the lowest point in her life, Lilli only left her apartment to go to work, until her mother threatened to come over to cheer her up. Not happening. So she'd thrown on an oversize T-shirt, baggy shorts and flip-flops to wander downtown, window shopping to get her mind off the sad state of her life.

She hadn't liked the lack of direction in her life, but couldn't seem to drag herself out of her funk. The scent of freshly brewed coffee had snagged her attention as she passed Cuppa Joe, so she'd ventured in. After placing her order, she'd taken a seat on the couch located in the corner just as Jewel breezed in. Before Lilli knew it, Jewel had engaged her in conversation and somehow managed to drag Lilli, kicking and screaming, back into the real world. For that, Lilli would be forever grateful.

After the horrible night when Rob left her, she'd questioned herself and her decisions. She knew he'd have preferred she stay home rather than work. He'd wanted someone to take care of him and had seen her job as competition. They'd had a few arguments about her quitting, but she'd attributed that to the wedding stress as the date drew near. The night of the wedding rehearsal, he told her the truth. The excuses about her working were a ruse. He didn't know what he wanted out of life, but knew he didn't want to get married. At least, not to her. It had taken her two-point-five seconds to realize she couldn't marry him, either. She'd finally found her identity after years of hiding in her parents' shadows. Finally found peace with who she had become. She wasn't going to give that up for any man.

If she did ever manage to fall in love, the man would have to prove to her, without a shadow of a doubt, that she came first in his life. Until then, her job gave her purpose, and when she'd found out about the promotion, she'd gone all-out after it.

The poking stopped. "You've been out of it all morning," Jewel said. "Ever since you got back from your meeting. How about we take a break? Go get some lunch?"

"It's lunch time already?" Lilli frowned. "I should skip. I haven't gotten much done, and Jim needs my report by the end of the day. He's finally on board with me going for the promotion and I can't blow it. Not with Nate after the same job."

And she wouldn't. She had all the qualities to make a good account executive.

She had a bachelor's degree in marketing. She was calm under pressure. Being well-organized and self-motivated was a plus when hunting for new clients. She communicated with skill, although her mother might argue that fact since Lilli couldn't get Max to volunteer as a groom. And lastly, she worked well with others. A team player. Until she got placed on her mother's team, apparently.

"What's up with you, anyway? You've been here in body, but your mind is elsewhere."

"Hmm? Oh, I have a lot of things to think about." Like brides and grooms and handsome private-security consultants, to name a few.

"Your mom's project?"

"For one. She's got this list and committees and…way too much for me to handle while working full time. Did you know my mom has a volunteer committee working for her? Working for her! And still she wants me to handle all the little details. Has she ever heard of delegation?"

Jewel's perfectly arched brow rose.

"Her lists are so detailed she must have spent hours putting them together. I have to admit, they're almost better than mine, and that's saying a lot. After seeing what she has in store for this show, I realize handling all this is a big deal." Blowing out a breath, she rested her chin on her upraised hand, sure she conjured up a picture of pure dejection. "Can I run a fashion show and go after that promotion without messing up? Especially when there are others in the office after it, too?"

"If anyone can do this, you can. The timing is perfect. It's been a year since, well, never mind. Look at this as your get-out-of-the-rut card."

Lilli laughed. "I hadn't looked at it that way."

"You should. And it's my job, as your friend, to be there for you. You know, to remind you to get out and have a life. To meet guys. Although I have to admit, you've been too picky in the men department, but I'll keep on trying."

"Along with my mother," Lilli said dryly.

"Well, you're not easy to work with. All guys aren't like Rob. If you'd give someone a chance you'd find out."

Yeah, her head knew that, but her heart hadn't made the leap—witness the wave of unwelcome memories plaguing her this morning. She realized she didn't want to go down that road again. Not if the ache in her stomach that had started at the mention of the country club became a permanent ailment. Eventually she'd have to step into that place, but not right this moment. Steering the conversation back to the present, Lilli told her friend, "You know, just for spite, I should make you help me out."

A flash of surprise lit Jewel's eyes, then a slow grin spread across her magenta lips. "This could work, you know. I do have an eye for fashion."

Lilli scrutinized the bohemian outfit of layered black and fuchsia tank tops matched with a flippy cotton skirt and sparkly sandals before glancing down at her own conservative outfit. What had happened to her sense of style? Standard blouse and skirt. Blend into the wall, why don't you?

"Hey, we all can't dress like we walked out of *Vogue*."

She loved her young friend. Jewel's fashion sense? Not always. But right now, her own wardrobe needed a major overhaul, so who was she to balk?

"I was thinking more of you helping me

here, in case I get behind or if Jim starts piling on the work." She flashed a pleading smile. "Please?"

Jewel laughed. "I can do that—as long as I get a shot at working the benefit."

Lilli thought about it for a few seconds, glancing at the file folder sitting on her desk. Getting Jewel to help might not be a bad idea. She nodded to the file. "There are all kinds of reception pictures in there. Why don't you take a look and put together some ideas for me?"

Jewel's eyes lit up. "You'd trust me to do that? I'm still an intern here."

"An intern who is about to be hired on as staff. You've proved yourself. Enough said. There's already a committee set up to do whatever I need, but give me some ideas and we'll go from there."

"I still can't believe Jim decided to hire me." Jewel grabbed the large file, hugging it to her chest. "And now this. Thanks."

"Well, that's two jobs down for today. Since I bombed on the first one, knowing you'll help has lessened my anxiety level."

"Two?" Jewel asked as she took a seat and explored the file.

"I'd hoped to get my number-one priority out of the way this morning."

"You mean getting your mother's stuff from the historical society?"

"Yes and no. I got the lists, but first I was supposed to talk Max Sanders into volunteering as one of the grooms."

Jewel's head popped up and her eyes grew wide. "Max Sanders? The hunky new P.I.?"

"Private security consultant," Lilli corrected. "You know him?"

Boy, did she know him. She wasn't ready to fill Jewel in on the details. She still needed to process the events of the morning.

When Lilli didn't respond, Jewel continued. "I met him at Cuppa Joe last week. You know me—never met a stranger."

Or a prospective date for Lilli. "You didn't mention him."

Jewel bent her head, busy searching the file. "Guess it slipped my mind."

Hardly. Good-looking guys never slipped Jewel's mind.

"Is there something wrong?"

Jewel's head jerked up again. "No! Why would you ask that?"

"Because you didn't try to introduce us."

A few beats passed before a knowing grin flashed across Jewel's face. "You're interested in him."

"I didn't say that." Nor would she ever admit

it because that would lead to heartache. She didn't do heartache anymore.

"You've never asked me about a guy before."

Lilli shrugged. "I kind of have to work with him for the fund-raiser. I'm curious."

"So am I. Now." Jewel dragged her chair to Lilli's desk. "Details."

"My mother wanted me to confirm Max as a volunteer groom. That's all."

"And…?"

"He refused. I used my strong powers of persuasion, and he still turned me down."

Jewel eyed her with skepticism.

"Okay, so my mother hired him to update the security system at the historical society office and provide security for the obscenely expensive jewelry she insists on showcasing at the benefit. But even if he hadn't already signed up to work for my mother, I was still persuasive."

Sure you were. Right up until he all but said you should take a hike.

He wasn't overjoyed at the prospect of being part of the fashion show. She couldn't blame him. She wouldn't want to model in front of all those people, either. Her mother hadn't gone as far as asking her to participate as one of the brides. Lilli would have refused. Wearing a wedding dress again would make the memories all too real.

But Max could look at this as a working gig. A great way to gain clients. So why turn down the opportunity? He may have been a bad boy years ago, but it looked as if he'd cleaned up his act and become responsible. She could give his business a boost by promoting Sanders Security around town, the least she could do for causing him trouble all those years ago.

She grinned when she remembered his appalled expression at the mention of wearing a tuxedo. It had been worth the visit to his office to see the look on his face. And when they shook hands… She shivered in memory. She couldn't deny the thrill when those smoky gray eyes focused on her alone. His clean-scented cologne and the promise of excitement hung in the air between them. She'd been mesmerized. And alarmed at her strong reaction to the man. The rugged tough-guy thing? Too much. So not Orlando Bloom. So not her type.

Maybe he should be, an impish voice taunted her.

Lilli caught Jewel grinning at her. "What are you smiling at?"

"Nothing."

Riiight.

"So, as of right now, phase one of mission 'Return Favor to Celeste Barclay' is a failure."

"You'll just have to come up with a better plan."

"Like what?" Lilli asked.

"I have no idea. That's your department."

Lilli thought back to their conversation. "He was adamant about not being a groom. I wonder if the vision of him and all those brides locked in one room made him nervous?" She paused a beat. "Oh, wait, that's *my* nightmare."

Jewel chuckled. "So, what's he like?" she asked, scooting closer to Lilli's desk so she could settle in to hear all the dirt. "I only got a few minutes in Cuppa Joe with him. Not a chatty guy. More interested in getting his morning coffee and heading out the door." Lilli knew perfectly well her friend wouldn't budge until she had her fill of information. "A real bad boy, right?"

"How would I know?" But yeah, a bad boy. She'd known that the first time she'd laid eyes on him. Today's meeting only confirmed her first impression. Because of that, she had a hard time loosening up around him and probably came off sounding very starchy. But he just oozed masculinity. Did he have to be so good-looking? And smell so good? Exceptionally good. When their gazes had connected over the desktop, she'd had to ignore the urge to ask what he'd done with his life since the summer they'd met.

Jewel continued. "So, we know he's gorgeous—"

Yeah, that, too.

"—if you like that kind." Jewel eyed her with suspicion.

"What kind?" Lilli had lost track of the thread of conversation.

"Tall, built, alpha attitude?"

Oh, yeah. All those things.

"You got all this at a coffee shop?" Lilli asked, busying herself with papers on her desk, hoping to hide her sappy smile.

"It's the vibe he sends out. Can't miss it." Jewel watched Lilli tidy up. "So that's why you haven't gotten any work done."

"Huh?"

"And you've got the look."

"What look?"

"Interested."

"No way." Did she? She hadn't been dwelling on him *all* morning, just snatches of time here and there. "And I can prove he's not my type. Not only did his clothing leave something to be desire—"

"What was he wearing?"

"What was he what?"

"Wearing? Obviously it bothers you."

"I don't know. Faded jeans. Tight black T-shirt. Five-o'clock shadow first thing in the morning."

Jewels eyebrows arched. "I didn't know shaving qualified as a fashion accessory."

"It's just unprofessional."

"He's a private investigator." Jewel threw her a look. "The last thing he wants to do is stick out in a crowd."

"I guess." Lilli pursed her lips, exasperated by her friend's interrogation. Cringing, she hoped she hadn't come across as uptight with Max, but she was very afraid she had. "Then explain this. When we were in his office, I noticed a wall calendar. Penciled in every Saturday is a woman's name. A *different* woman's name. Cards with Terri. The gazebo with Margaret. Drive with Carolyn."

"Which means what?"

"I don't know. He's a player?"

Jewel laughed.

"What?"

"That sounds so funny coming from you."

"Hey, I can be hip if I want to."

Jewel continued laughing. "Keep telling yourself that, but I know better."

"You know I don't go out with guys like him." Even to herself Lilli sounded uppity.

"Problem is, you don't go out at all," Jewel muttered, then flushed at Lilli's hurt expression. "I'm sorry. I call 'em like I see 'em. And you've got Max on the brain." Jewel placed the wedding file back on the desk. "Let's go eat. You need a break from all this charity-event talk and I want to check out the new place downtown, Pointe Café."

Lilli glanced at her computer screen again, knowing she wouldn't get any more work done. Max Sanders had captured her thoughts, thanks to Jewel's prodding. She needed a change of scenery. After saving her work, she stood. "Let's go."

Lilli grabbed her purse, knocking over the accordion file Mrs. Rumpold had given her earlier. Wedding gown photos spilled to the floor. Exasperated, Lilli knelt down to collect the pictures, her eye catching on an image of a beautiful gown. The white strapless creation hugged the model's body before flaring out in an embroidered trumpet skirt and train.

"Coming?" Jewel called.

"Be right there." She took one last look at the gown before scooping up the remaining pictures, securely placing them in the file and out of her sight before her resolve to stay un-affected by weddings unraveled.

CHAPTER THREE

Max held the printout with the particulars of the Wingate collection in his hand. He perused the information, realizing this collection was not just fancy jewelry. The pieces, which showcased several diamonds and sapphires, were more like artwork, he noted. His eyebrows rose when he saw the estimated value of the collection. Unbelievable. Why on earth would Clare Wingate loan her collection to a friend? Benefit or not? Thankfully, the collection had full insurance coverage. That lowered his heart rate some.

He'd do everything in his power to keep the collection safe, but couldn't deny he'd be glad when the pieces were returned to their owner.

Tossing the fax onto his desk, Max leaned back in his chair and stacked his bootheels on the windowsill, taking a moment to contemplate the scene from his office window. From here, he had an unimpeded view of the beach and the Gulf waters. If he'd realized all the stress that went into starting his own security firm, he might have had second thoughts. He'd loved police work, being something of an adrenaline junkie, but when word of his grandmother's bad heart had reached him he decided to come back to Florida.

Laverne Sanders had raised him after his father died and his mother couldn't deal with a son who tended to get into mischief. He grinned. His grandmother's kind description of his actions. Most people had plain-out called him trouble.

His old friend and mentor, the town police chief, called to inform Max that he'd assisted Gram after a fainting spell in the produce section of Winn Dixie. Apparently she'd been dealing with some health issues and hadn't told Max because she didn't want to worry him. He also found out her finances were a mess, so he came home to pitch in and help, whether she wanted him to or not. Each was all the family the other had. She'd always been rock solid for him, now he would take care of her.

Another reason to make sure his business became successful here in Cypress Pointe. Folks of this fine town might remember him as a hoodlum, but Gram knew better. The burden of proving he'd changed would be tough, but he'd always liked a good challenge.

She'd be miffed when she found out he'd

turned down the groom position for the charity function, since she'd been telling him he needed to get out and meet people. Women people, to be exact.

Right now he had to concentrate on his security business. The longer he was in town, the more he realized the need here. And he would make himself indispensable. *Even if it means volunteering for the wedding fashion show?* The thought made him shudder, until one particular bewitching redhead came to mind.

Max had to admit, working undercover might be his only option to guard both the jewelry collection and the vintage gowns, but he wouldn't give in easily. He ran a hand through his hair and drank the last of his coffee. Gone stone-cold again, along with his mood. The more he thought about Miss Barclay—which he'd done pretty much nonstop since she'd waltzed into his office, dragging the past with her—the more he vowed to prove himself to the folks of Cypress Pointe. He rose and walked to the outer office to get another mug of coffee just as Blanche breezed through the door.

"I'm back, boss."

"I could have used you about two hours ago."

"Why?"

"I had a visitor try to talk me into volunteering as a groom at that charity function."

She stopped just inside the threshold, closing the door behind her. The middle-aged control freak with short, spiky blond hair regarded him with an amused tilt of her lips as he explained Miss Barclay's visit. "I'm gone for the morning, and this place falls apart."

"You don't even know the half of it." He told her how he turned Lilli down flat. "She pretty much ran out of here."

"After such a heartfelt refusal? What a shocker."

Max scowled at his secretary, not missing the sarcasm in her tone.

"Hey, I agreed to security. Nothing more."

"Even if it means spending time with a pretty, young, *single* woman?"

"How do you know all that?"

"Please, you've forgotten that this is a small town." Blanche grinned. "Remind me never to leave you alone again."

He scowled at her.

She shook her head as she crossed the room to her desk. "Really, though, you should take advantage of these events. Look at it more as a business opportunity and less as getting wrangled to volunteer for Celeste."

"I suppose you're right."

"Max, you were under the mistaken belief that you can say no to this event. I know those historical society ladies. They're going to figure out a way to con you into volunteering, and they won't stop until you give in. And the chief warned you. Celeste Barclay expects results."

"She didn't ask me. Her daughter did."

Blanche shrugged. "Doesn't matter who did the asking. It's town tradition to volunteer and we all know what happens when you buck tradition."

"I don't."

"You don't get any business. Trust me on this."

"Like I have time for ridiculous stuff like escorting fake brides down the country club aisle," he grumbled. "I'm going to be working that night."

Blanche ignored him. "Think of Jake Riley and the animals at the shelter. How would he feel if you refused?"

He stared at her. "He's a dog. He doesn't care."

"Honey, there's just some things that are implied and this is one of them."

Shaking his head, he raised an eyebrow at the petite, bossy secretary. "This is crazy."

"This is Cypress Pointe."

No matter what he decided, this had all the signs of a disaster in the making.

Blanche crossed her arms over her chest. "Sorry, Max. You'll have to go."

The finality in her words made him cringe. She wasn't sorry. Not in the least.

"Okay, but I don't have to tell her right away."

Blanche shook her head in resignation at her boss's stubbornness.

Refusing to talk about it any longer, he handed her his mug in defeat. "More coffee?"

"Sure thing, boss."

He returned to his office and sank into the chair, closing his eyes to once again picture Miss Barclay with her cool smile and cooler eyes. Dressed in something that reminded him of the shade of summertime. A summer that had changed his life.

He couldn't back down. Not so quickly. He may still have trust issues with the woman— okay, major trust issues—but dressing up as a groom? He shuddered.

He glanced at the wall clock and jumped up when he saw the time. Grabbing the tools of the trade he needed to go undercover, he sprinted through the office. "Gotta take care of that surveillance case."

Blanche held up his mug. "What about your coffee?"

"Hang on to it until later." He stopped and

stared her down. "And please don't volunteer me for anything before I get back."

Blanche chuckled. "Sure. And you keep your mind on the job and off a particular pretty woman."

Easier said than done. Max hurried down the stairs and stepped into the late-morning sun.

ONE MORE MOVE, BART. Then you're mine.

Max folded the newspaper he'd been pretending to read, placing it on the bench beside him, his eyes never once leaving his quarry. Muscles tense, he waited patiently. Bad Bart, the town pickpocket, was about to mess up. Max could feel it in his bones. And when he did, Max would catch it all on tape.

"C'mon. Just do it," Max muttered under his breath while he waited for Bart to relieve his unsuspecting victim of his belongings.

If anyone had told Max that small-town life held as much drama as the big city of Atlanta where he had worked as a detective, he wouldn't have believed them. He'd been involved in undercover stakeouts in the most dangerous sections of the city, where he didn't dare take his hand off his firearm for safety's sake. He'd dealt with demanding bosses, low-life criminals and every type of perp who claimed he didn't do it. He'd taken it all in stride, until two cases, coming on the tail of each other, made him rethink his career.

He'd been called to assist a multiple homicide. A mother and her two sons. Victims of domestic abuse. Max hated family violence. Long estranged from his mother, he couldn't help but think he could have ended up like one of those boys had fate not intervened.

Max had been on hand for many of the calls to the apartment. He'd always hoped the mother would leave the guy, for the boys' sakes as well as her own. He'd encouraged the brothers to help their mother leave and had struck up a tentative friendship with them. From time to time, he stopped by the park near their building to watch them play baseball.

The mother finally decided to leave her boyfriend after he'd managed to mess her up pretty badly, and not just her that time. Once the guy went after one of her boys, she'd wanted out. Thinking he'd be gone all day at work, she'd gathered the boys and their few belongings. She'd made it as far as the car when her boyfriend came home unexpectedly. He went into a rage and shot them all, including himself.

The next case had hit even closer to home. A teen with an already growing record had stolen from his neighborhood convenience store and been caught on tape. Max and his partner went

to the teen's apartment, only to find him arguing with his mother. She told Max to take the
kid away. She was done worrying about him.
Hadn't Max heard those same words, only from
his own mother? Too many times to count.

They'd taken the kid to the station and
booked him. As he always did, Max talked
to the teenager, hoping he could get the kid to
see the error of his ways. He never knew if he
reached any of the young people he spoke to,
but he hoped they would listen. Max visited
the boy a few times, thinking he'd made some
headway. Then, shortly after, Max learned that
while in lockup the boy had been killed in a
gang attack.

Max's story had played out differently after
he came home from juvenile detention. His
mother had packed up and gone, leaving Max
homeless. If not for his grandmother, who
knew where he might be today? In jail? Or
worse, like the teen he'd tried to help?

Max had wondered what he could have done
differently to help the boys in both instances.
Logically, he knew he couldn't have done more.
Still, the memories had haunted him enough
that he knew he had to leave the city. That's
when he'd begun thinking about starting his
own security business.

Life in Cypress Pointe promised to be calm,

serene, even. Getting the security business up and running would take time, but he was eager to get going. Until Bad Bart.

Cliché? You bet. Bad Bart Bradbury had named himself and the nickname stuck. Pick-pocket Bart was more appropriate.

He was a thorn in the side of the Cypress Pointe Merchants Association, Max's current client. They wanted this scourge of society off the streets. When Max heard this description, he wondered what kind of menace terrorized the streets and why on earth his grandmother hadn't warned him about the criminal element. Then he'd gotten his first glimpse of Bart. A scourge? Far from it. Slippery? Oh, yeah. But Max hadn't met a criminal he couldn't capture and bring to justice.

Determined to close the case file today, Max sported his new spy-cam sunglasses. A perk in his line of work. He loved playing with high-tech gadgets. When Bart proved to be a worthy adversary, Max had purchased the surveillance kit. With the camera mounted on his belt, he resembled another tourist jamming to an MP3 player when he was actually recording Bart's movements. When Bart slipped up—and he would—the proof would be given to the association, his job done and a check sent to him in the mail.

Max regarded his subject, shaking his head. A nice enough kid, Bart worked as a busboy on the breakfast shift in a downtown restaurant. Five-eight, shaggy hair, maybe all of nineteen. Somewhere along the way he'd grown tired of his ho-hum life and decided picking pockets made him the center of attention in an invisible life. He didn't keep the money or the items he pilfered—a wallet here, a cell phone there. Max knew the items "anonymously" appeared on the counter at the police station before anyone could nab Bart. He just wanted people to acknowledge him.

Maybe he needed a girlfriend.

Or an hour with Max's grandmother. Laverne would fuss over him, urge him to stop his pickpocket ways and turn his life around. She'd given Max a talking to on more occasions than he cared to remember, and when he'd thought he'd burned his last bridge with her, he'd finally listened.

Squinting against the bright April sun, Max focused on Bart as he headed toward the new eatery in town. Max had observed that Bart finished his shift in the early afternoon, then mingled with the tourists who were out in large numbers looking for a place to eat or shop. Instead of following a mark, which was his normal M.O., today Bart waved at two women as they turned the corner to join him on the sidewalk. Max's eyes narrowed and surprise kicked through him. *No way.* Miss Charity Coordinator herself.

He shook his head, not sure if he should growl or groan. Not wanting his quarry to escape without getting the action on tape, Max jumped up from the bench. With a determined stride, he crossed the pavement, edging closer to what he hoped would be the end of this assignment. So far, Bart's elusiveness had proved to be a wrinkle in his plans. Max was so close to catching Bart. He couldn't let Lilli Barclay interfere with his goal.

Oh, yeah, he'd remembered her name once the shock of seeing her had worn off. Then he'd dug around for more. What kind of self-respecting security consultant would he be otherwise? He'd called the historical society office. The lady answering the phone had told Max everything he wanted to know, from Lilli's family, to where she worked and what coffee shop she frequented. Like he needed to know her coffee preference. But at this point, gaining the upper hand in every situation was the name of the game. And this pretty, pesky society babe constituted a situation.

Now he had to deal with her again, in a most inconvenient scenario.

Weaving through the tourists milling around the shop windows, Max focused on his target, stealthily moving closer, working hard to keep his distracted gaze from resting on Lilli. What was wrong with him? He loved this part of the action. The takedown. The adrenaline. But with her nearby, he found it impossible to concentrate.

Zooming the lens in closer to catch everything on tape, he saw Bart chatting with the two women as if they were all old friends. What was the guy up to? Putting his mark at ease so he could steal a purse when least expected? Could Lilli be his intended mark? He experienced an unexpected wave of protectiveness toward her.

Only Bart didn't do anything. He stood with his hands at his sides, in the open, talking to a young woman with…pink streaks in her hair? Lilli stood beside them, listening to their conversation, her eyes going wide when she spied Max. He held one finger up to his lips. She barely nodded before turning her attention back to Bart.

Relieved she understood his signal, Max walked right past them, ducking into the first open door he found. He scanned the store, recognizing the cluttered gift shop as Milly's Gifts and Things. A tourist haven, but a bad place to hide.

He strode to the large storefront window to continue his surveillance. Watching. Waiting for Bart to do something incriminating. But Bart just continued to talk. Max's blood pressure spiked every time Lilli sent worried glances around her. She had no way of knowing she stood with his quarry.

Please don't give me away.

"You need something, hon?" a cheerful voice asked behind him.

He glanced over his shoulder at a woman smiling at him. "No, just browsing," he told her, turning back to peer out the window, trying to see through the array of dream catchers and crystal pendants reflecting the bright sunlight.

"Can't do a good job of it if you're looking outside," she told him. "If you'd give me an idea of what you're looking for, I'd be more than happy to help you find it."

He turned to face the proprietress, an ample woman with her hands on her hips. He didn't need this attention right now. He sidled to the exit, apologizing to the woman. "Uh, wrong store. Sorry. I'll be leaving."

Stepping out the door to the sidewalk, Max came face-to-face with Lilli. She opened her mouth to speak but he clamped a hand on her arm to lead her away and explain the situation. Her eyes rounded and a clip dropped from her thick hair, leaving it to fall around her face.

He leaned down, his mouth close to her ear. "Now is not a good time to talk. I'm working." He couldn't afford an obstacle. Especially an attractive one.

She frowned up at him, pushing her hair from her eyes. "Working?"

"Undercover," he said, glancing over her shoulder. Bart still stood engrossed in conversation, unaware of the surveillance focused on him.

Her eyes grew wider. "Who are you after?"

"I can't say," Max said, still holding Lilli close.

His fingers brushed over the soft skin at the edges of her short-sleeved blouse. She hadn't pulled away yet, her gaze still locked with his. All over again he felt the heady rush he'd experienced that night at the beach when she'd looked up at him with those wide, gorgeous eyes. The light from the bonfire had cast a shimmering glow over her face and he'd been sucker-punched right then and there.

He blinked away the memory and the dizzying connection between them broke. With reluctance, Max loosened his grip. A light blush covered her cheekbones and she fussed with her hair, moving back to put some distance between them.

Max bent down to retrieve her hair clip, his line of vision to Bart broken. He straightened and held the clip out of reach. "Here you go, *Lilli*." He grinned. "Yeah. I remember."

She snatched the clip from him. "Thanks."

As Max looked around her again, he noticed the young woman with Bart peering in their direction.

She turned, following his line of vision before a surprised gasp escaped her. "You're following Bart?"

"Shh."

"What do you think he's going to do?"

"Right now I'm worried about what he's *not* going to do."

"And that is?"

"Commit a crime."

"Oh, please." She snorted. "Bart?"

"He's a criminal."

"Well, clearly you don't know him."

His sharp gaze pierced hers. A mistake. Her beguiling eyes held him captive. A sea green the same striking shade found in the calm Gulf waters bordering Cypress Pointe. His breath left him in a rush as he tried to cover his reaction. "And you do?"

"Sure. Everyone does. This is a small town."

How had he lost control of this situation? The green-eyed siren had to be the cause. "Here's the deal. I have a job to do here. So please go back to whatever you were doing and forget you saw me."

Jostled by a passing couple, Lilli's purse slid down her arm. As she grabbed for it, Max caught hold of the strap at the same time. Their fingers touched and the same dizzying jolt from moments before zapped him again. She must have felt it, too, because her eyes grew wide and she shuddered, taking a step back. He still held his hand out toward her. "I was trying to help."

She hugged her purse close to her midsection. "I'm fine."

He lowered his arm. Shoppers passed them, oblivious to his plight. Another tourist brushed by Lilli and she moved out of the way, closing the distance between them again, distance he needed so Bart wouldn't notice him. "You're missing the whole concept of undercover," he told her.

"Then enlighten me."

"Maybe when I have more time." Max moved toward the gift store, hoping to blend in with the crowd. He noticed the shop woman watching them through the window before she turned away. So much for going unnoticed.

"Please, go back to your friend and forget I'm here."

"It's too late," Lilli informed him.

Before Max had a chance to slip away unnoticed, Bart and the other woman joined them. If Bart suspected anything fishy, he didn't show it, beguiled by his smiling companion.

"Hey, Lilli, is that who I think it is?"

Lilli looked back and forth between Max and the woman, not sure how much to give away.

"Hey, Jewel. Um, yeah, it is."

Max groaned. *Just shoot me now and get it over with.*

Jewel frowned, sizing Max up. "I thought you were kidding about his clothes. He's—"

"Working." Lilli spoke the word with emphasis. Okay, she might not like his clothes but at least she didn't give him up.

"Leaving," Max corrected, looking at Lilli to relate his secret thanks. "We'll talk later."

Lilli opened her mouth to respond, but not before a uniformed police officer approached them. Max watched Bart's eyes flare in panic. Had the officer caught Bart in the act before Max?

"Excuse me," the officer spoke to Lilli. He

thumbed in Max's direction. "Is this guy giving you a hard time?"

She stared at the officer for a moment, stunned. "No. We were talking."

"We received a call that you might need help."

"A call?" She glanced up at Max, confusion knitting her brow.

The woman from Milly's Gifts and Things appeared at her door and pointed at Max. "That's the man, officer."

Great. Max couldn't nab Bart if the police wanted to question him.

"He's been skulking around," the woman continued. "He came into my store, casing it. I just knew he was going to rob me until this young lady stopped him."

"That's not true," Max told the officer.

"Then, clear as day, I saw him grab that woman's purse," the shop lady added, on a roll of accusations.

Max read a guilty verdict in the eyes of the people who stopped to watch the unfolding drama. He sure looked the part of a shady character. If he was a cop—and he had been—he'd believe the store owner in a heartbeat.

"No," Lilli assured the officer. "He stopped to help me."

"Help himself to your belongings," the store

owner countered. "I saw him grab on to her purse strap not five minutes ago."

Lilli tried to defend Max, but the store owner didn't believe her.

Max scrubbed his hand over his face, wondering how his simple surveillance had gone haywire. Trying to make his case to the officer, who tried to get everyone to stop talking at the same time, Max pleaded innocence. No one listened. The store owner started yelling about a bad element plaguing their town. By the time Max realized his stakeout was a lost cause, he'd taken his attention from his suspect for too long. Bart had disappeared.

"Where'd he go?" Max asked no one in particular. He turned in a circle on his bootheel, running a hand through his hair, frustrated no end.

He turned to face the crowd gathered around him. The officer frowned at him.

Max held his hands up. "I can explain everything."

"Sir, let me see some ID," the officer said, unimpressed with Max's urgent declaration.

Max groaned. He went to pull his wallet from his back pocket. Only it wasn't there. Stunned, his eyes locked with the pesky woman who'd disrupted his world twice today.

"Bart took my wallet."

CHAPTER FOUR

STANDING IN AN OFFICE at the police station, Lilli watched Max as he paced in front of the police chief. The chief had suggested they all move from the sidewalk to the station to straighten out the misunderstanding. Especially when the crowd grew bigger.

Every so often Max cast a frown in her direction. While that should've bothered her, instead, her heart beat rapidly. If anything, Max had caused her nothing but trouble today. First, by refusing to be a volunteer groom, then when she'd inadvertently got caught in his stakeout. Shouldn't she be upset with him? Her stomach flip-flopped. From all the excitement, she reasoned, not because of totally gorgeous Max. His dark, unruly hair kept falling over his forehead after he unsuccessfully brushed it back. Could he be any more adorable?

No. He's making your job more difficult, remember? Because of him, she'd have to find another suitable volunteer groom. Her mother would not be happy that Max hadn't jumped on board with her idea, which meant an earful for Lilli.

Yep, Max Sanders had made her life complicated. Again. But she did feel bad that he'd lost his wallet.

When they'd arrived at the station, Max had removed his sunglasses and glanced at her. She'd gotten up close and personal with those stormy gray eyes. For a fleeting moment his annoyance had vanished, replaced with…what? Curiosity? Interest in her, perhaps?

She'd tried not to react, but how could she not? He was seriously good-looking. Throw in the broad shoulders, six feet of muscular build—obviously the man worked out—and long denim-clad legs and…well, she noticed.

Yet she had to ignore his undeniable appeal and how it affected her. Even if she had wanted this tug of awareness to go somewhere, the unresolved past between them would make that impossible.

"I can't believe he's been spying on Bart," Jewel fumed as she shot the hunky Max another glare. "Why would anyone want Bart tailed?"

Bart came across as a nice enough guy, but had trouble with his "confusion of ownership" issues. Amused by Jewel's passionate defense,

Lilli listened, letting her friend vent. She'd never seen Jewel this charged up before.

The chief, a tall bear of a man, with distinguished gray hair and a ready smile, moved their way to join the tail end of the conversation. He hadn't changed much since the night he sat her in the squad car while he called her parents. At least this time she wasn't in trouble. "Max was doing his job," the chief explained.

Jewel simmered down, but her lips pursed in mulish displeasure.

"This is all just a misunderstandin'," he assured them.

"Bart would never hurt anyone," Jewel insisted. "Sure, he's a little different, but that's his appeal. Not everyone follows their inner voice."

Not everyone's inner voice told them to pick pockets, either. Lilli glanced over at her friend. "Since when did you become so interested in Bart?"

Pink covered Jewels cheeks. "I've run into him around town a few times. We went to high school together," she explained. "Recently we reconnected. I even invited him to join us for lunch today…before we were interrupted. But he turned me down."

Interrupted by Max. Lilli peeked over at him again, her stomach fluttering. For the second time in her life, Max Sanders caught and held her attention, but she resisted the lure. She had a lot on her plate, which didn't include getting tangled up with Max again.

"The officer has your statements, ladies, so if you'll excuse me, I should probably get back to Max." The chief excused himself.

"Isn't that peachy," Jewel grumbled.

"He knows what he's doing," Lilli told her friend.

"Bart's not even here to defend himself."

Lilli decided not to point out the fact that his disappearing act looked suspicious. While Jewel complained, her attention went back to Max.

He stood only a few feet away, so she couldn't help but hear the chief laughing while Max spoke in a low tone. He frowned and seemed put out, while the chief enjoyed the entire situation, especially when he handed Max a square brown object that could only have been the pilfered wallet. Max's neck grew red as he shoved the billfold into his back pocket. Lilli chuckled at his disgruntled expression.

He headed in her direction. *Uh-oh.*

"Look, things got out of hand. Thanks for not blowing my cover."

"Are you appreciative enough to be a groom?"

"No way."

"You know, I could have told the officer you were causing trouble."

"I still would have ended up here. Like the last time the police brought us both in." His eyes narrowed. "You seem to have a special ability for getting me in hot water."

"Hey, I didn't plan to."

"Today? Or years ago?"

"Neither. And I resent the implication."

"You're trouble, pure and simple."

"And you're not?"

The chief chuckled. "Should I leave you two alone to work things out?"

She grimaced. "No, thanks."

The chief still grinned. "That's good, 'cuz Max here doesn't like being cornered."

By his scowl, Lilli knew she'd managed that. Twice in one day.

"I still lost Bart," Max groused.

"Are you implying it's my fault he got away?" Lilli planted her fists on her hips. Max leaned toward her and she couldn't deny the sparks flaring between them as they squared off. Every flash of potent energy threw off tantalizing heat, yet she didn't back down.

"No, I'm flat-out saying it."

They were still glaring at each other when the chief stepped between them.

"Bart's a slippery one, I'll give you that. But I have no doubt you'll get the job done." He slapped Max on the back, as if giving Max his cue to leave. Max's neck grew red again. He sent Lilli a curt nod and strode off.

"Our lunch hour is completely blown." Jewel told Lilli as they left the station. "But watching you push Mr. Security Consultant's buttons? Worth not eating."

"Did I do that?" Lilli asked innocently while batting her eyelashes.

"Like a pro." Jewel held up her hand for a high five. Lilli slapped her hand against Jewel's. "So really, what's going on between you two?"

Lilli adjusted her purse strap, her gaze following the path Max had taken. "Nothing."

Jewel snorted. "Yeah, right."

"I sort of know him."

Jewel's eyes went wide. "Explain 'sort of.'"

Lilli squirmed. "We met twelve years ago. Just once. At the beach." She laughed. "I got him into trouble with the police."

"Do I even want to know?"

"It's a long story. Suffice it to say, he's still holding a grudge."

"And now you've reconnected. Interesting."

Lilli frowned. "There's nothing to be interested in."

"So you say."

Okay, so maybe she missed their verbal skirmishes already. She squirmed under Jewel's smug scrutiny, not wanting to delve too deeply into the matter here in the middle of the sidewalk. Bad enough she'd provoked the guy. She didn't want to uncover the reasons why.

"Let's not go there," Lilli said.

"I knew it. You're totally crushing on Max."

"Am not."

"Are, too. Why are you denying it? What are you afraid of?"

Flashbacks of the night on the beach were quickly overshadowed by the catastrophe that had been her wedding rehearsal dinner. The pain and humiliation. Afraid? Yes. But she'd never admit it out loud.

"My relationship with Max, if you could call it that, is difficult."

"Looks like it."

"He's infuriating."

"That's half the fun."

Lilli glanced down the empty sidewalk. "I knew you'd say that."

BACK AT WORK, Jewel continued her running commentary about Bart while Lilli tried to concentrate on the Natural Puppy account. She'd hoped that Jewel's evaluation of Lilli's attraction to Max would prove wrong, but with reluctance, admitted she might be right.

What was she going to do about it?

As the question swirled around in her brain, an annoying chime sounded from her purse. Digging through the tan leather bag, she found her cell.

She squinted at the caller ID, sighing heavily. Her mother's timing could be uncanny. "Mom, I'm in the middle of a deadline," Lilli said by way of greeting. "I can't talk about the benefit right now."

"Of course you can," Celeste Barclay informed her only daughter in her cultured tone. "It's for the good of the society."

Lilli gripped the phone tightly. "I don't even belong to the society."

"Of course you do. I added you to the roster years ago."

Lilli clenched her teeth. *Of course she had.* With her mother, every answer started with, *of course you do.* Or *can.* Or *will.* Of course you can swim, just pump your legs. Of course you'll attend the ballet, we bought you a ticket. Of course I can upset your life, I'm your mother and I love you.

"You promised you'd be back in plenty of time for Tie the Knot," Lilly reminded her.

"No, dear. I promised to do everything in my

power to get back in plenty of time. My ladies are counting on you."

Her ladies. Lilli rolled her eyes. Just because they were her mom's ladies didn't mean Lilli should inherit them. "So are you saying you won't make it back in time?"

"If your father hadn't left his tennis bag on the floor right by the balcony of our suite, I wouldn't have tripped over it."

"Dad is with you?"

A slight pause. "He was."

"Why?"

"I told you. Aunt Marian got herself into a little legal entanglement. Your father came here as her attorney."

That made sense. But still, her parents, together?

"As I was saying, I nearly pitched right over the railing. I could have died. Instead I only hurt my arm."

"Your arm?"

"It's a sprain. I told that man a thousand times not to leave his things in the middle of the floor. He never listened. Briefcase, gym bags, shoes, you name it. It's been like this—"

Lilli had heard these complaints before and knew if she didn't cut her mother's tirade short, she'd go on all afternoon.

"Does it hurt?"

"Does what hurt?"

"Your arm."

"My arm? Oh, my arm." She paused on a well-timed moan. "My wrist hurts and there is some swelling, but I don't need a cast. Could you imagine trying to accessorize? The sweet doctor taped my wrist and said I need to stay put for now so I don't aggravate it. Although I can't complain—even though your father abandoned me to go back to work. Between you and me, I think your father is trying to kill me."

"I doubt it."

"It seems that way."

Yeah, it always did with them.

"Mom, you should be here. The fund-raiser is your baby."

"The prep work for the fund-raiser is already done. I have lists and committees all set up. All you need to do is step in and take over. Oh, have you read the information about the Wingate collection yet? I can't believe my old friend Clare came through for me. Especially since I asked her on a whim. It's the pièce de résistance of the benefit."

And an additional responsibility to take Lilli away from her job.

"Her late husband presented her with this antique jewelry collection the night before they were married at St. Patrick's Cathedral in New

York. It is rumored to have been smuggled out of Russia by one of the last royal family members of Czar somebody-or-other. I've seen the necklace myself, just once, and it is stunning! We're not only going to display the necklace, but also the matching earrings, bracelet and ring, as well. After the benefit, Clare is letting us show the collection at the historical society office."

Celeste stopped to catch her breath. While her mother saw another successful event, Lilli saw a logistical nightmare go from bad to worse.

"Now, Lilli, as I was saying—" On her mother's end, a knocking sounded in the distance. "Hold on, dear. Someone is at the door."

Lilli held on while her mother put the phone down. From now on she vowed to let her mother's calls go to voice mail.

An untimely growl sounded from her stomach. Lunch had been a quick stop at a to-go burger joint and Lilli hadn't made much of a dent in the burger before they'd returned to work, hurrying inside so Jim didn't make a scene. She scanned the office. With Jim safely ensconced in his office, she slid open her top drawer, snuck a fry from the box tucked away inside and nibbled.

Her mother finally came back on the line. "I

called for fresh towels. Did I tell you they have the most extravagant amenities here? Why, yesterday—"

"Mom, where are you? You said Aunt Marian needed you."

"She did. We rendezvoused at the spa."

"That's your emergency?"

"We didn't come here until after her troubles. Now she has some personal issues we needed to discuss."

"At a spa," she reiterated in a flat tone.

"What better place?"

Lilli tried to ignore the throbbing in her head. "I need to get back to work."

"Oh, of course. Well, then, one last thing, dear. Did Max agree to be a volunteer groom?"

The question sent a chill through Lilli. "Not yet."

"What do you mean 'not yet'?" her mother asked in her steely tone.

"He wasn't exactly receptive to the idea."

"And you explained why he should volunteer?"

"Yes, but he still refused."

"Hmm. That's hard to believe. Police Chief Gardener assured me he's a lovely man to work with. And he was perfectly pleasant when he came to set up the security system."

Max Sanders? A lovely man? "I wouldn't go

that far." Handsome, yes. Focused, most definitely. But lovely? No possible way. And she couldn't imagine a man's man like the chief using the word *lovely* to describe Max. Or anyone else, for that matter.

"Keep working on him. I don't have any other single men to choose from."

"I can give you a list."

"No, Lillian. Get Max to commit. I hired him for security and he has to be there now that we have the jewelry collection. Don't let him get away."

Suddenly Lilli heard a muffled voice on the other end of the phone, sounding suspiciously like a PA system announcing some sort of activity. "Mom, are you still there?"

"Lillian, I must run now."

"Run where? Aren't you supposed to be resting?"

"Mud wrap. It's good for the spirit and the body. And my arm, of course."

"Mom, what's really going on?"

She talked to dead air. Dropping her shoulders, Lilli looked up at the ceiling and took cleansing breaths.

"Celeste?" Jewel asked, plopping down into a vacant chair beside her.

"How could you tell?"

"Your face is red."

"This is crazy." She flipped her cell phone closed. "If she needed time away, why didn't she just say so? I would have understood. But to make it sound like an emergency and leave me with all this responsibility? As usual, she just assumed I would help her. And I fell for it. What does that say about me?"

"That you're gullible when it comes to your mom?"

An understatement if there ever was one.

"And from what I heard from your end of the conversation, she still wants you to convince Max to be a groom."

"Yes." Lilli rubbed her eyes.

"After this afternoon? Good luck with that."

"You do realize how complicated this is, right?"

Jewel shot her a sympathetic shrug.

"Some help you are."

AT SEVEN O'CLOCK Lilli turned in her project, much to her boss's relief. Jim stayed at the office so she wouldn't be alone, although he usually worked late anyway. He depended on her way too much, not only for her ability to make account holders happy with her ideas, but because of her organizational skills, as well. Yeah, because she nearly ran the place. That's why getting this promotion had to happen.

She always finished her projects on time. At least, she had until tonight, when visions of lace, tulle, seed pearls and white, white, *white* had invaded her mind. Throw in a tall, dark and scruffy security consultant and she'd had enough for one day.

The fluorescent light hummed over her as she straightened up her desk for the night. She stared at the accordion file from Mrs. Rumpold. She'd asked Jewel to leave it on her desk until tomorrow so Lilli could look through it first. Almost reluctantly, she reached for it and then hesitated. If she started looking at the material her mother had collected, she would be totally committed to the event, though realistically she knew there was already no going back.

Wouldn't it be nice if her mother showed up tomorrow, good as new and ready to take the job back? She suspected there was more to her mother's story than Celeste was letting on. But Lilli couldn't force her to reveal whatever she was hiding. Why couldn't her family be normal? Just when she'd finally managed to move beyond her mother's drama, she got sucked back in again. When would she have her own life?

Her mother had only been gone a few days, and already Lilli been had thrust into working on a historical society function, reluctantly dredging up the past and reconnecting with a man who definitely caught her attention. What next?

Lilli refocused on the file filled with every bride's hopes and dreams. She didn't want to decorate for a wedding with all the glamour and bells and whistles that went with the event. A designer gown and lavish reception? Not for her. She'd almost had it once. She didn't need it now.

"Great job," Jim told her as he locked up his office. "I only glanced over the proposal, but it looks solid. Natural Puppy should like it."

"Thanks. I know I'm usually finished by five, but since I came in late this morning, it couldn't be avoided—"

"It was due Thursday. Today's Thursday. We're good."

"Today's been rather...eventful."

Jim narrowed his eyes. "This thing your mother roped you into isn't going to infringe on any more of my time, is it?"

Just the thing Lilli had been worried about, her mother's request causing problems with her actual job. "Don't worry about me taking too much time to work on the benefit. Everything's in order." *I hope.*

"Not a problem as long as you get your

work done here. The Danielson account is a big deal."

Robert Danielson owned three of the biggest car dealerships in the area. He'd recently started shopping for a new marketing firm and set KLC high on his list. "I need to see how you handle it."

A test. Okay. She would pass because, first, she'd grown up with Cindy Danielson so she had an in with the family. Second, she'd already been to the dealerships and spoken with the owner numerous times. And third, if she wanted the promotion she'd have to bring in new accounts. She'd do whatever it took.

"I appreciate it, Jim. I will get the account and I won't let the fund-raiser get in the way."

"Good. Good." He shifted his stance, staying on the far side of her desk. Not good. Jim liked to stir things up before making a quick escape and leaving her to take care of the fallout. That's probably what made him a skilled motivator. "I asked about the benefit for a reason."

"And that would be?"

"Hear me out. You're my best producer and I wasn't too thrilled about you splitting your time between KLC projects and your mother's fancy party. But after some thought I realized maybe this charity event can be used to KLC's advantage."

Warning bells clanged in her mind. "How, exactly?"

"Since you're making the decisions, it wouldn't be out of the realm of your coordinator capacity to advertise our company. You could make company literature available to the people attending the benefit. You're clever enough to find ways to showcase our name without knocking people over the head with it. Just think of all those rich…I mean, generous… businesspeople who might want to use our services."

Lilli gaped at her boss. Who knew Jim could be so devious?

"Look, I would never *tell* you that you had to advertise, but as a loyal employee…"

"And, of course, KLC will make a generous donation to the cause?" Lilli asked, playing his game.

"I'd hoped we could let that slide."

"Not if you want exposure at the charity event and around town."

"Around town?"

"Sure, at the historical society offices, small businesses downtown… You know, all the places I advertise the event."

Admiration glimmered in his eyes. "You're good."

"So you're going to make a donation, right?" she asked sweetly.

He went quiet for a drawn-out moment before his calculating expression gave him away. He held out his hand. "We have a deal."

She shook his hand. "So you won't hassle me if I have to attend to historical society business?"

"Not as long as you get your work done here."

"Thanks."

"Work it hard. If we land new clients, we'll all have more job security."

So much for Jim's philanthropy.

"And, of course, I'll want free tickets to Tie the Knot."

Free? Good old Jim and his frugality.

"It's the hottest ticket in town right now. And my wife wants to go."

Ah. The real reason.

"I'll see what I can do," she said, hiding a smile as she gathered her belongings and walked with Jim to the door.

"By the way," he said as he shut off the lights before they stepped outside into the clear, fragrant spring night. "Have you finished the business forum program? We're only a few days away."

Four, to be exact.

Twice a year the Cypress Pointe Merchants Association held a business forum in St. Luke's gymnasium. In the spring, the focus stayed mainly on the businesses themselves, with workshops on how to run more efficiently, how to attract customers, anything business related. Later, in the fall, the forum opened to the public, focusing on what the community wanted as the tourist town grew larger and busier.

This year, Jim had decided KLC needed to be more visible, so he'd volunteered company resources and time to get exposure. Translated: Lilli's time and ideas. She hadn't minded because she looked at the extra work as an opportunity to show her commitment to the company.

"Pretty much. I have a few changes to make, but every business has confirmed with room for last-minute attendees." Including a call from Sanders Security a few days earlier, before she knew Sanders was Max. "All the speakers are lined up. We're good to go."

"Great. We don't need any hiccups. You know how important this is."

"I do." She said as they reached their vehicles. "I'll see you tomorrow."

As Lilli settled into her vintage Mustang, her cell phone rang. "Lilli speaking."

"Hey, Lilli, it's Donna at the shelter. Did you forget you're scheduled for tonight?"

Oh, great. With everything going on, she had indeed forgotten. She turned the key in the ignition. "Be right there."

Ten minutes later, Lilli stopped in a parking space outside the Creature Comfort animal shelter. The sun had almost set, leaving a warm evening in its wake. A perfect night to let the dogs out for a run. She locked her car and hurried inside.

"I'm here," she announced as she stepped through the door.

"Good timing," Donna told her, as she came around the corner. "I was about to take the dogs out myself."

Lilli noticed Donna wearing a dress instead of her usual shelter T-shirt and shorts. "That's right, your son has the spelling bee tonight."

"If I leave now, I'll get there in time to see him wow everyone with his mad spelling skills."

"I'm so sorry. I got caught up at work."

Donna handed Lilli the keys to the kennel. "You're here now. Lock up when you're finished." She grabbed her purse from her desk. "And Doc's office is still open, but they'll be leaving soon. A client called in late to pick up a boarded pet."

"Gotcha. Now go," Lilli shooed Donna out the door. She took a minute to acclimate herself then got busy with the task at hand. She headed to the kennel, where she was greeted by a dozen barking canines.

"Hey, guys. Get ready to work off all your stored-up energy." She retrieved the leashes from a nearby closet and went about hooking up the first four dogs. She'd learned not to take out more than that after her first ambitious walk with six energetic animals pulling at the leash. Needless to say, not pretty.

Once set, she followed the excited animals to a side door that led to a large fenced yard where the dogs could run freely. A latched door at the far end led to a pathway winding to a park. At the opposite end of the yard was Doc Williams's office. The vet's office and the shelter shared an open area of grass. The two entities worked together to board and make appointments for the animals, and to educate the public about animal health and safety. Normally Doc's office closed by six, but Lilli could still see the inside lights as she led the dogs out.

The beginning shadows of dusk enveloped the grounds, so Lilli elected to keep the dogs on the property. Normally she arrived earlier and would walk to the park, but not tonight.

As it was, she'd be here for a while yet, making sure all the dogs got exercise.

She'd removed the leashes and had just headed back to collect another group of dogs when, from the direction of the vet's office, a large canine ran toward Lilli, jumping up and nearly knocking her over. She steadied herself and rubbed the friendly dog's head. "Hey, where did you come from?"

"He's mine."

She jerked her head up to see Max's strong silhouette in the light mounted by the shelter door. Surprise, and a pleasurable jolt of anticipation, raced through her blood.

"Spying on me, Mr. P.I.?"

CHAPTER FIVE

"Private security consultant." Max stared into Lilli's pretty green eyes, which were made soft by the muted light. "More like wondering what you're doing here."

"Why? You haven't seen enough of me for one day?"

"Obviously not." The fact that he had been thinking about her had nothing to do with their paths crossing again. Although he couldn't say he was disappointed.

"Well, to answer your question, I'm volunteering. Hint. Hint."

He grimaced. "Touché."

"I told you the animal shelter is a good cause. I've worked here since high school." She straightened the leashes in her hands. "You're here because…?"

"My Lab has been at the vet's office all day. Came by to pick him up."

She tilted her head toward the Lab obediently sitting at Max's side. "Ah. The jumper."

"I like to think of Jake Riley as friendly."

"Good quality in a pet."

"I've always thought so." His gaze caught hers and he couldn't break the connection. Didn't want to.

She blinked, then said, "And since I'm working, you'll have to excuse me. I have a few more dogs waiting to get exercise."

He followed her. "You've volunteered since high school?"

"Except when I went to college. My parents wouldn't let me have a pet when I was a kid, so coming here was the next best thing."

"Pretty loyal."

"What can I say? I stick with what's important."

She corralled the next group of dogs and ushered them outside.

"Is your dog okay?"

"Now. Close call with a poisonous frog."

"Poor baby. You probably want to get him home."

"Looks like Jake Riley has other ideas." His dog scampered off to join the others. Jake would be getting a treat when they got home, because honestly, Max didn't want to take off just yet.

"Are you here alone?" he asked.

"Yep."

Now he definitely couldn't leave her.

"I think I'll stick around and help you out."

"Um, thanks." With a nod, she hurried back inside. He watched her disappear, a slight smile tugging at his lips. A bark snagged his attention and he looked out over the yard, finding Jake. The Lab loved to be in the middle of things, and he hoped there wouldn't be any unnecessary mischief. A few minutes later Lilli returned, holding a squirming puppy in her arms. The pup took one look at the action in the yard and jumped from her arms.

"Sampson, be good," she called after the frisky pup. Puffing her hair from her eyes, she sighed as she brushed multicolored dog hair off her skirt.

Max looked at her outfit. "Haven't been home yet?"

"Long work day. Starting with you."

He chuckled. "Yeah, you mentioned you were new to the charity-event coordinating job."

"My first day."

"Busy first day."

She raised a perfectly arched eyebrow. "If you would agree to volunteer, the day could end on a better note."

"Sorry. You'll have to find another groom."

"That's what I figured." She sent him a sideways glance. "Any suggestions?"

"Doesn't your mom have other names on the list to choose from?"

"No. You're it."

"I don't know whether to be flattered or terrified."

"What can I say?" She peered over his shoulder. "Sampson. No." Never close to teetering off her high heels, Lilli jogged over to the puppy busy digging and making a mess near the fence. Impressed that she didn't turn her ankle, Max followed.

She clapped her hands. "Sampson. Stop."

The puppy ignored her, his tail wagging with happiness as he dug to freedom.

"Please," she reasoned with the pup.

"I think he's got plans."

"I swear, that dog acts like a convict trying to break out of prison." Lilli pursed her lips before rolling up her sleeves and moving to the puppy. "Okay, buddy. You asked for it."

"I don't think that's a good idea."

As his words trailed off, Lilli tried to get close enough to the busy animal to grab his collar. Instead, the puppy jumped, his paw throwing up clumps of earth. Lilli tried to side-step but ended up with a face full of dirt. She froze, gasped, then lifted her hands to gingerly remove good old Mother Earth from her face.

Max couldn't control a chuckle. "Told you that wasn't a good idea."

"You'd think I'd know better. This isn't the first time Sampson and I have gotten into it."

Max walked to the puppy, snapped his fingers and pointed to the ground next to him. "Okay, buddy. Let's give the lady a break." At his strong, firm voice, the pup looked up, wagged his tail and strolled over to sniff Max.

Lilli closed her gaping mouth. "What? How?"

Max shrugged. "It's my cop tone. Works every time."

Sampson grew bored and moved on to another adventure while Lilli walked to an outdoor spigot to clean off her hands and face. Max went inside, found a clean towel and brought it out to her. She accepted it, a slight grin on her lips.

"And I thought helping my mother was messy."

"The fund-raiser?"

She patted her face dry. "I have a day job, but I promised to help my mother."

"Sometimes that can be inconvenient."

"Especially with all the things she's scheduled for the benefit. Between the loaner gowns and the jewelry, this has become bigger than I expected."

Working full time, helping her mother with the fund-raiser and still making the effort to volunteer at the animal shelter? Did she have to be so likeable? "Since, you brought it up, I should tell you I'm still waiting on the delivery time of the jewelry. Once I have confirmation, I'll let you know where we go from there."

She sighed. "This is going to be a logistical nightmare. You know, it would be a lot easier for both of us if you'd work undercover at the benefit."

Add pushy to the list.

"And I'll be the one to decide my role. It's what I'm good at. I don't let anything get in the way of doing my job."

"I never questioned that, Max," she said quietly.

True, she hadn't. But in one day she'd managed to turn his life upside down. One day? It seemed like he'd been picturing the ocean green of her eyes forever. And he couldn't help but notice again—okay for maybe the fiftieth time today—how she'd grown up to become quite a looker. Her quiet, classic beauty drew him in, against his better judgment.

Despite their clashes, he found himself intrigued by her. Just as he had been that night on the beach.

She stared at him for a long moment. The

skin under his collar grew warm. He cleared his throat. "It's nice that you do this."

"My mother always volunteered when I was growing up. Guess it's in my blood."

That, or she had a generous heart.

Max noticed that while they'd been talking, the sky had turned a deep blue with a few stars popping out. Lilli looked up and rolled her shoulders.

"I think the dogs have had enough fun time. I'm going to start rounding them up."

"Let me help."

She hesitated a moment. "Thanks."

Thirty minutes later the dogs were back in the kennel, the food bowls filled, and Lilli was turning out the lights in the office. Jake Riley sniffed around Max's truck and they stood by their cars, ready to head out.

"Thanks again," Lilli told him.

"I'll be in touch. About the jewelry."

Lilli nodded and unlocked the door, ready to climb into her sedan.

"Wait," he said.

She raised a brow.

"What happened that night?"

"On the beach?"

"Yeah."

After a long pause, she said, "Things got out

of control." She tilted her head. "You know. You were there."

Yeah. He remembered as if it was yesterday.

He'd noticed her at the bonfire, the new girl off to the side, alone, looking out of place around the regular troublemakers. He'd caught her gaze and she'd sent him a timid smile. Before he could talk himself out of it, he walked her way. His stomach jittered with nerves, unusual for him.

"I haven't seen you around here before," he'd said when he stopped at her side.

She'd shrugged. "Maybe you never looked."

"So you're saying I'm blind?"

"Could be."

He'd laughed. "If you'd been here before, I'd have never missed you."

She'd glanced up at him, her expression saying she didn't buy that line. "So what are you doing here?"

He'd jammed his hands in his shorts pockets. "Hanging out."

"Lucky for me."

His chest had hitched. "Yeah. Lucky you."

She'd looked away, then back again. "I'm Lilli."

"Max."

After the stilted introduction, they'd talked and laughed with ease, as if they'd known each other for years. It had all seemed a blur, until he led her away from the crowd to the edges of the firelight. She'd raised a brow, silently questioning his actions.

Not able to help himself, he'd leaned in to brush his lips over hers. A shock wave had hit him. This kiss, unlike any other he'd ever stolen, stirred his rebel soul.

She'd wrapped her arms around his neck. He'd circled her waist with his hands, dragging her closer as the kiss grew deeper. Lost in her arms, he'd barely noticed when everyone around them starting yelling. Lilli had broken the kiss, eyes wide in alarm. "What's going on?"

Only then had he heard the sirens.

"C'mon." He'd grabbed her hand, heading away from the beach. After a few feet Lilli had stumbled, breaking their connection. He'd tried to grab hold again but lost her in the crowd. Frantically searching, he couldn't find her, so he doubled back just in time to see her take a miscalculated turn straight into the police chief.

Max's memories faded out. He saw the question in Lilli's eyes. "We were a bunch of teenage boys out to impress cute girls by blowing stuff up at a prohibited bonfire."

"Which you had to know would alert the police." Her eyes narrowed. "You left me behind when everyone ran."

"Not on purpose. We got separated."

"You could have come back."

He ran a hand through his hair. "I was already in lots of hot water. One more mistake and I'd have been on the first bus to juvenile detention." He continued, "I did double back, but by that time the chief already had you."

"You came back for me?"

He nodded.

Her pert features softened a degree. "Still didn't help."

"Is that why you turned me in? Because I left you?"

She fiddled with her car keys. "After we were separated, I ended up with some of the other kids from the bonfire. I overheard them talking about how hanging around with you would get them all in trouble. So I decided to follow the group, but suddenly they took off and left me standing there, with the chief's flashlight shining on me. I couldn't run at that point."

"So why drop my name?"

"He started talking about calling my parents and having them pick me up from jail. I panicked. Max, I was sixteen. I'd never done anything like that before. Going to jail scared me, so I blurted out your name." She looked him straight in the eyes. "I didn't do it maliciously."

"Maybe. But you went home. I had a longer stay."

Yeah. She'd been a kid, just like him, making decisions without thinking them through. Except that night, her turning him in almost ruined his life.

"Look, Max, it's the past. I can't change anything." She glanced at her watch. "I haven't had dinner yet. Why don't we finish walking down memory lane when my stomach isn't growling?"

What could he say? He was spoiling for a fight and she didn't want to participate. Which made him even more aggravated. He didn't know what he wanted. An apology? Answers? Whatever it was, Lilli didn't seem inclined to oblige him.

When he didn't answer, she said, "See you around, Max."

He stood by the truck, watching her car ease down the road before the red lights turned out of sight. Edgy, tired from being cooped up in the office working on reports all afternoon, he didn't want to head home. A walk on the beach might settle him down.

He whistled for Jake Riley and headed the few blocks to the shore.

When it came to Lilli, he'd be crazy not to be wary. Women with lists, especially ones who took copious notes, always scared him. She'd be talking him into running around town in a tutu if he wasn't careful. You'd think after all their run-ins today, the way she'd expertly put him in his place, he'd be immune to this woman's charms. Nope. Just when he figured he'd inched under her skin, she turned it around on him. A phenomenon he didn't want to analyze, because if he did, he might do something idiotic like change his mind and volunteer for her fund-raiser. Silently, he called himself all kinds of crazy.

He strode from the concrete sidewalk into the softly shifting sand, his bootheels sinking deep. Salty air cooled his flushed skin. As he neared the shoreline, the foamy tide lapped over the sand in small waves. The bright moon shone on the undulating water.

He'd known coming back to Cypress Pointe wouldn't be easy. Hadn't wanted to dwell on it, not exactly proud of the wild teen he used to be. He hadn't been using his head back then, driven by pure emotion. Which hadn't worked out too well, especially when school officials or the local authorities called him on his truancy and mischief making.

He kicked sand into the calm water, intend-

ing to churn it up like the unwelcome feelings
swirling inside him. As much as he tried to
squelch them, memories bombarded him one
after another.

His father had died when Max turned ten.
Max had adored the man, shadowing his footsteps endlessly. Once he'd realized his father
was never coming back, Max had taken on the
role of family protector.

Single parenthood took too much out of his
mother, and a couple of years later she'd up and
left him. At twelve years old, Max had been in
danger of going into foster care until his grandmother took him in. Max, hiding the hurt of
his mother's abandonment, had generally made
life unpleasant for his grandmother, much to
his regret now. He'd wanted to take care of his
mother, but she'd walked out on him. Expecting the same treatment from his grandmother,
Laverne, he'd cut loose and done his own thing,
waiting for the day she'd turn her back on him
just as his mother had.

During his senior year in high school,
which he'd rarely attended, he'd met Denise, a
spoiled-rotten rich daddy's girl who went slum-
ming with the bad boys just to make a point to
dear old Dad. Max never could resist a challenge and had started dating her. They'd stayed
together a lot longer than he'd expected. For

a while, she'd made him forget the anger that had built up inside him after his mother left, the anger that had continually gotten him into trouble.

It had been good, until she'd started getting all clingy and whiny. When he'd wanted to slow things down, she'd ignored him. Sure, she'd achieved her goal of making Daddy mad, but she didn't want to let go of Max. He'd known her game all along, but realized too late that, deep down, he greatly resented being used.

So he'd broken up with her. She didn't take it well.

"I've put a lot of time into our relationship," Denise informed him when the crowd went to hang out at the beach.

"By using me? Not a great relationship."

"According to you, we have no longer *have* a relationship."

He clamped his mouth shut.

"I'm warning you, Max. You'd better change your mind."

"Not gonna happen."

"Fine." With a furious stomp of her foot, she glared at him one final time and sashayed off to her friends.

He'd intended to head home, tired of the drama. He went to tell his buddy, Dane, good-bye, and when he turned around he'd seen Lilli in the firelight. Of course, he didn't know her, but that didn't stop him from hanging on her every word. They talked as if only the two of them existed. And before he knew it, he'd taken her face in his hands and kissed her. He'd kissed other girls, but it had never felt like that.

He shook his head, burying the memory. He didn't want to examine how much that kiss still affected him.

Things had gone downhill after that night. The chief had him thrown in juvenile detention to make a point. The vandalism, boosting of cars and petty theft were about to catch up with him. Close to getting a permanent record, he'd decided he needed to make a change.

A few days later, the final straw came when the chief found him in the parking lot of Winn Dixie, standing next to his grandmother's car, observing a cracked windshield and slashed tires. The damage was courtesy of Denise and her crowd, who didn't appreciate him dumping one of their own.

"Is there a problem here?"

"Yes, sir."

There'd been a few times when the chief had to question him about some mischief complaints. Standing beside a car with slashed tires probably matched up with his mischievous activities in the chief's eyes. He might be wild, but he wasn't an idiot. This was Laverne's car.

"You do this, son?"

"No, sir."

He'd excluded Max as a suspect. Why the chief believed his story, Max was never sure. Maybe because the chief knew Max lived with his grandmother. She, on the other hand, had had enough and gave Max a tough-love ultimatum: straighten up or you're out.

Just as he'd expected. His grandmother didn't want him, either.

So he'd packed his things, only to find the chief waiting for him in the driveway when he tore out of the house. The older man had talked him into giving his grandmother another try. Where else was he going to go? From then on, the police chief had taken him under his wing. Probably a good thing, or he'd have ended up in jail. Later he found out Laverne had never wanted him to leave, but had believed Max needed to make a change.

So Max had turned himself around. He'd made a better life for himself. He didn't see a wife and family on the horizon—he wasn't cut out to be a family man—but he would continue to help people, as he had in the navy and on the police force. He wouldn't let little Miss Lilli Barclay or the past make him question his decisions. He'd come to Cypress Pointe to help his grandmother and build a successful business, and he didn't plan on reverting back to being that troubled kid again.

LILLI DROVE DOWN Main Street, passing the gift store where she'd bumped into Max just that afternoon. Had it only been a few hours ago? His face flashed in her mind and she didn't bother holding back a smile. Then she groaned. What was wrong with her? After their most recent conversation, how could she possibly feel the old attraction surfacing again?

A horn blared, bringing her attention back to traffic. As she eased along, she noticed all types of people lining the sidewalks, filling the trendy restaurants that had popped up since tourism increased. She cruised past Pointe Café and on impulse circled the block and turned into the parking lot adjacent to the restaurant.

Clutching her purse, she hurried inside to read the menu and order dinner when she noticed the yummy-looking desserts featured in the glass display case. On impulse, she placed an order for baklava. Sticky and sweet. Her weakness. Sighing, she sucked in her tummy to loosen the waistband of her skirt. She'd worry about her muffin top tomorrow.

She stepped outside, and had just reached a

bistro-style table when she heard, "Lilli Barclay? What are you doing here?"

She set her food down before forcing a smile and turning to the woman who'd spoken. "Marisa. Imagine running into you here." And how she wished she hadn't.

"Chandler and I decided to take a break from the wedding planning and grab a cup of coffee. He's parking the Corvette." Marisa dropped her purse on the table. "It's a good thing I ran into you. We need to discuss society business before our meeting at the country club."

Lilli didn't need any more complications tonight. Especially from her lifelong nemesis.

Before Marisa had a chance to dive in with her complaints, Chandler joined them. Handsome, rich and a successful financial investor, he was Marisa's perfect fiancé.

"Hey, babe." Chandler leaned down to brush a kiss over Marisa's high cheekbone. "Ready to get that coffee?"

Marisa smiled up at her fiancé. Boy, she could go from cranky to lovey-dovey in thirty seconds flat.

"I need to talk to Lilli first. Would you mind ordering for me?"

"Sure. No problem." He nodded at Lilli and strode away.

"So, is your mother coming home anytime

soon?" Marisa asked. Snarky personified. Snarky, but beautiful. Tonight she wore a pink silk T-shirt, ridiculously expensive designer jeans and killer heels. While Lilli still wore her work clothes covered in dog hair.

She sighed. "I'm not sure."

"It's so ironic your mother's emergency occurred right before the benefit."

Okay, dig taken. "My mother is away on family business."

A waitress approached Marisa with a mug of coffee. "Your fiancé found a table and will meet you inside when you're finished."

Preening, Marisa took the cup into her hand. "How sweet of Chandler. He's always doting on me." Marisa raised the cup to her lips to blow on the hot beverage. "So, what's this about family business?" she asked in a tone that said she didn't believe it.

How had Lilli ended up here, at this moment, talking to her worst enemy?

"Marisa, it's late and I—"

Just as Lilli spoke, Marissa choked and cried out, "This isn't what I ordered." A thundercloud formed in Marisa's eyes. "I'll be right back," she said and stomped into the café.

First Celeste and the historical society. Now Marisa. Soon enough, the club. Lilli shuddered. After practicing careful avoidance for a year, all paths were converging together into her complete and total nightmare.

She bit into the sweet dessert and sighed as it melted on her tongue, taking with it the stress of the day.

Marisa soon returned with a new coffee. "Are you looking forward to working at the club? We shared so many good times there."

Good? Miserable, more like it. Lilli had always felt out of place and dorky with the other kids at the club, strong-armed into activities that forced her to pal around with polished Marisa Vandermere. How many behind-her-back snickers had Lilli endured from a clique she didn't belong to? Too many to count.

When they were teens, Marisa had gone out with a new boyfriend every week, usually one she stole from another unsuspecting girl. Marisa had always loved a challenge. Even now, Marisa caught the eye of a young man a few tables away sitting with a date. Some things never changed.

"So, what do you want to discuss?" Lilli kept her tone light but firm. Not that she wanted to engage in this conversation, but she knew Marisa well enough to suspect the woman wouldn't leave until she'd had her say.

"I'll reschedule our committee meeting for sometime next week," Marisa blithely continued, as if her announcement was a foregone conclusion. "With your mother gone, I'll get the itinerary from Mrs. Rumpold and check the ongoing progress to find out where we are with the planning. I can take over from—"

"No."

Marisa blinked. "Excuse me?"

"There's no need. The meeting is scheduled for Saturday morning. I've been brought up to speed on the progress so far. I'll handle it."

"But…" Marisa stammered, uncharacteristically at a loss. "You aren't technically a member."

"Sure, I am." *Thanks, Celeste, for signing me up.* Lilli smiled brightly. "I've been on the roster for years."

Marisa's eyes narrowed. She clearly hadn't expected trouble from Lilli.

"My mother is in charge and she passed the job on to me. I appreciate your help, but I'll be fine."

"And you expect the ladies to follow?"

Time to draw the line in the sand. "Yes, if they want to continue being part of the fundraiser."

Marisa stared her down. Waiting for Lilli to back down? Oh, no, Lilli would not give her the satisfaction.

"We'll see about that." Marisa rose and

waved at the restaurant window. Shortly after, Chandler exited the building. Marisa took his hand to lead him away, but he paused.

"Have a nice night," he told Lilli.

"Thanks."

At least one half of the duo had manners.

With a slight smile, Lilli watched her nemesis storm away. Marisa may have had the last word, but after this run-in, Lilli decided to take the fund-raiser more seriously. What could Marisa do about that?

CHAPTER SIX

"Mom, you told me fifteen times. I can handle it."

"Remember, don't let the Vandemere women give you a hard time. They're waiting for an excuse to throw you under the bus."

"Nice visual."

"I'm just saying, watch those two. Don't let Marisa take over. She's not the coordinator, but she'll still try to run the show. Along with her mother."

"She's already tried that tactic."

"You can't let her."

"Don't worry, I have it under control."

"Those two have been trying to take over for years. Last time Marisa headed a committee she dumped all the work on everyone else. I don't want to see that happen to you."

"If she runs true to course, she'll lose interest soon. I'm not worried." Lilli paused. "Or you could come home."

Celeste went uncharacteristically quiet for a moment. "Not right now, dear."

So, something was wrong. Lilli had suspected it all along. Let's face it, her mother had never run out on a fund-raising benefit before. Why would she now?

"Mom, what's going on?"

"I need time, Lillian. Just time."

"But—"

"Let's focus on the task at hand. If you have any logistical problems, ask for Klaus, the club manager, or his assistant, Tom."

"Got it."

"Then that's everything for today. What do you think?"

"You're asking me what I think?" That never happened.

"Why, yes. You're handling things during my absence. I know it's a lot of last-minute work, but you're more than capable."

Wow. She'd never heard that, either. "It's all under control. No worries, Mom."

"Good. Show them the Barclay backbone."

"I'm getting ready to walk into the club, so I have to run. I'll let you know how it goes."

The bright Saturday morning sun blinded Lilli as she slipped out of her parked car in the Cypress Pointe Country Club parking lot. She donned her sunglasses before grabbing her overflowing tote bag. She had a million things to juggle, as well as a stomach full of butter-flies.

She hadn't slept well last night, having vi-sions of the gruff adult Max melding with the rebellious teen from that night on the beach. The same man, yet so different now.

No matter how much she wanted to deny it, she had Max Sanders on the brain. With his alluring five-o'clock shadow and smoky eyes, he'd taken up residence in her mind ever since she'd walked into his messy office with the piles of boxes, names of women on his calen-dar and his emphatic refusal to volunteer for the benefit.

The benefit. Right. She could do this while juggling her real job. Prepared and competent. The fearless leader of the ladies waiting inside.

This morning she'd taken more than a few minutes to throw an outfit together. She'd cho-sen a hot-pink pullover, white cropped pants and low-heeled sparkly sandals. Applying her makeup hadn't been a five-minute job. She'd taken her time with the cosmetics and styled her hair in a breezy, flowing style. Image was everything with these women. She'd opted for the country club look, and from what she'd seen reflected in the mirror, she'd succeeded.

Until her ruined wedding rehearsal flashed through her mind and her heart started racing.

She hesitated on the brick walkway to catch her breath, staring out over the golf course. The morning haze was burning off as the day grew warm. Lingering humidity dampened her skin and the hum of a golf cart zooming by roused her from her sinking mood. Straightening her shoulders, she marched through the etched glass front door, right into the location of her wedding nightmare.

Instead of going directly to the meeting room, she made a detour to the restroom for a last-minute check on her makeup. She'd looked fine when she left the apartment, but she couldn't chance any visible flaw or these women would pounce.

Effectively procrastinating with her side trip, she found her makeup in the same shape as when she'd left her apartment. No more excuses. *Bite the bullet and get to the meeting.* Glancing at her watch she saw she had about five minutes to spare.

Enough. Just do this.

On her way to the meeting room she passed the main event room where the benefit would be held. The same room as the rehearsal dinner. As if pushed by an invisible force, Lilli found herself entering the dim room. Scattered tables and a few chairs littered the space. The back wall of floor-to-ceiling windows was flanked by thick drapes, showcasing a beautiful view of the golf course.

A chill ran over her as she drifted back to that night....

Lilli had beamed in delight as the dreamy, romantic images of the slideshow flashed on the overhead screen. Images of her with Rob appeared in a collage set to the theme song from the movie *Titanic*. Overlapping photos featured their childhood then moved into the year they dated. Teary-eyed with happiness, Lilli had taken Rob's hand in hers, resting her head on his shoulder. The most perfect ending to their rehearsal dinner, to be followed by the most perfect fairy-tale wedding the next day.

"Lilli, we have to talk," Rob had whispered urgently in her ear.

She'd squeezed his hand with excitement. "Just another minute. Mom went to so much trouble to put this beautiful tribute together. We have a lifetime to talk after all the celebrating."

"But, Lilli, I've been trying to talk to you all night, please—" Rob had begun until Lilli hugged herself closer to him. She'd breathed in the scent of his musky cologne. The fine fabric of his suit brushed against her cheek. The months spent planning this wedding were finally proving worthwhile as the inevitable drama receded into relief, then celebration. After tomorrow, she and Rob would enjoy their new lives together without bickering over every little life decision.

"Shall I compare thee to a summer's day?" Celeste had recited Shakespeare's famous sonnet after the music stopped. The words to the romantic poem appeared on the screen while her mother spoke into the microphone she'd been holding.

Rob had stirred beside her. "Lilli, please."

She pulled back, frowning. "Can't it wait?"

Rob had responded with a sigh and sat, rigid. He'd been preoccupied and moody all week, blaming his behavior on wedding stress. What with the year-long planning and his recent job promotion at the law firm, she couldn't blame him. She'd been caught up in the whirlwind herself. In fact, they hadn't talked in weeks. Wasn't that to be expected when emotions ran high as the big day drew closer?

"Okay, Lilli. I'll let you have your moment," he'd muttered.

He'd let go of her hand to sip his iced tea just as the opening strains of "Spring" from Vivaldi's *Four Seasons* began. Lilli turned her attention back to the screen. Her heart swelled at the picture—the two of them at the beach, arm in arm, silhouetted against a dramatic apricot-hued sunset.

Images of wedding gowns, roses and chocolates had appeared on the screen, leading to the grand finale of the presentation. Lilli turned back to Rob, startled that he'd disappeared. She looked over her shoulder. Scanning the room, she'd finally spied him beside her mother, deep in heated conversation.

"Well, why didn't you say so?" Celeste admonished, not realizing she still held the live microphone close by. "Of course, go right ahead."

Rob shook his head.

"Everyone," Celeste said. "The groom-to-be would like to say something to the bride-to-be. Apparently, they haven't had a moment alone for him to say what's in his heart."

The room had filled with hushed excitement as Lilli leaned back in her linen-covered chair, waiting to see what kind of romantic surprise Rob had in store for her.

Rob's gaze had met hers and he paled. Letting out a groan of frustration, he sidled past his future mother-in-law to the keyboard used to run the presentation.

The screen went blank.

Rob typed furiously.

Lilli, along with everyone in the large ballroom, waited in anticipation for the heartfelt words that would appear on the screen.

Lilli, you are a wonderful girl, the words began, making everyone in the room sigh simultaneously. Lilli had felt a lump of emotion rise in her throat.

But, came the next word.

Followed by, *I have to beak up with you.*

"Beak?" her mother asked directly into the microphone. She exchanged a confused glance between the screen and Lilli, who sat frozen in her seat. "What does *beak* mean?"

Lilli frowned. *Beak?* Did he mean…?

"Break," Rob belted out. "Lilli, I have to break up with you," he said from across the room. "Before our family and friends, I have to break up with you."

Lilli stared at him in horror as excited murmurs rose throughout the room. Her mind went blank until Rob had managed to pull Lilli to a corner of the room.

"Why?" Lilli had asked, her chest tight, her eyes hot with unshed tears.

"I can't do this."

"But we have the church reserved. The reception hall booked. Our whole future ahead of us."

"That's just it, a future with you working."

"What are you talking about?" she'd asked, truly confused.

"I thought I wanted a wife. A family. But instead I just feel pressured."

"Is this about me working? I can cut back for a while, until we get used to—"

"That's just it. I don't know what I want right now. The pressure of this wedding is just too much."

She'd glanced around the room full of rapt faces hanging on the engaged couple's every word. "And you've decided that right now is the time to discuss this?"

"What better time? After we say our vows? You've been putting me off, what with all the wedding lists and plans. Everything has to be just so, according to your timetable. What about what I want?"

She'd blinked and looked at him. Really looked at him. Is this how married life would be? Rob changing his mind about their lives when the pressure became too much for him?

"So this is your decision?" She refused to go back to a life where other people dictated her every move. Her parents had done that most of her life. Her husband would not.

Rob straightened his shoulders. "I'm sorry, Lilli."

"I know, Rob." She hadn't understood, but knew he meant those words.

Rob had turned on his heel and walked out of her life, leaving her with a room full of people who wanted answers, a wedding to undo and facing the realization that she'd almost made a huge mistake.

Now, a year later, Lilli slowly backed out of the room, her palms damp, disturbed by her memories. Rob may have taken off after embarrassing her, but she'd learned one thing for sure. Never, ever again would she allow herself to be that thoroughly humiliated.

She shook her head, removing the lingering visuals and pulling herself together. When she finally entered the room to conduct the meeting, the chatter faded. Lilli faced the women before her, suddenly at a loss for words. Each face held a different emotion. Curiosity. Doubt. Disdain. Now that she had to actually run this meeting, she couldn't think of a thing to say.

It only took one condescending look from Marisa to get her mind in gear.

She took a deep breath and said, "Thank you so much for meeting with me this morning. I have reviewed my mother's initial lists, which Mrs. Rumpold kindly put together." She paused as the ladies gave the older woman much-deserved applause. "I wanted to touch base with you all and review some items."

She pulled out the master list she'd made last night with all the information Celeste left her along with some ideas of her own.

"From what I can tell, the committees are full and we still have a lot of work ahead of us to make Tie the Knot a success."

"The committees were filled long before you came on the scene," Sissy Vandermere, Marisa's mother, informed Lilli before she could say another word. Just as Celeste had warned her.

Unruffled, Lilli said, "Yes, I see that, so I'd like to get a status report today."

"Status reports? Really, Lilli, I've been involved with this project from the start. I know more than you do about the lists and committees." Sissy crossed her arms over her chest and pouted. Lilli half expected the woman to stand up and stomp her feet in a childish tantrum, screaming, "My way or the highway!"

Lilli cleared her throat, trying to ignore the interruption. "Humor me." She scanned the list. "I have decorations, donations, club liaison and publicity."

"I can take care of the details as well as you." Sissy straightened, fussed with her hair and took her bossy attitude up a notch. "I'm club liaison, since everyone knows we're members here."

No one needed the reminder.

Lilli continued. "The club has posted the date and time of Tie the Knot." She glanced at her notes then asked Sissy, "When can we have access to the event room?"

Sissy looked around the room, then at Lilli. "Excuse me?"

"When will they let us in to get the room ready for the benefit?"

Sissy nearly sniffed her answer. "I didn't ask. I assumed we'd have it whenever we wanted."

"We need to know so we can plan accordingly, especially if there is another event scheduled close to ours. We need to have the tables in place in order to set the stage, decorate and position the silent auction table—"

"Your mother takes care of that," Sissy said, a red bloom to her cheeks.

"My mother isn't here—I am. And your job is to coordinate with the club, unless you can't handle that."

Silence filled the room as the tension ratcheted higher. The ladies looked from Lilli to Sissy and back again.

Sissy's back went up and her eyes narrowed. "I'll get back to you with those details."

"Thank you. Now, let's move on to decorations."

A petite woman raised her hand. "I'm Mary Gibbons. That's my committee, but I'd like to talk to you later, if possible."

Lilli glanced at the worried frown on the woman's face. "No problem. We'll get together after the meeting." She gave Mary a reassuring smile before looking at her list. After checking her notes, she said, "Silent auction?"

"That would be me." The polished voice sounded from the back of the room. Lilli groaned when Marisa coyly raised her hand. Just what she needed. The Vandermere mother/daughter tag team.

"Marisa. How are you doing with donations for the auction?"

Marisa shifted in the seat beside her mother. Dressed to the nines, she sported designer jeans and an expensive top, not a bleached hair out of place, her makeup artfully applied. "I have some wonderful items lined up."

"Can I have your list?"

"List?"

"Yes, so we know exactly what is being auctioned off."

Marisa glared at Lilli. "It's all in my head."

"I need a list."

"Fine," she snapped. "I'll get one to you."

And I won't hold my breath waiting. "Thanks." Lilli smiled politely and moved on. "Mrs. Rumpold and I will be working on matching the models with the volunteer grooms. I also arranged for a harp player. It will add to the atmosphere." When no one argued with her, Lilli hid a smile. Except for the Vandermeres, so far so good.

Mrs. Rumpold clasped her hands together and addressed the ladies. "The display wedding dresses are to arrive at the historical society office this afternoon. Let's not forget that we have them due to Lilli's connection."

The ladies murmured their thanks.

"Are all the grooms accounted for?" asked a woman Lilli didn't know.

"Not yet," she hedged. "I still have a few calls to make." To whom, she still hadn't figured out.

The women began to chatter about the lineup of men slated to play groom.

"I know the mayor volunteered. Who else?" another woman asked.

Mrs. Rumpold stood up. "There's the fire chief, the owner of Pointe Café, Tim from the insurance company, Dane Peterson and the police chief, of course. But I'm holding out for Max Sanders."

"Max Sanders? That name sounds familiar." Mrs. Weston said.

"He a security consultant," Lilli told her.

"No, it's not that."

"Yes, that's his business."

"No, I mean that's not where I know him from."

"He's been gone from Cypress Pointe for many years."

Mrs. Weston sat straight in her chair. "I remember now. He tried to steal my husband's car."

"That was years ago," Mrs. Rumpold told her.

Mrs. Weston shot Mrs. R. a dirty look. "And you think he's an appropriate choice?"

"Oh, he's more than appropriate," Mrs. Rumpold gushed. Lilli mentally rolled her eyes. "He's a security consultant now. I don't see a problem."

"Problem? He's a known thief."

"Reformed," Mrs. Rumpold piped in, defending her man.

"Please, ladies." Lilli tried to calm them down. She couldn't tell them he'd be working security at the benefit, because she hadn't convinced him to be a groom yet. And when, not if, he agreed, she didn't want to blow his cover.

"Max has been vetted by my mother and the chief. I don't think we have to worry."

The women volleyed questions at Lilli that she had no answers for. When had she lost control? At the mention of Max's name, that's when.

Sissy spoke up again. "My husband would love to be added to the groom list."

Lilli jumped on this change of topic. "I'll add him to the stand-by list."

Marisa raised her hand. "Chandler and I have already been selected as the final couple, you know, since we'll be married soon."

"Isn't it bad luck for the groom to see the wedding dress before the wedding?" Mrs. Rumpold asked.

Marisa glared at the woman. "It's not my actual wedding dress for the big day with Chandler. It's the other one."

The "other one" meaning the dress from the previous engagement. Yes, Marisa had been engaged. Twice. Before Chandler. The one she would wear for the fashion show had been created from antique lace and satin, so it fit the theme of the fashion show.

Marisa continued. "You won't be changing the lineup, will you Lilli?"

Lilli's teeth hurt at Marisa's sweet-as-molasses tone. Okay, she could argue on principle or choose her battles. Letting the couple remain the finale was a concession she could easily make. "The lineup will stay the same, Marisa."

Marisa's eyebrow angled. In suspicion? If she expected a fight, Lilli decided not to give it to her. She needed all her energy for another battle on another day.

Fortunately the topic of Max never surfaced again. After discussing several more items on her agenda, Lilli declared the meeting adjourned. The ladies mingled and chatted before leaving. Most of them came up to tell Lilli she was doing a good job in her mother's place. Finally, she met with Mary Gibbons.

"I have to say, I'm a bit overwhelmed with the decorations. I'm not sure where to start. Your mother envisioned the room decorated like a wedding reception. She is very particular, and I don't want to let her down."

An idea popped into Lilli's head. "I may have a solution."

Mary nodded.

"My good friend Jewel has expressed an interest in helping us. She's very artsy and I think you might work well together. I'll set up a meeting. How does that sound?"

Mary took Lilli's hand. "Now I know why your mother asked you to run things while she's away."

"Thanks."

"Marisa has been circling like a vulture since the moment your mother left town, but thankfully Celeste had the smarts to bring you in. Honestly, if Marisa had her way, this benefit would be a catastrophe."

The compliment warmed Lilli's heart.

Finally the room emptied out. Lilli pulled her cell phone from her purse and dialed Jewel. "You're officially in."

A whoop sounded from the other end.

"Get busy with your ideas. Remember, classic wedding." Lilli explained that Jewel would work with Mary. "Gotta run. I'm off to meet the curator who is delivering the designer wedding dresses. I'll call you later."

Lilli gathered her belongings and stopped by the club office, asking to speak to the events coordinator. Sure enough, Sissy hadn't made arrangements for the group to come in and decorate prior to the benefit. Lilli talked to the savvy woman and felt more secure that things would indeed go well.

"Is Klaus in his office? I want to touch base with him before the benefit."

"He's not there right now, but his assistant, Tom, can help you."

"That's okay. I'll make arrangements to see him next time I'm here."

She headed for the exit, only to see Max walking down the hallway with Klaus. He stopped before her, his tangy cologne invading her senses. Dark hair fell over his forehead and his lips formed a kind of crooked smile.

"What are you doing here?" she asked.

"Business."

She stared at him blankly.

"You know, for my security company."

"Oh, yes, right." *Stop talking!*

Klaus, a tanned, impeccably dressed man in his fifties, held out his hand. "Miss Barclay. Your mother has been in touch."

Of course she had.

Max stood beside her and she noticed he had abandoned the usual T-shirt and jeans for a pair of black slacks matched with a white button-down shirt. She was glad she'd taken a few extras minutes dressing this morning, even though he probably wouldn't notice.

"Something wrong?" he asked.

"Why would you ask?"

"Because you're frowning."

"I am?"

"Can't you tell?"

She frowned harder. "Apparently not."

Klaus discreetly cleared his throat. "Max, call me if you need anything."

"Thanks, Klaus. I'll be in touch when we get closer to the event."

Klaus nodded to Lilli. "I'm free to talk now."

Lilli smiled at him. "Give me five?"

"Of course. I'll be in my office."

As Klaus walked away, Lilli let out a long breath. Bad enough dealing with the Vandermeres, but running into Max? Frosting on the proverbial wedding cake.

"Tough morning?"

"Gee, how'd you guess?"

"Wasn't that hard."

"Then pat yourself on the back for such an in-depth piece of investigating."

He chuckled. "Did you know your cheeks get all flushed when you tell me off?"

"Which would be almost every time I run into you."

"Yeah. We need to work on that."

"Look, I'm sorry Max. I have a lot on my plate right now."

His eyes narrowed.

"What?" she asked.

"You're getting all prickly again."

She rubbed her temple. "I'm going to call it a day."

"That's going to be a problem."

"Why?"

"I have the details you'll need about the Wingate collection."

"Is that why you're here with Klaus?"

He hesitated. "Partly."

"If you were meeting him to talk about the collection, why didn't you include me?"

"You were in your own meeting."

"You still could have told me."

Max ran a hand through his hair. "Lilli, it's not like I'm running off to meetings and purposely leaving you behind. I had the appointment set with Klaus on a completely different matter. The information about the collection had just become available so we talked about it. It's my job, remember?"

How could she forget? "Okay. Fine."

"Listen, I have some work here, but I'll be finished by one. Why don't you come by my office and we'll talk about security for the event."

"One o'clock." She turned to walk down the hallway, but not before she heard, "Pesky woman," muttered in Max's deep voice.

CHAPTER SEVEN

TORN BETWEEN WALLOWING in memories of her emotional wedding rehearsal and driving far, far away from the country club to escape the heaviness around her heart, Lilli finally calmed down enough to grab lunch before heading to her appointment with Max.

As she climbed the stairs to his office, her stomach fluttered. Great. Maybe she was coming down with a case of food poisoning.

She opened the door to find Max at his secretary's desk reading some papers. He looked up, his easy smile making her stomach flutter even more.

"Thanks for stopping by."

"You said you had an update?"

"Yes. C'mon back to my office."

She followed, her steps slow, trying to convince herself she could talk Max into changing his mind about the volunteer groom job. Since she'd been striking out in that area, she needed him to say yes before time ran out to find a replacement.

"Have a seat."

She moved to the same chair she'd sat in mere days before. The good old days. Before her Tie the Knot coordinator duties got more complicated. "So," she said in her clipped, business tone. "Bring me up to speed."

"Let's start at the beginning. Initially your mother contacted me to evaluate security for the bridal gowns to be exhibited at the historical society office, and requested an upgrade on the existing security system at the office. I put together a report, she signed off on it and I installed the new system last week."

"Makes sense."

"With the jewelry being displayed at the country club," Max continued to explain, "Klaus needed club security evaluated. I didn't involve you because I knew you were holding your committee meeting and didn't want to bother you."

"Fair enough." Still, she felt like he was holding back.

Stop. He has a job to do. That's all.

"The Wingate collection will be delivered to the club a few days before the event. It will be kept in the safe at the country club until the benefit. After that, if your mother insists on displaying it at the historical society office, I'll make additional arrangements for a full-time security guard. I'm hoping your mother, or Mrs. Wingate, will realize that keeping the collection here in town is not a great idea."

"Sounds like you have every scenario accounted for."

"Always."

"Except for one thing."

He gave her a doubtful look. "Which is?"

"Since you're the only security business in town, won't guests think you're working at the benefit as some kind of guard, watching the collection?"

"And I will be."

She shook her head.

"You have a better idea?"

Oh, yeah, she did. "You need a guard, but not you."

"And why is that?"

"Because people expect that. What they don't expect is for you to show up as a volunteer groom. Anyone who might consider stealing the collection will think your attention is elsewhere. But really, you'll have a better feel for the crowd if you are one of them.

"I know we already talked about you going undercover. You could move around, mingle, talk to guests and get a feel for who you might need to watch while another guard stands watch beside the collection all night."

His eyes narrowed but he didn't say a word.

"Even better, what if you're a groom and you have a date?"

"A date? Won't I be paired up with a bride?"

"Yes, but she doesn't necessarily have to be your date for the entire evening. We just match you up with a bride to walk with down the runway during the fashion show. But if we go together, you can think of it as us working as a team."

"You're kidding, right?"

"Nope." She held up three fingers. "Am I desperate to get you to be a groom? Yes. Concerned about the collection? Yes. Willing to pretend we're together for the night? Yes, again. All in the name of making the night go smoothly."

"And if I say no? Again?"

"You're a smart businessman, Max. Despite our past, this is a perfect option. Please don't let your grudge against me keep you from securing the collections."

He rolled his chair away from the desk at an angle to stare out the window behind him. Lilli folded her hands together, squeezing hard as she hoped he'd see her point. It made sense. Surely he'd see that, too?

Finally, he faced her again. She tried to quell her excitement at the resigned look on his face.

"You're right, Lilli. Undercover is my best shot at surveillance." He stopped. Ran a hand through his hair. "As much as it pains me to say yes, I'll do the volunteer groom thing because it does work best."

Lilli bit her lower lip to keep from saying "I told you so." She'd gotten him to agree. That's all that mattered.

"I'm glad you could see this my way. It's only one night, but it will be worth it in the end."

"One night that will feel like forever."

"Maybe you can have a little fun at the same time?"

"Fun? I take my job very seriously, Lilli."

His somber eyes met hers and she tried to backpedal. "Of course you do. I would never presume otherwise."

"Fine. As long as we have this straight. It's only business."

"Right. Business. Mutually helping each other out."

"So, we're officially working together." He didn't sound thrilled.

"That would be correct," she said, infusing her voice with enthusiasm. "Well, I should get going." She stood on shaky legs. Talk about being out of her comfort zone. Now she was going to work closely with Max, the most attractive man she'd seen in…forever. And she had a date…sort of.

But what happened after the benefit? Did they go back to being polite business acquaintances who said hello when they passed on the street, but nothing more? Her glum reaction told Lilli she was getting way ahead of herself.

"Listen," Max said, stopping her before she had a chance to escape. "About the other night."

"The other night?"

"At the animal shelter."

"Yes?"

"Thanks for clearing up what happened the night we met at the bonfire. It'll make things easier as we move forward in the work process."

Work process. Why did that distinction bother her?

"Sure," she answered, pasting on a fake smile, ready to make her getaway. "Anything else I should know about? I don't like going into any business arrangement without all the facts."

"That covers it for now."

Max rose and she followed him to the outer office. He opened the door and she brushed against him as she passed by. His body heat made her flustered all over again.

Her eyes met his, and she could have sworn

she saw heat flash there before he schooled his features. Gone was the cute, dangerous boy she met years ago. The teasing, maddening Max. In his place stood a very capable, very concerned male. A male who, by his sheer presence, made her heart pound and her good sense fly out the window.

She stepped away, putting much-needed distance between them. She had to get to the historical society office anyway. The curator would have arrived with the display wedding dresses and Lilli wanted to talk to her old friend and personally thank her for delivering the collection.

With a curt nod, she hurried down the stairs and walked to the next block. Her heart pounded as though she'd run a marathon. This physical response only happened around Max. She needed to get a grip, especially since she worked with him now.

She had to deal with this crazy attraction, be professional as they came, if she wanted to earn his respect.

Having made that determination, she entered the historical society office to find Mrs. Rumpold speaking to a woman holding a garment bag. She smiled and walked their way.

"Lilli, you're here for the unveiling." Mrs. R. waved her over.

"Gab," Lilli said to her friend. "So good to see you."

The attractive woman with sleek black hair and sparkling sapphire-blue eyes hugged Lilli. "It's been way too long."

"It has. We need a girls' night out to reminisce."

"And catch up on our current lives."

"It's a date." Lilli nodded to the rolling clothing rack holding multiple garment bags. "So, what have we got here?"

"Some of Renata's all-time favorite designs, as well as other designer gowns she's acquired for her own personal collection through the years. She personally selected each one." Gabrielle finished unzipping the bag she held. "I think you'll be pleased."

Lilli watched as Gabrielle and Mrs. R. removed the delicate gown and placed it on the dress form. White satin and flowing tulle.

Hiding her distress at yet another painful wedding reminder, she hurried into her mother's office with the excuse she needed to make a phone call.

"Pull it together," she muttered. Lilli grabbed a tissue and collided with the tidy well-organized desk. A lone picture frame toppled over. Afraid she might have broken the glass, Lilli righted it, expecting to see a photo of Pookie, her mother's bow-toting Pekinese. Instead, she nearly dropped the ornate frame in surprise.

The picture of her was taken about two years ago. Lilli had hired a professional photographer to take pictures before her wedding. Her mother had liked the pose, so Lilli had given her an eight-by-ten, never expecting that Celeste would place it on her desk. Since the picture had been taken, Lilli had darkened her shoulder-length hair from blond to a rich reddish-chestnut with chunky golden highlights.

Lilli angled the frame back on the desk, just as it had been before. With a sigh, she realized that although Celeste's fund-raising forays were important to her, so was Lilli. Sure, they'd had their ups and downs over the years, but she had to admit that her mother keeping a picture of her at work touched her heart. With that came the resolve to work this benefit hard so her mother would come back to a success.

Realizing she'd stayed in the office too long, Lilli straightened her shoulders and walked out to the main room. Gabrielle had placed another gown on a dress form. And still the sight made Lilli's chest ache.

She stayed for another half hour, catching up with Gabrielle. Finally, she said, "Ladies, I'm afraid I have to leave. I have so much work to catch up on."

Gabrielle looked her way. "On a Saturday?"

"Yes. But I promise to get back soon to see the full display. You're right, the pieces are incredible."

Gabrielle glanced at the gowns, then met Lilli's gaze. Behind the other woman's smile, Lilli noted sadness in her eyes. What was it about weddings that brought out angst in people? If Lilli asked, she'd probably get another brokenhearted wedding story. Having lived that story once was more than enough.

"Just sign off on the collection and you're good to go."

Lilli hesitated, the full impact of being responsible for the beautiful dresses making her think twice. Then she remembered how important this was to her mother and signed the paper.

"Before you leave, I have something for you," Mrs. Rumpold said. She hurried to her desk, searched through the mess and came back to place a small item in Lilli's hand. "I had a key made for you. Now you can come and go from the office anytime you please."

Lilli's fingers closed around the cool metal. Mixed emotions swamped her. On the one hand, she felt honored. As if she'd been accepted into a special club and now belonged.

On the other, she felt the never-ending burden of responsibilities for the benefit grow heavier.

"Thank you."

"You've earned it, my dear."

Before she could tear up again, she left the building, wondering if she'd ever regain her love of weddings.

SHE'D REELED HIM IN. Hook, line and sea-green eyes.

As much as he wouldn't admit it to Lilli, she was right. He did need to keep watch on the collections at the benefit, and acting as a groom would solidify his cover. He'd resigned himself to that before the meeting, but there was no way he'd let her think she won this little battle.

As a volunteer he'd have access not only to the guests, but also fellow grooms and brides, and the country club staff, just as Lilli had pointed out. They'd let their guard down, making it easier for Max to watch for any suspicious behavior that posed a threat to either collection.

He'd already asked one of the chief's officers to work with him the night of the event, so he'd have his obvious security guard in place.

He also had a date. Not that he couldn't get one himself, but Lilli made that part easy for him. She must be excellent at her job, given the ease with which she'd talked him into her plan, so sure of herself.

He could appreciate that, but his admiration went hand in hand with a big dose of wariness. He needed to stay focused on the plan, not on how good Lilli smelled, especially when she passed him in the doorway and all he wanted to do was kiss her.

Nope. No matter how alluring she was, he had to work with Lilli, and he couldn't afford to get distracted. He needed to build a name for Sanders Security, and allowing the jewelry collection to be stolen while he drooled over a beautiful woman was not the way to accomplish his goal.

Max spent the next few hours writing up an analysis for a new country club security system for Klaus. This was really his first big job, and he had Lilli and her mother to thank for that. If he hadn't been involved with the charity event, he never would have gone to the club to discuss storing and displaying the jewelry collection.

Klaus informed him that the board had decided to upgrade the club security system after a recent rash of thefts. Klaus wondered if it was an inside job and wanted Max to present a new security plan to the board. Max couldn't be happier about the opportunity. Between that and the potential client he'd met through Klaus the same day, his business prospects were looking up.

Klaus had introduced Max to Ned Rawlings, a local resident who owned a nationwide shipping business. His business had grown quickly in the past few years, and with it, security concerns at his various warehouses. Max had pitched Sanders Security right on the spot. Liking what he heard, Ned had given Max his card and told him to call his office and set up an appointment. If Max landed Ned as a client, this would move his business to the next level sooner than he'd anticipated.

Finishing the report, he glanced at his watch. Too late on a Saturday for any new business. He swiveled in his chair, propping his booted feet on the windowsill. It didn't take long for Lilli to enter his thoughts.

When was the last time a woman had grabbed his attention so completely? *That night, twelve years ago. Face it*—Lilli had gotten under his skin. Then and now.

She'd looked great today, in a cute outfit that highlighted her curvy body, her hair framing her pretty face, her floral scent setting his senses on fire. He lost all rational thought when she was around.

Women. Couldn't live without them, couldn't forget their perfume.

He gathered a bunch of papers together, trying to dispel the images of Lilli that continued to tinker on the edges of his mind. He needed a diversion.

Time to go Bart hunting.

He hooked up his spy-cam equipment before leaving the office. His interest in technology went way back, so when he'd decided to go into business for himself, security and surveillance had seemed like the obvious choice, especially with his experience in law enforcement. Chasing after Bart might earn him a paycheck and a reputation, but that end of the business didn't interest him any longer. He'd chased enough criminals in his years as a cop. Now he wanted a different challenge and hoped to find it in Cypress Pointe.

He exited his office building, stepping into another picture-perfect spring afternoon. Odds were pretty good that Bart would be busy relieving the tourists of their personal belongings. This close to dinnertime, he should be right in the thick of things, especially while folks went out for a bite to eat and meandered down Main Street to window-shop. With a determined stride, Max left his office and stepped onto the sidewalk, smack into tourist central.

Making his way along the thoroughfare, Max searched for his target. Bart's MO was to chat up unsuspecting marks as they made their way to the numerous restaurants dotting the street. It took him all of ten minutes to find his man. Bart sat on a sidewalk bench, stopping folks to talk. As a couple strolled by, Max saw the moment Bart focused on his next target.

Max moved closer as Bart began to stroll behind the man and his wife. The couple stopped at an ice cream vendor. Max saw the man pull his wallet from his back pocket. Bart bumped into him. A classic pickpocket move. Only Bart didn't take off. He stopped and bent down, as if retrieving something from the ground.

At this point, Max came upon the scene. Bart looked over. His eyes grew wide and he started to rise. Too late. Max's clapped his hand on Bart's shoulder and pushed him away from the couple. In the old days, Max would have yanked Bart by the shirt collar and dragged him to headquarters, not worried if the guy went kicking or screaming, but he wasn't a cop anymore. Despite the trouble Bart had been giving him, Max restrained himself. Especially now. He had a professional reputation to maintain.

"Don't even think about it."

"But I—"

He snatched the wallet from Bart. "The buck stops here, my friend."

Bart grabbed at it. "What're you talking about?"

Max opened the leather billfold searching for ID. "You're Walter P. Klingman, fifty-three years old, from Pontiac, Michigan?"

Yeah. Bart had to be a whole nineteen years old.

"You got it wrong. The guy dropped his wallet and I picked it up for him."

"Helped yourself is more like it. I should drag you over to the station right now."

"I didn't do anything."

"From where I was standing, you were holding the wallet."

Bart squirmed.

"Look, the Merchants Association wants this to stop. You've managed to tick off the wrong people."

"So why are you telling me this instead of hauling me to the station?"

"I'm going to in a minute. I wanted to give you a friendly warning to stop bothering folks." He paused for a moment, choosing his next words carefully. "Bart, you've got to get a life. Something else to focus your attention on. A better job. School. A girlfriend. Something other than the way you're headed."

Bart turned red.

"You have a girlfriend?"

"No girlfriend." Defensive. "Do you?"

Lilli's pretty face flashed in his mind. *Not going there.* "We're talking about you, Bart. Look, I'm telling you this because you need a new direction."

"Like where? On a bus out of town?"

"Is that what you want?"

Bart's lips closed tight.

Why did the guy's reaction matter so much? Maybe Max wanted to help Bart because he saw a little of his old self in the younger man. Max had run wild, when what he'd needed was someone to care about him. He'd been so bent on destruction he hadn't listened to the one person who loved him unconditionally. Gram had loved him no matter what he did. When that finally sank in, he took the first step toward changing his life. Once pointed in the right direction, Max had done well. Bart could certainly do the same.

"I've heard about you," Bart said. "About how you used to be a troublemaker. So I checked you out and found out about your cool security business."

"It is cool. And I got there by working hard. How can I get you to see you're headed down a dead-end road?"

Bart stared over Max's shoulder for a long time before giving Max an answer. "How about you take me to the church?"

"Excuse me? Did you say the church?"

Bart's shoulders squared. "Yeah, I did."

Of all the things Bart could have said to him, this never even would have made the list.

He sighed over the corner he'd painted himself into. "I guess that would be the place to learn you aren't supposed to steal."

Bart blinked. "Not for the service. For the business forum at St. Luke's gymnasium tomorrow afternoon."

Max started at the younger man. "Business forum?"

"Don't tell me you haven't heard about it, since the Merchants Association is your boss."

Max knew. He'd had his secretary register him last week. In light of his need to network, he wanted face time with the community. "I know about it. So?"

"We should go together. Show people you're good at your job. I'm like free publicity."

"I don't think they'd see it that way."

"They would if I was part of your business."

Max raised his eyebrows. "You're not part of my business."

"Sure I am. Think of me as your first success story."

"After I put you in jail?"

"I thought we could skip that part."

Max wondered when he had lost control of the conversation.

"You just said I need something more exciting in my life. Like working for you. You know, to give me direction. Keep me out of trouble."

"I'm not hiring,"

"I could intern."

Hmm. Max took a good look at Bart. The earnest expression on the young man's face made him consider the possibility. "Intern?"

"The chief told me all about how you were opening a security business, and I've been thinking that your side of the law is better than what I've been doing. I could learn the ropes from you. And I'm a whiz on the computer. No one can top my skills."

Max had his own skills, but extra help might come in handy.

"So we'll go to the forum?" Bart asked.

"I haven't said yes yet."

"But you will, because like it or not, you're looking out for me."

"What makes you think that?"

"If you weren't, you'd have hauled me in without all this talking. Besides," he said almost shyly, "there's this girl."

"Huh. So there *is* a girl."

"She'll be there. I haven't had the nerve to ask her out, what with my reputation and all, but if I set a new course for myself, she might take a chance."

Max blew out a long breath. If he agreed to this internship, he'd have to work with Bart on a daily basis. Someone had to cut the guy a break, just like the chief had when he'd helped an angry teen realize trouble would never get him anywhere good in life. Max had listened. Maybe Bart would do the same. Still, the prevailing question lingered. Could he trust Bart?

"Here's the deal. I'll go along with this internship as long as you're on time and ready to work every day."

The younger man's eyes lit up. "I can do that."

"No more following tourists around."

"Okay."

"Attending the forum is out, though. You're going to have to prove yourself, and that takes time."

Bart went silent, as if pondering the weightiness of his decision. Max remembered the same moment in his life, when he'd finally made the right choice. When he walked away from trouble and began his journey down a better path.

"Now, let's go to police station."

Bart's face fell. "But you just took me on."

"Yes, but you have a wallet you need to return."

"I'm telling you, I wasn't stealing. The guy dropped it and I was gonna give it back to him when you stopped me."

"Like I haven't heard that before." Max grabbed Bart's arm, pushing him down the sidewalk. "I need proof, so my client can see I did my job by nabbing you in the act."

They'd walked a few yards when two boys on skateboards careened down the sidewalk. Max veered out of the way, but Bart stayed put. As the boys skimmed by, one decided to cut directly between Max and Bart. Max jumped back and the wallet fell from his hand. Once the boys passed, Bart bent down to retrieve the wallet then turned to run in the opposite direction.

"So much for a new leaf," Max muttered as he took off after Bart, rounding the nearest corner. Nothing. "This is not happening."

Hands on hips, he stood there, shaking his head in disbelief. Trying to decide his next course of action, he heard someone yell, "That's my wallet, officer."

Max turned in time to find Bart handing the wallet to the older man.

TEN MINUTES LATER Max explained his story to the on-duty officer at the police station. The chief showed up, trying hard not to laugh.

"I'm done with this Merchants Association gig," Max groused in way of greeting.

The chief waved off the officer interviewing Max and led him to his office. "Bart again?" he asked after closing the door.

"Yeah. Almost had the goods on him."

"Enough proof to close the case?"

"If he really picked the guy's pocket."

The chief sat behind his desk, rested his elbows on the arms of his chair and steepled his fingers over his chest. His shoulders shook in a hearty chuckle. "You know why you can't catch him, don't you?"

Max shrugged.

"Same problem I have. You like him."

"Talk about a conflict of interest."

"So how did you get hauled down here?" the chief asked as if he didn't know. The man knew everything that went on in Cypress Pointe.

"I had to confirm his story. When Bart picked the wallet up from the ground, he told me he was going to return it."

"You believed him?"

"'Course not. But we started having this conversation and, long story short, he ended up doing the right thing."

Silence filled the room for several moments while Max tried to figure out if Bart really had planned to return the wallet as he claimed. Bottom line: he did the right thing. Max should be happy, but couldn't help wondering if he'd made a mistake making Bart his intern.

The chief's perceptive eyes pinned Max. "Looks to me like you've got something on your mind."

Max hesitated before saying anything to the Chief, but knew the older man would weasel Max's thoughts out of him sooner or later. "I told Bart he could intern for me."

"Didn't know you were lookin' for an intern."

"I'm not."

Surprise lit the chief's eyes. "Didn't see that coming." He picked up a pen and drummed it on the desk. "Intern, huh?"

"What do you think?"

"We've tried to get him involved in some programs to turn him around, with no success. For whatever reason, you've made an impression on him."

"I didn't do anything."

"Can't always explain things. Just gotta go with 'em when they work." He caught Max's gaze. "Bart needs to focus his energies elsewhere. Interning with you is a good place to start."

"I see some of me in Bart. I want to help him."

"I understand."

"What's the worst that can happen?"

"You sure you want the answer to that?"

"Not really. I'll hope for the best."

The chief settled back in his chair. The aged leather creaked as he moved. "Looks like you're settling into life in Cypress Pointe."

"It's a good place to start my business. I'm close to Gram. Making connections in the community."

A twinkle gleamed in the chief's eyes. "Thought maybe you were preoccupied by a woman."

"Why would you think that?"

"Son, I've got a few years on you. I've seen that look on countless young men's faces."

Max grunted. "I suppose it ain't pretty."

"To tell you the truth, it's about time a good woman got your attention."

"How do you know it's a good woman?"

"After seein' the two of you in action the other day, I figure your mind is focused on Lilli Barclay." The chief nonchalantly straightened the files on his desk. "So, you thinkin' about asking her to the Merchants Association fish fry next weekend?"

"Hadn't planned on it."

"Why not?"

"Because we're working together. Nothing more."

"Working together? Since when?"

"A few hours ago. We were discussing the Wingate collection. I need to work undercover and the volunteer groom thing will allow me to do that."

"Let me guess…. You let her think it was all her idea."

Max shrugged.

"You should take a chance, Max. Lilli is a good person."

Max eyed him suspiciously. "Why does it matter to you?"

Now the chief shrugged. "Just sayin'."

"Meddling is more like it."

"Can't help it if I take an interest in your life."

"As much as I appreciate all you've done for me, keep your advice about my lack of a love life to yourself."

"Seems the mention of Lilli Barclay gets you all riled up."

"Poking into my private life gets me riled up."

When Max didn't say anything more, the

chief continued. "Face it, Max. If Lilli hadn't turned you in that summer night, your life wouldn't have turned out this good." The chief leaned forward to rest his arms on the desk, a serious expression eclipsing his usually merry eyes. "Didn't you ever wonder what happened the night you first met Lilli? Why I hauled your sorry behind to juvenile detention after the light show on the beach?"

"Too prove a point?"

"Exactly. I needed to do something. You were headed for serious trouble. I couldn't let that happen, so I called in a few favors and locked you up to make a point."

The chief had always had his number. And his back. Even when he didn't deserve it.

He supposed the man was right. He and Lilli getting caught that night had changed his direction. Maybe he should start looking at her turning him in as saving his life, not ruining it.

"All I know is that Lilli's walking back into your life is a sign. Where you take it from here will make the difference."

Max narrowed his eyes. He would not let the chief bait him. The older man always knew which buttons to push. "Are we finished here?"

"Yes. We informed Mr. Klingman about the mix-up. He left after thanking Bart for being an upstanding citizen and returning his wallet."

Max snorted then rose and crossed to the door.

"One more thing," the chief said before Max left.

"What?"

"I know for a fact that Lilli will be working one of the volunteer booths at the fish fry."

Max stormed out, shutting the door to the chief's office harder than necessary. The man had made it more than clear he wanted to get him and Lilli together.

That was not going to happen.

CHAPTER EIGHT

"I DON'T THINK this is a good idea."

"Yes. It is," Jewel said as she dragged Lilli to the beach where a huge bonfire served as a beacon to the people of Cypress Pointe. "You put too much pressure on yourself. You need to get out and enjoy yourself, not sit home on a Saturday night."

"But I have—"

"That's your problem. You always have an excuse. No lists. No worrying about the benefit. Tonight we're going to have some fun."

Lilli had to admit, it had been a long time since she'd been out, socializing and having fun. And to be honest, leaving all the business of the benefit and the promotion behind for a few hours took an enormous weight off her shoulders.

As Lilli drew closer to the fire, her muscles relaxed. Her mind cleared of the ever-present lists, worries and responsibilities. Being a type A personality had its disadvantages.

The flaming wood snapped, and sparks

sailed into the dark night like fireflies escaping a jar. Smoke rose and drifted in the wind, leaving a pungent scent in its wake. She stood there, reminded of another night. Another bonfire.

That summer had been challenging, to say the least, with her additional summer studies and reading assignments for advanced classes the next school year. When Max had caught her attention, he'd taken her mind off her worries.

Something about him had gotten to her. Cute, yes, but beyond that. Maybe the aura of excitement surrounding him. So different from her staid life. She was tired of being the good girl, always following the rules, and that rough-around-the-edges guy had made her feel alive. She'd decided to see what would happen.

What she hadn't expected was getting hauled off to the police station.

A young man ran by, jostling Lilli out of the past. Laughter and loud voices surrounded her, drawing her back to the present. Realizing she stood much too close to the heat of the fire, Lilli stepped back, looking for an out-of-the-way spot free from chatting people. Making her way to the outskirts of the rowdy group, Lilli sank down onto the cool sand, cooling her memories, as well. She hadn't thought about the events of that night for years. Until Max had turned up in her life again.

Shaking her head, Lilli glanced over at Jewel, the life of the party, holding court with a group of her friends. So unlike Lilli.

Earlier, Jewel had showed up unannounced at her apartment, insisting Lilli accompany her to the beach. Every month the city allowed a public bonfire and Jewel had wanted Lilli to go along. Lilli had already settled in after a busy day, but Jewel wouldn't take no for an answer. Throwing on a T-shirt, jeans and a lightweight jacket, Lilli had tagged along. So here she sat, in the sand, surrounded by people, many she didn't know, relaxing for the first time in days. Between work and the charity event, she'd been on permanent fast-forward.

She glanced across the water. Moonlight trailed over the waves. A smattering of stars twinkled in the night. The comfortable temperature made it perfect bonfire weather. Even though there were plenty of people to talk to, Lilli hung back. Before long, a sense of loneliness enveloped her. Not exactly a new sensation. She'd battled this feeling all her life. Tonight it seemed more pronounced, like a clock counting down to some unknown future.

Securing the new account at work would help her move ahead in the company. But was that enough? Did she want more in life beyond the promotion? She'd been working toward the one goal for so long, she hadn't had time for anything outside of work. The only extra activity in her life was the animal shelter. Now that her mother's actions had immersed her in the historical society business, she realized she'd closed herself off from other activities. She missed being involved with other people.

Pulling her legs up, she circled her arms around them and rested her chin on her knees. She might be in the midst of coordinating the charity benefit, but face it, once that ended Lilli would be back at square one. Good at her job but no social life to round out her days and nights.

She was so caught up in her revelation, it took a few seconds to register a pair of boots in the sand beside her. She glanced over, her eyes moving from the boots, to worn jeans, up over the UF sweatshirt, to meet the eyes of Max Sanders.

He handed her a bottle of water. "Thought you might be here."

"Good guess." She took the water bottle he offered, surprised and pleased to see him.

Max nodded to the fire. "Been a while since I came to one of these gatherings."

"Probably because the last campfire we were at together ended so abruptly."

"That and the resulting trip to juvenile detention."

"And I apologized for that."

He lowered himself beside her, stretching his long legs out before him, crossing his ankles and leaning back on his elbows. "And here I'd figured I'd made a positive first impression."

"A little." More, really, but Max didn't have to know that.

He turned his head to her.

"You and your buddies were up to no good that night," she reminded him.

"I remember we started out the night joyriding. There's only so much driving around you can do until boredom sets in, so we got this brilliant idea to come down to the beach. Bad enough we started a fire, against city ordinance, but then we had to make things worse by tossing firecrackers and cherry bombs into the flames. Not our smartest move."

"Except it wasn't your move. You had nothing to do with it."

"Because I was kissing you at the time."

Heat that had nothing to do with the fire warmed her face. "Yes, you were. It was a memorable kiss."

"Yeah?" A crooked smile curved Max's lips.

"I guess it'll always be a night to remember," she said.

The wavering firelight cast his face in shadows. A shiver ran through her. Lilli couldn't deny her attraction to this man. Not only his good looks, but the raw confidence he exuded. That, more than anything, kept her attention.

Max laughed. "The chief was not happy with us. I gotta say, the man is usually pretty even keeled, but you wake him up in the middle of the night over mischief like that, he can be downright ornery."

"Especially when he had to deal with my parents."

Max nodded. "Or when he came to find me. He camped outside Gram's house until I came home. Caught me when I tried to sneak in." He shook his head. "He pulled out the cuffs and made a big deal about putting me in the squad car."

"I remember when he dragged you into the station. You were not a happy camper."

"No, I wasn't. Later, when we drove up to juvie, he told me it was for my own good. He definitely scared me straight. Once I got out of the detention center, we had a long conversation about my future. For the first time, I listened."

"Your relationship goes way back."

"Yeah. We've worked things out over the years." He untwisted the cap from his water bottle and took a long drink.

"And here I thought I had you beat with my story of skipping out of lunch period with kids from the National Honor Society right before the induction ceremony. Guess not."

"Induction ceremony?"

She grinned, remembering how scared and excited, she'd been. "My senior year, the school had this candlelight ceremony planned. Kind of a big deal. But before that, some friends wanted to go get lunch off campus. I went along. Guess who I ran into on the way back into school?"

"The principal?"

"Logical guess, but no. My parents. They'd come for the ceremony."

Looking back on it now, Lilli realized she'd been shocked that day, but not by getting caught for skipping out of school. She'd been a good student and her leaving wasn't a big deal in the grand scheme of things. Besides, she'd left with National Honor Society kids. Not exactly a gang of thugs.

No, her surprise stemmed from the fact that her parents had come to a function together.

"The chance of getting caught skipping class was part of the appeal," Max told her.

"Yeah, well, it was my first, and last, time."

His eyes widened. "You're kidding me, right?"

"Afraid not."

"Edgy woman."

"I may not have skipped a lot, but I had my share of moments."

"Yeah, like I said, edgy."

He grinned the grin that told her he was messing with her and enjoyed it. The bonfire flames lit the humor in his eyes. And once again, her stomach fluttered in a way only Max could make happen.

She shrugged, trying hard to ignore her attraction to Max and failing miserably.

"Lame story," she muttered.

"Nah. Gives me hope."

"For what?"

"That you're not entirely the prim and proper good girl you want the world to believe you are."

"That's what you got out of that story? That I'm prim and proper?"

He shot her look that said, "You think?"

Okay, it was a given. But maybe she missed that girl at the beach who'd kissed a strange boy and liked it. "What if I'm tired of being the good girl? The responsible girl?" she asked herself as well as Max. "Maybe I want to prove to everyone I can be bad."

"Slow down, tiger." He chuckled. "In my experience, there's always a bit of mischief buried in people. The secret is figuring how to channel it."

Maybe that bit of mischief in her explained why she'd wanted to be his date for the benefit.

"So, you have experience helping people channel their mischief?"

"Definitely." He stared at the fire. "But not anymore. Taking risks doesn't appeal to me unless it's business related."

So much for hoping this reformed rebel might teach her a thing or two.

"I know one thing, though."

She looked at him, noting the serious gleam in his eyes.

"Sanders Security comes first. I need to focus on getting it up and running, and making it successful."

Just the way she felt about getting the promotion. Seems they had one thing in common.

MAX DIDN'T SLEEP WELL with one particular woman invading his dreams—visions of Lilli dressed to the nines, informing him he'd been banned from the benefit because he didn't own a tuxedo. She turned on her fancy high-heeled shoe and slammed a giant oak door behind her, leaving him outside the club, miserably calling her name. That brought him bolting up in a tangle of sheets.

He ran a hand over his face. "Get a grip."

That had been 1:00 a.m.

After that, he'd tossed and turned until the early hours of the morning. Even Jake Riley had abandoned him, unable to get any sleep due to Max's restlessness. When the alarm finally went off, he growled and knocked the clock radio off the nightstand. "Not now," he muttered to no one.

He took a quick shower, dressed in charcoal-colored slacks, a striped shirt and black loafers, and straggled into the kitchen in search of caffeine to clear his head before heading to his grandmother's house.

Gram had bacon sizzling in the pan when he and Jake Riley came through the back door. This morning she wore a sunny yellow dress, her short, gray hair set in soft curls. Her dazzling smile greeted him, the wrinkles around her cheery eyes a testament to years of laughter. She stood about five and a half feet tall, but loomed larger than life in Max's memory. And she could still scare him straight with a few well-spoken words.

"Feeling okay?" he asked, as he did every day.

"Yes. I think that new prescription is finally working. I feel better than I have in ages."

"You said having me around was the best medicine."

She chuckled. "Of course it is. You know I love having you here."

"I hear a *but* in that."

"But I'm better. You don't have to hang around here and worry."

"Gram, I know I don't have to. I want to."

"I appreciate all your help, but I'm stronger. Start focusing on your own life. It's time."

"I have a life."

"More than just work."

Gram had been after him to get a more active social life. He explained over and over that the business took priority, but his words fell on deaf ears. Gram wanted more for him, even if he enjoyed doing security work and hanging out with Jake Riley. She made no bones about the fact that she wanted great-grandkids, which he figured had to be a grandmother thing because all her friends were the same way, constantly asking if he was seeing anyone and offering up their granddaughters as potential dates. Now that he and Lilli were working together on the charity event, he decided not to mention it for fear of Gram having visions of Lilli and him walking down the real marriage aisle.

"You're sure your health is better?"

"I'm sure." Gram broke eggs into a bowl. "What are you up to today?"

"Business forum," he said before taking a gulp of coffee.

"It's a beautiful day outside and you're going to waste it on business?"

"It won't be a waste. It's called networking. I hope to get more security jobs to keep my new intern busy."

"Intern? That's new. Anyone I know?"

"Bart."

She stopped, midwhisk. "Excuse me?"

The corner of his mouth quirked.

"What brought this on?"

"I was about to drag him to the police station yesterday and I remembered what I was doing at his age. Long story short, he's going to straighten up."

She stopped stirring the eggs, considered what he said and then continued with the job. "I think that's a good idea."

As usual, Gram surprised him.

"You do?"

"Yes. I think your influence will be good for Bart."

"That's what the chief said."

"You do have plenty of experience getting in trouble, so you should be able to relate to the boy."

"I can't believe you just said that."

"It's the truth, honey." She patted his cheek. "Bart's a good boy. He'll figure it out. Just like you did."

"Not before he makes me crazy."

"It's called payback."

Max grinned. Gram had nailed it, as usual.

She set out the food and they ate quickly, both heading out in opposite directions. He had a few things to tie up at the office before going across town.

Before long he arrived at the forum. Searching for a place to park in the rapidly filling parking lot, Max found an empty space and quickly steered the truck in.

He sat for a few minutes, scanning the people walking toward the building. Was this a good idea? Max stared at the building, uncertain.

Because of his past, he needed to meet this challenge head-on. He entered the building, the first hurdle in mixing with the mainstream. He approached a young woman with pink streaks in her hair, greeting people at the door. He recognized her from the day he'd seen her with Lilli after his pursuit of Bart.

"Welcome," the young woman smiled. "I'm... Max?"

"No, I'm Max. You're Jewel."

She blinked in surprise. "What are you doing here?"

"What, no open arms?"

"Just surprised is all. Lilli didn't mention you'd be here."

Why would it matter to Lilli? He shoved his hands in his pockets. "I'm here for the forum, just like everyone else."

"You're not here to cause trouble like you did with Bart, are you?"

"No."

"Good, because the jury's still out," Jewel informed him.

"I'm going to find a seat," Max said, moving out of the line of fire.

He wandered into the gym. Waiting for the first speaker to take the podium, people milled around, introducing themselves and shaking his hand. Trying not to act like a fish out of water, he spoke to people, hoping they wouldn't notice his unease. He kept waiting for his past to catch up with him.

A deep, familiar voice, greeted him with genuine pleasure. "Max Sanders. Long time, buddy."

"Dane." The two men shook hands and Max said, "Heard you'd moved to Tampa."

Dane smiled. "I did for a while, but I'm back now. Bought the old Grand Cypress Hotel."

"No kidding."

"Yep. Been living there while I remodel the place. Right now only the restaurant is open."

Max had been tight with Dane Peterson during high school. The two had become partners, of sorts, in vandalism. They'd taken turns being on lookout while the other guy boosted a car. Committed petty theft. They'd been young and known it all. Or so they'd thought. Them feeding off each other's troubles and encouraging each other's bad behavior had made both families tear their hair out in frustration. When Dane had suddenly gone to live with an uncle and Max had enlisted, they'd lost touch.

Dane regarded his friend with a serious expression. "I have to say, this is the last place I ever expected to run into you."

Max laughed. "Ditto."

"We stirred up a lot of trouble."

"Who woulda figured we'd end up respectable business owners?"

"Not our families, that's for sure." Dane shook his head, a ghost of a smile playing over his lips.

Max found himself relaxing.

"I heard you've set up shop in town. I'd like to make an appointment with you about security at my hotel."

"How about tomorrow?"

"Sounds good. I'm free in the morning." Dane shook his head, chuckled. "You. Doing security work."

"Looks like we both turned our lives around. I appreciate you considering Sanders Security."

"Hey, we always had each other's back."

"We did." Max said with a grin.

"It'll be great to catch up."

Before Max had a chance to agree, another voice interrupted their conversation. "Max?"

He spun around to face Lilli, who was looking very put together, having abandoned her casual style of last night. Today she'd pulled her hair back in a sort of wispy updo and wore a flattering pastel-pink dress. Understated gold jewelry glittered at her ears and around her neck.

"Hello, Lilli."

"I'm glad you could make it to my forum," she said in a tight voice. On closer inspection, she looked a bit harried.

"I guess I missed your name on the sign out front," he teased, hoping to lighten the mood.

She had the good grace to look chagrined. "The town forum. I planned it this year." That explained Jewel's earlier remark. "I'm glad Blanche called to reserve a space. Networking will be good for your company."

As if just noticing another person present,

Lilli smiled distractedly at Dane. "Good to see you, too."

Dane only nodded. His glance traveled from Lilli to Max and back again.

"If you'll excuse me, I have to be, um, somewhere," she said, before hurrying to the back of the gymnasium.

"Something I said?" Max muttered.

Dane chuckled. "Still smooth with the ladies, I see."

"Only the pain-in-the-neck kind."

"Yeah, you always did go for trouble." Dane shook his head. "Let me guess. She roped you into the Tie the Knot charity benefit."

"Yeah. You, too?"

"I'll be there in a tux, escorting brides. Barclay women are very persuasive."

Didn't Max know it.

"Look at it this way. We're doing our civic duty. All we have to do is get into a penguin suit and show up."

Which, as he sized up Dane's fashionable clothes, wasn't a hardship for him.

Max told Dane he'd see him tomorrow and made his way toward the nearest empty seat, wondering where Lilli had run off to. Telling himself it didn't matter.

LILLI STOOD BEFORE the restroom mirror, eyes wide, face flaming. Why had she reacted to

Max Sanders that way? She didn't begrudge him being here—he needed connections as much as the next business owner. Her reaction had to do with nerves, nothing more, she assured herself. She needed this day to go well. To wow her boss.

In the past few months, she'd put a lot of time and energy into making sure today would be a hit, hoping the success of the forum would go a long way toward getting her that promotion. She'd been in constant contact with Mr. Danielson, hoping to sway him to sign with KLC. She even stopped by the dealership this morning, checking in, making nice and keeping herself visible. He'd promised an answer by next week.

Now she had to wait and worry.

So she'd pasted on a sunny smile and greeted the attendees, using the nervous energy in a positive way. Until she'd laid eyes on Max.

Okay, this was selfish of her. She'd encouraged most of the town's business owners to attend, so why wouldn't she want the same for Max?

Because he flustered her? Brought out the prickly in her? *Wrong,* her inner voice taunted. *Because you're attracted to him. Which is a thousand times worse.* She frowned at her reflection. Okay, she had to be honest with herself and admit that she was more than a little attracted to Max. Working with him for the fund-raiser excited her in a way she hadn't felt in a very long time, even though he'd made it clear he wanted their relationship to be business only. Fine, really, since she had her own job to focus on. But still, she couldn't deny the spark between them.

With a final shake of her head, she pulled herself together and retraced her steps to the gymnasium. As she crossed the room, her boss, Jim, pulled her aside.

"I made myself clear. No problems today."

"There aren't any."

"Then how do you explain the entire town frowning at Sanders?"

"I don't think you have to worry about Max."

"You'd better be right," Jim warned and headed in the other direction.

Great. She didn't need Jim questioning her ability to plan and run this event.

Lilli made her way to her seat, noticing a tense buzz charging the room as the first speaker made his way to the podium. Not the kind of anticipation you'd expect for a speaker, though. More like a sense of pending disaster. She smiled and waved to people she knew as she crossed the room, but most seemed preoccupied.

Joining Jewel, she took a seat before noticing Max across the aisle, calmly reading a brochure. Did he feel the tension, too? If he did, his body language said otherwise. She had to admire that since her stomach had turned to knots.

As the speaker advised the business owners on better techniques to draw foot traffic into their shops, Lilli noticed people throwing looks over their shoulders. Concerned, she studied the movements, realizing the looks were for Max. Oh, no. This couldn't be good.

Finally, time came for a fifteen-minute break. Lilli started to work her way to the front of the room when Mrs. Lyons, the shop owner from Milly's Gifts and Things, stopped her.

"What is he doing here?"

Lilli stifled a groan and looked in the direction of the pointed finger at Max.

"Mrs. Lyons, this forum is open to all the businesspeople in town. Mr. Sanders is one of them."

"More like a criminal element, I say."

"No, he owns a business to stop criminals."

The woman narrowed her eyes. "Are you in cahoots with him?"

Cahoots? She almost laughed. "No, we aren't in cahoots."

Another person in the group pointed to Max and said, "I heard he hired the pickpocket."

"Doesn't anyone around here use names?" Lilli heard Max mutter behind her. She glanced over her shoulder to find Max frowning at the group.

"Bart is my intern," he clarified.

Surprised, she blinked, then turned back to the crowd. "Max is a guest today, just like every one of you."

"I remember Sanders running with a bad crowd," someone else added.

"He vandalized my home," said another.

Lilli held her hands up. "Everyone, please. Mr. Sanders is not a threat to the community. As I pointed out, he has a security consulting business. If anything, we need his services."

"Has anyone hired him?" Mrs. Lyons asked.

"Yes, as a matter of fact," Max answered. "The Merchants Association, of which most of you are members."

Mrs. Lyons frowned.

"And the historical society," Mrs. Rumpold announced as she made her way into the throng. She batted her eyelashes at Max then spoke to the others. "We're looking forward to having him spend time at the office."

The entire community of business owners started talking at once. Lilli tried to calm them down, but couldn't yell over all the arguing. She silently counted to ten.

"I warned you about this," Jim said as he materialized beside her.

"It's not like I planned it."

"Get this thing under control."

Before she had a chance, someone tapped on the live microphone at the podium.

"If everyone would quiet down, I'd like to say something."

The crowd turned as one to find Max at the podium. Lilli's stomach dropped. As a group, they all stood in the center aisle.

"Hello, everyone. I'm Max Sanders. Some of you remember me from my teen years. I'll admit, I did cause some trouble in town, and for that, I apologize. Call it lack of guidance or a kid acting out. That would be both for me."

Lilli swallowed, her heart aching that Max had to stand there and prove himself. Proud that he did.

"But I won't apologize for coming back to Cypress Pointe to start a business. I'm good at what I do and there is a definite need here. I also won't apologize for taking Bart on as an intern. I haven't seen one of you step up to help him instead of complaining. In time, I hope you find that I'm not mistaken, that Bart will become a vital part of our town, just as I plan to become an active part of the Cypress Pointe business community."

He paused and when no one spoke up, he continued. "Most of you know my grandmother. And you all know the chief. They trust me. I'm asking you all to take a chance and know that Sanders Security is here to help you." He held up the itinerary in his hand. "Now, let's get back to business. Mr. Ronson is up next to talk about…" he paused, raising an eyebrow as he read from the program "…the town working together as a team."

Lilli watched the townsfolk make their way back to their seats. As Max passed Mrs. Lyons, she stopped him. "I'll be watching out for you."

Max didn't miss a beat. "Then you should have one of these." He reached into his shirt pocket and extracted a business card before making his way back to his seat. As he passed Lilli he winked.

Lilli shook her head. Disaster averted, thanks to Max's honesty and willingness to address the crowd. Another reason she admired his business skills. And his integrity.

As Mr. Ronson spoke, she noticed glances sent Max's way, only this time the looks came from some of the younger, single women. Lilli ignored the tingle of jealousy.

"Awesome business forum," Jewel whispered in Lilli's direction.

Lilli rolled her eyes at her friend. Could this day get any more bizarre?

By the time the speakers had finished, it was four o'clock. Volunteers began to clean up while attendees mingled, exchanging ideas and business cards. Lilli noticed a group around Max and hoped they were asking about his services, not griping at him about crime in this town. Needing air, she gathered her things and headed outside to take a seat at a picnic table on the lawn beside the gymnasium. The temperature had warmed up, and it was another lovely Florida spring day. She didn't want to be cooped up inside any longer.

Preoccupied by the many thoughts bombarding her, she stared into the distance for a while before fixating on the upcoming charity event. She had her lists with her, as well as some of the wedding magazine clippings, hoping she and Jewel could brainstorm after the forum.

She dropped her tote bag on the table and some photos spilled out. Gathering them together, she noticed a sticky note attached to the corner of one picture. *One true love.* She squinted for a moment, trying to remember why she wrote that. Then it came to her. Just before she'd dozed off to sleep a few nights ago, she'd gotten the idea to personalize the wedding theme. Take one great love story and feature it during the benefit. Let those in attendance get the feel of more than a fashion show. Let them experience a story of true love from a real couple.

A glossy picture cut from a magazine caught her eye. A couple, probably at their wedding reception, perched on a balcony with a gorgeous sunset as the backdrop. The bride's veil lifted in the breeze. Her dress, a silk A-line gown, sparkled with embroidered sequin swirls dotted with seed pearls. The groom, in a dark tux, wound his arms around her waist, as if protecting her from the world. Together they would face whatever came, from that point on.

Fanciful thinking on her part. Even though she recognized a staged pose for a magazine spread, she couldn't help but wonder what their story could be. What great love affair they might embody.

That was the idea she wanted to focus on for her love story. Well, not her story, of course, since she didn't have one, but the theme threaded throughout the benefit. She couldn't decide between using a fictional couple or a real-life couple. She didn't know any real couples who fell into this category, but a fictional couple wouldn't give the same feeling of intimacy.

She'd drawn several question marks on the sticky note when she heard footsteps behind her. She turned to look over her shoulder.

Max stopped beside the table. "Should you be working on the charity thing when you have the entire business community of Cypress Pointe inside?"

"My part in the forum is over. Besides, I can't get my mind off all I still need to do."

He took a seat beside her, looking very suave dressed in business attire. He cleaned up nicely, and while she should be impressed with his transformation, she realized his usual casual look had slowly grown on her.

She shook her head, thinking, *I'm in trouble here.* His very nearness stirred a blend of delight and apprehension. He said he only cared about getting his business off the ground, so why did he still hang around?

A gust of wind caught the edges of the pictures, and Max grabbed the glossy images before they fluttered to the ground. As he handed them back to her, their fingers brushed. Warmth spread up her arms and settled in her heart. She wondered what it would be like if they were a real couple, going on dates or hanging out with friends. Doing daily things couples did together.

Lilli shifted her thoughts to a safer topic. "So, Bart?"

A ghost of a smile curved Max's lips. "On a trial basis. I'm trying to help him make better decisions."

"As your intern?"

"Someone needs to give him a chance."

With those words, Lilli's admiration for Max grew even more. His piercing gaze captured her eyes. She couldn't look away.

After several long, charged seconds, Max craned his neck to look at her pile of photos. "So, what are you up to?"

Jewel was clearly still busy, so why not get a male perspective? She needed a sounding board and he'd asked.

"The event date is getting close and I have some loose ends."

"Like what you're going to wear on our date?"

Why would he care? It's not as though he really wanted to attend the event. "You mean our arrangement?"

"Whatever you want to call it."

"Honestly, I haven't gotten around to finding a dress. Between work and the fund-raiser, I've been busy." And she'd scoured several stores and couldn't find anything she liked.

He chuckled. "Right."

"And what about a tux?"

"I'll get one. When you tell me you have a dress."

"I have too many other *important* things on my mind."

"Like?"

Like, did her "real love story" idea point in the right direction or was it too hokey for words?

"I've been going over the info for this vintage wedding idea, but I feel like a piece is missing." She pointed to the picture of the young couple decked out in wedding regalia, gazing into each other's eyes. "I mean, it's wonderful to showcase all these fabulous dresses and have couples model, but what ties it all together? I've been racking my brains and then it hit me— what about one personal love story to weave the wedding theme around? A strong thread to connect it all?"

"So you're looking for a great love story?"

"Exactly." She felt her cheeks heat. "Is that lame?"

He picked up the photo, regarding it for long moments before shooting her a cheeky grin. "I guess everyone enjoys a good love story."

"Even you?"

He slanted her a glance. "If it's the right one."

She let out a shaky breath and turned away. "Well, um, I haven't sketched out all the details yet. I guess I wanted to say it out loud and see where the idea goes." She glanced at him slyly. "Any chance you're a secret wedding planner on the side of your security business?"

He visibly cringed. "No way."

"Then I'm out of luck."

He shrugged. "I don't get to many weddings, but what you're trying to accomplish makes sense."

"The only problem is I don't know whose story to use."

"Have you contacted any local people?"

She told him she hadn't, because she couldn't think of a couple who inspired her. And while the idea of featuring a romantic couple from fiction or cinema would work if all else failed, she hoped a real love story would elicit heartfelt emotion as well as drawing a few tears.

"What about your love life?" he asked.

"Mine?"

"Sure. Haven't you had that one great love?"

Was that interest or sarcasm in his question? She scoffed, covering her insecurity with this man. "Hardly. That's why I need someone else's." She paused for a moment. If he was fishing for information, why not return the favor? "Got a love story you want to share?"

"Personally, no." He stared down at the photo once again, rubbing his chin. "But I think I know someone who might be able to help you."

"That would be great."

He glanced at her. "Are you free now?"

She nodded, her curiosity getting the better of her.

"I'd like you to meet someone."

At his serious expression, she found herself growing even more curious about the man. As much as she tried to convince herself otherwise, she wanted to get to know Max. What better way than to go listen to this mystery person's story, with the side benefit of maybe finding a solution to her problem? Nothing wrong with that, right? "Sure. Let's go."

Max stood, holding his hand out to help her up from the bench. "Besides, the sooner you wrap up loose ends, the sooner you can concentrate on finding a dress for our date."

She shook her head even as her heart lifted. This man spelled trouble with a capital T.

CHAPTER NINE

"So where are we going?" Lilli asked after they'd settled into Max's truck.

"My grandmother's house."

He drove them to an older section of town, away from the swanky, expensive homes to smaller, older, more down-home ranch-style houses.

"She's your source?"

"I think your meeting each other will be mutually beneficial. You need an idea and she needs something to be involved in."

"So you're playing wedding broker, here?"

He chuckled. "Gram was sick for a while. She's been getting better, but I think your project will really put her back on track."

"So you're doing it for your grandmother."

"And I'm hoping if I help you, you won't talk me into any more volunteer duties down the road."

"Sneaky man."

"We all have skills."

He turned onto a quiet street, traveling about

halfway down before pulling into the driveway of a small, tidy house. The front yard, overgrown with a profuse collection of mature tropical foliage, greeted her. Pink bougainvillea grew wildly along a trellis by the side of the house and soft white impatiens lined the walkway to the front door.

"Wow."

"Yeah. She usually gets that reaction. You should see the backyard."

She'd just started walking up the sidewalk when the front door opened and a big dog loped out, picking up speed as he saw his master. Lilli sidestepped as the Lab jumped up on Max.

"Hey, buddy." Max scratched behind the dog's ears, a genuine smile tilting his lips. Lilli found herself enjoying his relaxed, handsome features.

The dog savored the attention for a few minutes then set his sights on Lilli.

"Oh, no." The dog beelined for her and before she knew it, his big paws rested on her. What was it about dogs jumping on her good clothes? She tried to redirect him but the dog had other ideas.

"Jake Riley. Down boy."

Lilli scratched behind the Lab's ears. "You're just a big ol' friendly one, aren't you, boy?"

An older woman joined them on the walkway. She wore a pink velour jogging set and sneakers. "Max, get that dog off the poor girl."

Max leaned over to the woman and kissed her cheek. "Hey, Gram. I brought you a visitor. This is Lilli Barclay. Lilli, Laverne Sanders."

Lilli held out her hand and it was enveloped by Laverne's smooth fingers. "I'm pleased to meet you."

"And to what do I owe this visit?" Laverne asked, clearly pleased by the prospect of company.

"I'll let her explain," Max told his grandmother. "Why don't we go inside."

They were headed for the door when Max's cell phone rang. He glanced at the screen. "Excuse me, ladies. I have to take this."

"Come in." Laverne led the way into the house while Jake Riley bounded off after some critter in the yard.

They entered a living room cluttered with books, knickknacks and pictures. A floral-patterned couch, flanked by two easy chairs, faced a television, which had to be Max's contribution judging by the sleek flat screen and sheer size. It had male written all over it. In fact, it was the only male item in a room filled with pretty hand-embroidered pillows and other girly touches tastefully exhibited.

"Would you like some iced tea?"

"I don't want to put you out."

"Nonsense. I just made some. Besides, I love company. Don't get anywhere near enough of it." She motioned to the couch. "Please, sit down."

Lilli took a seat, continuing to survey the room until Laverne returned with two tall glasses.

"Now, what can I help you with?"

Lilli explained the Tie the Knot benefit and the concept of featuring a beautiful love story.

A dreamy expression flitted over Laverne's pretty face. "You've come to the right place." She crossed the room to a curio cabinet, removing one of the many framed pictures inside. She handed it to Lilli before sitting down beside her. "My husband, Clifford. We were married nearly forty years before he passed away."

Lilli glanced down at the distinguished gentleman smiling back at her. He wore a military uniform, the cap sitting at a jaunty angle on his head.

"He was quite a looker." Laverne smiled with the same charm Max possessed. "So many of the girls had a crush on him, but he only had eyes for me."

Lilli could see why. Laverne had retained her pretty features in her twilight years, but also the sweetness Lilli sensed would attract anyone. Especially a man used to the stringent world of the military. "How did you meet?"

"He relocated here with a friend after being discharged from the army. They had this great plan to open an auto repair garage. They needed a bookkeeper and I wanted to work to help my family financially.

"My parents didn't think I should work, but at the time, women were moving into the work force out of necessity. Believe me, we had plenty of arguments over my decision." Laverne chuckled. "I'll never forget the first time I walked into his office. Clifford smiled and offered me the job right on the spot. It was love at first sight.

"My parents didn't like that Clifford hired me and that caused some tense moments when we started dating. In the end, it all worked out." She winked at Lilli. "Sanders men usually get what they want."

Lilli lowered her face, hoping Laverne wouldn't notice her heated cheeks.

"We got married six months later. We waited that long because my mother wanted a fancy church wedding. I was the first girl in the family to get married, you see, so my mother scraped together enough money for a big to-do." She chuckled. "I had a grand gown and a fancy reception at the church. It made everyone happy."

Laverne went to another cabinet along the wall and pulled a large book from one of the drawers. When she brought it back, Lilli recognized it as a wedding album. The older woman lovingly ran a wrinkled finger over the worn edges before handing it to Lilli.

Slowly, Lilli paged through the album, lingering on pictures featuring the couple. Had she ever seen anyone that much in love? Only in pictures. And these pictures spoke volumes.

In her mind's eye, she imagined placing framed photos from the album around the event room. She'd start with a collection of wedding pictures beside a bouquet of fresh flowers displayed on a lace-covered table as the guests entered the room. Smaller photographs would be displayed on the silent auction and historical society information tables. Maybe even the actual gown Laverne had worn—Lilli was certain she'd still have it somewhere safe—either modeled in the fashion show or on a mannequin, displayed at a pivotal point in the room.

Now that she imagined the Sanderses' love story, the next question to enter her mind had to be: would Laverne go for it?

"Laverne, I have a question for you."

The older woman brought her loving gaze

from the album. Tears shone in Laverne's eyes. Lilli had to swallow hard not to tear up, as well.

"What is it, dear?"

"Would you let us use your wedding dress and pictures during the fund-raiser?"

Laverne leaned back against the cushion, her hand over her heart. "These pictures aren't anything fancy."

"They are to me. There's a world of love encapsulated in this album."

Laverne glanced back to the closed book, her fingers lightly tracing over the lace design of ringing bells adorning the cover.

"And the dress would be perfect. It's exactly what I'm trying to capture. A love that transcends time. I promise anything you lend me will be treated like gold," Lilli assured her.

Laverne glanced over at Lilli, her insightful gaze exactly like one Lilli had received from Max on occasion. "Only if I might make a suggestion."

"Anything."

"Will you allow me to write the love story as it progresses along with the pictures?"

"Are you kidding? I'd love it." With a sense of rightness, Lilli knew the photos connected to the story would be a hit. "And the gown will be the finishing touch to the story."

"All right. Let's do it. The gown is in storage, but I'll get it out." Laverne beamed. "In the meantime, I can start working on the story and give you portions as I finish it."

"Finish what?" Max asked as he sauntered back into the living room.

"Lilli wants to feature my love story with your grandfather at her event."

Max grinned at Lilli as if to say *I told you so.*

"This is wonderful," Lilli told Laverne, pointedly ignoring Max's gloating smile.

"I'll have Max deliver the photos once I gather them all together."

Yet another reason to get together with Max. Funny how that made her heart beat a little faster.

Max eyed Lilli, a glimmer of promise shadowed in the smoky depths. "This keeps getting better and better."

Lilli visited with Laverne awhile longer before Max took her back to the church to pick up her sedan.

"I can't thank you enough for taking me to meet your grandmother. She's exactly the right person for my idea."

He shrugged. "When you're right, you're right."

"And modest, too?"

He didn't hide the heat in the depths of his eyes. Her stomach dipped. Instead of growing immune to the man, her reaction was only growing stronger.

"I have a full schedule this week, so I'll check my calendar and see when I can drop the pictures off."

The calendar with a bunch of other women's names penciled in on different days? Yeah, she remembered. Frowning, she wished she hadn't noticed the names the first time she'd gone to his office. He claimed to always be working, but who knew? Not that it mattered to her. She was too busy to worry about his social life anyway.

"You're okay with that, right?"

"Hmm. Oh, yes. Fine," she muttered, torn between the displeasure at becoming another one of his calendar women and the dissatisfaction of being just another person he worked with. Why were things never easy with this man? And what did she really want from him, anyway?

THE NEXT MORNING, Max walked into his office to find Blanche behind her desk, as usual, typing away.

"Heard you created quite a stir at the business forum."

He paused beside her desk. "I got our name out."

A smile quivered on Blanche's lips. "People noticed, that's for sure."

"And since you weren't there, who is your source of information?"

Her smiled blossomed into a wide grin. "You'd be surprised, but mostly I know from the calls I've already gotten this morning." She pointed to her monitor screen. "Typing up your schedule now."

Max took a look. He had appointments scattered throughout the week. "All that from one meeting?"

"I'd say it's because you stood up for yourself. Folks around here like that."

"Huh."

He knew he'd taken a chance, but if he wanted to establish Sanders Security in this town, he had to do it right away. When Mrs. Lyons had given him the evil eye, he'd figured he was done for. Guess he'd figured wrong.

"The bulk of calls came from businesses on Main Street. A few homeowners. Also," she said, glancing down at a memo pad, "a Mr. Rawlings's office called to confirm." She looked up at Max. "Is he the man you met at the country club?"

"Yes. He's interested in using Sanders Security. I don't have all the details yet, but I do know I'd have to travel."

"But you just got to town."

"I know, but this client could put us in the black."

"If you travel, how will we run the office?"

"I've been in touch with a friend in Atlanta. I told him he has a job here if I get the Rawlings account."

"Another man I have to train?"

Max chuckled. "Don't get ahead of yourself. I haven't even met with Rawlings yet."

He didn't miss her concerned frown. "Don't worry, Blanche. Sanders Security will stay here in Cypress Pointe. Maybe with a different focus than I planned, but you'll always have a job."

"I'm going to hold you to that."

"I wouldn't expect it any other way."

"Good. Oh, don't forget, Dane Peterson said to come by anytime. He's free all morning."

Max glanced at his watch. Besides business, catching up with his old friend ranked as a top priority. "Great. I'll head over there now."

"You can't."

He raised an eyebrow. "And why is that?"

"You have someone in your office."

Max frowned. "Were you going to tell me anytime soon?"

Blanche continued to smile.

Switching to his business face, Max entered

his office. "Good morning." He stopped short when he glimpsed Bart seated in front of his desk. "Bart?"

"Hi. I know we didn't set up a time for me to get started, but I wanted to talk to you first thing this morning."

Max moved to his chair, quickly glancing around the room to note everything in its place.

"I didn't take anything."

"I'm not taking any chances." Max eyed his guest. "What's up?"

"I heard you stuck up for me at the forum. No one's ever done that for me. Thanks."

Flashbacks of his teenage years filled his mind. When he'd been out of control and needed a mentor. Just like Bart, he'd made mistakes. Plenty of them, but for some reason, the night on the beach when he kissed Lilli flashed through his mind. Why did that take precedence?

"I thought about what you said, about making changes in my life," Bart went on as Max brought his mind back to the present. "I'm a fast learner and I plan on taking criminal justice classes at the community college."

"That's a good start."

"Look, I know we didn't start out in the best way, what with you surveilling me, but since we've become friends—"

"Friends?"

"Okay, maybe not friends, but I heard you were kind of wild and you changed. I can, too."

Is this how the chief had felt when he first took Max under his wing? The sense of responsibility? The pride in knowing he could help a young man who needed his advice?

"Since you'll be tied up with groom duties for the benefit, why not let me help you? I'm going to be there anyway." His face went red. "Jewel invited me. She's working with Lilli on the decorations."

Max grinned. All it took was a girl to make Bart rethink his life choices. "Would you excuse me for a minute?"

Bart sat straighter in his chair. "Sure."

Max left his office, closing the door behind him. "You heard all that?"

"Yep," Blanche replied.

"What do you think?"

She eyed him with all seriousness. "I think Bart is you twelve years ago. You had the chief. Bart has you."

"I don't know if I'm up for this."

"You are. Give him a chance."

Max walked away from Blanche's desk to stand before the window, staring down at Main Street. Deep inside he knew helping Bart was the right thing to do. And if he could help Bart make positive changes in his life, maybe people in this town would see he'd changed, too.

He returned to the office. Bart stood as soon as Max entered.

"Okay, here's the deal," Max informed him. "We'll start out slow so I can teach you the basics. When we pick up more cases, I'll see about paying you. You will take classes and you will stay out of trouble."

"I can do that," Bart assured him, relief and happiness lighting his face. "I promise. You won't be disappointed."

"I better not be."

"So, when do we start?"

"I've got a few appointments today. You stay here and go over the upcoming schedule with Blanche. Make notes about what kind of security the customer is interested in. We'll go over it later."

"Sure thing, boss."

Boss. Max hoped he wouldn't regret this.

MILD WAVES LAPPED the sand as seagulls dipped and dove in the shallow water. Max stood on the expansive pool deck of the newly remodeled Grand Cypress Hotel. He remembered this place, since he'd hung out here from time to time the summer Dane worked at the hotel. The elegant feel of the place had been missing back then—it'd been run-down and past its prime. Dane had modernized the entire hotel and breathed in new life.

"The hotel looks great," Max remarked as Dane joined him at the railing separating the deck from the sprawling, manicured lawn leading to the beach. "I'm impressed."

"It's been a lot of work, but worth it."

Max rested his lower back against the rail, crossing his arms over his chest. Intensely bright noon sun reflected off the pool water. Max squinted behind his dark sunglasses. "I'm surprised you don't already have a security system lined up."

"I do, but the company I'm using isn't as on top of things as I'd like. I need a second opinion."

"No problem."

"Let's have coffee out here on the terrace and discuss it." Dane led them to the outdoor restaurant, spoke to the hostess then picked out the table farthest away from other diners. A waitress took their orders and after she left, Dane laid out his concerns.

Twenty minutes later, Max had a good idea of what Dane needed. He hoped for a chance to implement those ideas.

Dane leaned back in his chair. "I'm glad you

came back to town. You know what you're doing."

Max laughed. "You seem surprised."

"Nah. I expected as much. When you put your mind to it, things always got done."

"Like causing trouble and getting us both in hot water."

"True, but this security business is a good fit for you."

"Thanks…I think. Designing or improving a system comes easy. Everything else?" he shrugged.

Dane scrutinized his friend from across the table. "So, Lilli Barclay, huh?"

No point in denying it. Dane must have noticed Max's reaction to Lilli at the forum. "You'd think I'd stay far, far away, wouldn't you."

"You could do worse."

Max didn't respond. He hadn't been great at picking out girlfriends and they both knew it.

"Things serious?"

"No. I'm keeping it all business between us. I volunteered for the wedding benefit, like she asked, but only so I can keep an eye on security without being obvious."

"A pretty woman asked for your help and you couldn't refuse. What's wrong with that?"

"Nothing, I suppose."

"The Max I knew would look at it as a challenge. He would have wanted to know pretty Miss Barclay better."

"The teenage Max would have been all over it, but now that I'm slowly getting business I don't want to mess things up."

"Then don't." Dane leveled Max with a searing stare. "Look, we got into trouble when we were kids. We both admit it. You straightened out. So did I. You can't change the past, buddy, but you can make a difference in your future."

"Sounds like you've had experience in that department." Max nodded to the now-elegant, sweeping two-story building. "It's a long way from working here to owning the place."

Dane shrugged. "I made some money so I invested in my dream. Trust me, in the beginning I wondered if I'd made a huge mistake. But despite my past, I dug my heels in and proved I could do this. Proved it to myself and others."

"A lot of that going on."

"Don't let anyone say otherwise."

Max nodded toward the hotel. "I guess if you can pull this off, I can handle a business and a simple charity event."

"Nothing worth having is ever easy."

"True."

Dane grinned. "I'm glad you stopped by. You

owe me for all the trouble you talked me into when we were younger."

"I did, didn't I?"

"You didn't exactly twist my arm. Still, if you hadn't come up with those crazy ideas…"

"We wouldn't have gotten into trouble. I know." Max leaned forward and rested his arms on the table. "I'm sorry, Dane."

"I had a choice."

"Yeah, but because of me, you got into scrapes with the law. And then you left without a word."

"Unlike your grandmother, my parents had had enough of my antics. Moving to Tampa to live with my uncle wasn't great, but it opened my eyes."

"Do you mind if I ask what happened?"

Dane looked over the water, his face devoid of expression. "Let's just say it had to do with a girl and a car."

Max thought back to that last summer together. Dane had been serious with a girl…. What was her name? Oh yeah: Nealy. Obviously a sore subject, judging by his friend's body language.

Dane turned back to Max and spoke with an even voice. "So, back to security."

Okay, topic closed. He understood.

"Give me a shot, Dane. After the couple of

cases I've worked on so far, I want to get out of the P.I. stuff and deal mainly with security concerns. I have experience with surveillance equipment and I like that end of the business." He grimaced. "Chasing after pickpockets, not so much."

Dane turned, humor lurking in his eyes. "Bart?"

"He's a decent guy. Needs someone to change his focus."

"Soft spot there?"

"Could be."

"I'll give you the blueprints of the hotel before you leave, along with the schematics of the current system. Since I've already told you my concerns, call me when you put a proposal together."

With business concluded, the men rose. Max fished in his pocket for cash to pay for the coffee.

Dane stopped him. "Not today. It's on me."

Max removed his hand from his pocket, holding it out to Dane. "Thanks. I appreciate it."

Shaking his hand, Dane said, "Just come up with a good plan."

Max rocked back on his bootheels. "No pressure, huh?"

"I know you can do this."

The two men walked back to the building. "Let's go to my office. I'll get you the prints."

Max followed Dane inside, for the first time noticing the man's attire. Dressed in a crisp white polo shirt, creased khaki slacks and brown loafers, he looked like he'd stepped out of GQ, a far cry from his rocker days when shaggy long hair had been the rage. Now, his short, styled hair held highlights. Max wondered if his buddy spent time in the sun or in a salon. Nah, he couldn't picture Dane sitting long enough to get his hair colored. Still, he had the look Lilli would probably go for. Glancing down at his own T-shirt, jeans and boots, he decided he had more of a *Guns & Ammo* look.

They'd both come a long way from long-haired, troubled juveniles, but he was still kind of dressing like one.

"Dane, can I ask you something?"

"Shoot."

"Where do you buy your clothes?"

One eyebrow arched. "Seriously?"

He nodded.

"Banana Republic. At the mall."

Max groaned. It had been years since he'd set foot in a mall. Too many stores with too many choices. But if he wanted to change his image, he'd have to suck it up and plan a visit. "That's what I thought."

CHAPTER TEN

"I THINK THIS is the color," Jewel said, passing Lilli yet another torn-out magazine page. The two had holed up at the historical society offices to go over Jewel's selections for the mock wedding reception. Mary Gibbons, the head of the decorating committee, had given Jewel the green light to jump right in after reviewing Jewel's ideas. With Mrs. Rumpold out for lunch, they were able to work in relative quiet.

Working on the details made her think about attending the event with Max. She still couldn't figure out why every time she met up with him she lost her usual cool. He seemed to drag out her inner prim and proper when in reality she wanted to show him she could be exciting and daring. Could she? Did she even want to try? More than anything. But she had to acknowledge that not being hurt by a man ranked high on her self-preservation chart. And Max was a man. Boy-oh-boy, a hunky man.

"Lilli. The color?"

"Tiffany blue. Very spring."

"It's rich and elegant. Plus, your mom will love it."

"That's true. Anything to do with Tiffany's makes Celeste happy."

"We should drape the chairs," Jewel said, "adding very sheer silver tulle over the blue material to give a luster effect."

They sat cross-legged on the carpeted floor before the wedding gowns from the Renata Ogilvy collection. What better place for inspiration? "Have we settled on the centerpiece?"

"Earth to Lilli. Hello? About ten minutes ago."

"Sorry." Lilli picked up the legal pad with her notes. "Clear vase filled with creamy white faux pearls to conceal the stems of the flowers. Paper-white narcissus, right?"

"That's right." Jewel sorted through another stack of pictures. "Let's add orange blossoms at each table setting. The flowers are small and the petals are white so they fit the color scheme we've picked. Plus, they're meant to symbolize good fortune to a wedding."

"We can use all the good fortune we can get."

Jewel chuckled. "Good. Now we have two decisions made."

"Hmm?"

"Where is your head?" Jewel looked up. "Let me guess. Thinking about Max?"

"I still can't believe we're working together."

"It's a good thing your mother hired him. These dresses are stunning."

"They are incredible." Lilli sighed as she took a long look at the priceless creations before her. She didn't know the dollar amount of their worth, or if you could even come up with an exact figure. Even with insurance, her mother had been right to update the security system—the dresses were irreplaceable. And since Max had installed the system personally, Lilli felt at ease keeping them here. After all, these dresses were her responsibility, not only because she'd arranged to have them showcased, but her friend Gab had taken a professional risk by talking the designer into loaning the dresses to the historical society. Then there was her mom, excited by the publicity the collection would draw. Celeste was counting on Lilli to maintain her reputation for high standards.

"Look, Max is doing his job. I don't know him, but he seems serious about his work."

And smart and professional. Nothing personal involved in the job. Is that what bothered her?

"I know it's all for the sake of the benefit."

She sighed. "I'll figure out how I feel about this after the event."

Lilli picked up another magazine clipping of a beautifully set reception table. "You know, I saw some table coverings in the closet when I arrived. Let me get one and see if it's in our color palette."

Leaving Jewel to sift through pictures, Lilli headed down the short hallway that led to the storage closet and back door. As she reached the closet, she noticed a spot of light shining on the floor. Had Mrs. R. forgotten to close the outside door tightly when she'd come in this morning? Inspecting further, she realized the door was closed, but there was light shining through a gap around the knob. She unlocked the door and opened it, peering cautiously into the back alley, but it appeared to be empty. When she stepped back inside and grabbed the handle to close the door securely, the knob nearly fell out of the door.

"What in the world?"

She looked closer, noted the knob jiggled when she touched it. She reopened the door to check outside. Scratches marred the wood around the outside knob.

"Jewel, come here."

"What's up?"

"Does this look weird to you?"

"The knob?" Jewel checked it out and nodded. "It's not fitting right."

"Exactly."

"Think Mrs. R. did something to it?"

"No. If she knew it was broken, she would have gotten someone to fix it."

Lilli exchanged an uneasy glance with Jewel. "Do you think—"

"—someone tried to break in?" Jewel finished.

"This is creepy."

"Mrs. R. was here all alone this morning. What if someone had broken in?"

Lilli hated to even consider the consequences.

"Better call Max. This falls under his job description."

Lilli pulled the door closed then hurried to the front of the office to find her phone. As much as she had hoped not to have to use it, she'd added his office number in her contact list for just such a situation as this.

"Hi, Blanche, it's Lilli Barclay. Could you let Max know someone might have tried to break in at the historical office? Thanks."

She ended the call and joined Jewel as her friend collected the scattered pictures. "He'll be right over."

"Lilli, this is serious. What if someone wanted the gowns?"

What would anyone do with a bunch of wedding gowns, even if they are priceless? "It could be nothing."

"Or it could be a problem."

"Let's let Max decide." She glanced around the office. "I'm sure he'll do a sweep of the place when he gets here."

Minutes later voices carried in from the front door. She turned in time to see Mrs. Rumpold let herself in, talking away, followed by none other than Max himself, dressed in the usual jeans and dark T-shirt, now sporting the Sanders Security logo. He'd gotten his hair trimmed, but the ever present five-o'clock shadow covered his jaw. She had to admit the look was growing on her. Just like him. His dark eyes met and searched hers from across the room, concern evident in the clear gray depths.

"I didn't come in the back way," Mrs. Rumpold said. "Or I would have called you."

Lilli walked across the room to join them. "Thanks for getting here so quickly."

"Are you okay?"

Her heart warmed over being his first concern. "Yes. No one was out back when I noticed the problem."

He nodded. "Show me."

As they began to walk down the hallway, Mrs. R. stopped Lilli. "I'm so sorry. I didn't check the back door this morning. The phone kept ringing and I had messages to answer..." Her voice caught. "I never went back there."

Worry etched the older woman's face. No point making her feel worse than she already did. "No problem, Mrs. R. I'm just glad you're okay. Max will take care of things now."

Mrs. R. smiled in spite of her tears. "He's a good man."

Lilli patted the woman's arm. "Let's go see what he's discovered."

Mrs. R. took a shaky breath. "Okay."

She returned to the hallway, Mrs. R. close behind.

"When did you notice the problem?" he asked.

"Right before I called your office. Jewel and I were working. I came to the closet and noticed something off." She angled her head toward the back door. "It looked to me as though someone tried to break in. The knob is rather cockeyed and loose, like maybe someone tampered with it. If it weren't for the dresses on display, I wouldn't worry so much."

"You didn't set the alarm?" Max asked Mrs. R.

The older woman's face fell. "I'm afraid not. To be honest, before the gowns arrived we weren't very good about setting the alarm every night. It's an excuse, I know, but I'm not in the habit yet."

He shot her a stern look. "You have to turn it on when no one is here."

"I know that. I'm… It's…"

Lilli placed her arm around Mrs. R.'s shoulder. "It'll be okay. I guess we needed a scare to make us aware of the importance of arming the system." Max opened his mouth to say more, but Lilli cut him off. "Just be sure to set the alarm every time you leave the office."

"I will," Mrs. R. promised. The phone rang and she scurried off to answer it.

Max's expression didn't reveal his frustration, but his jaw flexed. "You have to make Mrs. R., and anyone else who has regular access to the office, understand how important it is to set the alarm."

"Max, I think she learned her lesson. You saw how upset she is. There's no point in making her feel worse."

He leaned against the wall, crossing his arms over his chest. "I didn't take you for a soft touch."

"Normally I'm not, but getting ugly with Mrs. R. wouldn't help matters."

Max turned to the back door. "You're probably right."

"I am right."

"Yeah, yeah, yeah," he groused, but she didn't miss his reluctant grin.

He opened the door, walked outside and studied the doorknob. He reached out and ran a finger over the casement, the frown growing deeper.

"What do you think happened?" she asked.

"Come and see." He motioned for her to join him. She stepped out into the warm air, catching a whiff of his tangy cologne as he stood close to her. Her heart beat double-time, but she focused on the door. He pointed to the scratches in the wood.

"The scratches are fresh. I'd guess whoever did this either got spooked or couldn't pry the door open. It wouldn't have taken much more work to get the knob off completely." He jiggled it. The knob fell out of the door and clattered to the ground. Max bent down to pick it up, examining it. "Definitely suspicious."

"Thanks goodness no one got in."

Max studied the doorframe and pulled at some splintered wood. "For whatever reason, the door held up long enough to discourage the intruder."

"It would have been horrible if someone had stolen the gowns."

Mrs. R. returned from her phone call. "Is it bad?"

"No. I can fix it."

Mrs. R. looked at Max with stars in her eyes, then said to Lilli, "Leave it to Max to take care of it."

He glanced at Lilli. "I have a toolbox in the truck."

She raised her eyebrow. The things she didn't know about this man.

"I'm kinda handy with tools," he explained, amusement twinkling in his eyes. Now that the worst of the situation had passed, everyone could rest easier.

"You don't say?"

The warmth of his gaze made her heart skip. It should have bothered her, this physical re-action, but more and more she looked forward to the way she felt around him. She either had to figure out what she wanted to do about her reaction, or walk away. Since her feet were firmly planted on the ground as he smiled that killer smile at her, her only option was to stick around.

"Give me a minute."

He brushed past her, lingering just a moment as their arms brushed, before heading back into the office and out the front door. She let out the breath she didn't realize she'd held on to and hurried to her mother's office.

Inhaling deeply, she tried to slow her heart rate. This was crazy. She had to get control over this…this…what? Infatuation? *Sheesh.* The benefit couldn't get here soon enough.

Girlish anticipation rose up and she checked her hair and makeup in the travel mirror she carried in her purse. She smoothed her new jeans and cute T-shirt with the sparkly crystals on the front. Finished fussing, she sauntered out of the office on her spike-heeled sandals, hoping to catch Max's eye. She only hoped she didn't come off too obvious, because there was more than infatuation going on here.

"I'll have this fixed today." He told Lilli as she rejoined him by the back door. He dropped a screwdriver back into the box. "I'll head out to the hardware store and get the supplies I need."

"Thanks, Max. I appreciate it."

"After I fix the knob, I'll still run a system check. Although it won't do much good if the alarm isn't set when everyone leaves."

"I'm sure Mrs. R. will be on it now. She's pretty upset."

"I don't mean to put it on you, but you are in charge of things. Make sure it happens."

Her shoulders went stiff. "If I had known, I would have taken care of the problem."

"Did Mrs. R. give you the code?"

Lilli hesitated, since he wasn't going to like her answer. "Not yet."

He ran a hand over his stubbly chin.

"I planned on getting it today."

He looked less than pleased. "Make sure you keep it handy. Have you seen the keypad yet?"

"On the wall by my mother's office."

"Come with me."

Max grabbed his toolbox and they walked back to the office. Max stopped by the keypad. "It's your basic model. Easy to use."

"I'm sure I'd have figured it out."

"Give it a try." He moved so close she felt his breath in her hair. "You don't have to put heavy pressure on the keypad when you enter the number, but make sure you press firmly."

Ignoring the jitters Max inspired, Lilli focused on the tiny green glowing button, indicating the system was turned off, then did as instructed. "Got it."

It might have been her imagination, but it seemed he stood beside her a little longer than necessary, his body heat invading her space, making her flush.

He finally stepped away. "If the alarm is

armed properly, we shouldn't have any more close calls."

Lilli nodded. From now on she planned to stop by the office on her way home from work every night to make sure the alarm had been set. "Is there anything else I should do?"

"As long as everyone follows protocol, both collections will be safe."

"After this, I'm even more concerned about the Wingate collection. Do you think keeping it at the country club when it arrives is wise? Should we get a safety deposit box at the bank?"

"Klaus and I went over the security system at the club with a fine-tooth comb and when I make the upgrades, you can rest assured that no one will be able to access the safe."

"Sounds like you have the situation under control."

"It's what I do, Lilli. Trust me."

She didn't have a choice, but he'd proved he was on the job. She couldn't ask for more.

"If your mother still insists on displaying the jewelry here after the benefit, Sanders Security will work overtime."

"Let's not wait until then. Hopefully she'll realize the risk isn't worth it."

Max raised an eyebrow.

"Because of the wedding dresses," Lilli explained. "They're a big draw for the event. Come look."

She led him to the dress forms displaying the vintage collection. "These really pull the theme of the benefit together. To me, they are at least as important as the jewelry and we need to keep them safe at all costs."

"We will, Lilli."

"I'm sorry, I don't mean to go on about this. It isn't about the money. If anything were to happen, neither the jewelry nor these gowns can be replaced."

"Either way, I'll make sure both collections are protected. Today I'll fix the back door and check all the locks. I'll file a police report and alert the chief to make sure this office is part of a regular patrol. I'll also stop by frequently to check on things."

"Thanks."

A few seconds of silence passed.

"So, this is why women get all crazy over weddings?"

"You have to admit, they are exquisite."

He reached out to touch the lace on one dress. His masculine hand should have seemed out of place beside something so fragile, but in the movement, Lilli saw the gentle strength Max possessed.

"I know men don't get excited about the

planning part of the wedding," she said in a soft voice. "But it's hard to ignore the look on a man's face when he gets the first glimpse of his bride walking down the aisle wearing a dress like this."

Max turned his head. Her blood warmed at the heat smoldering in his eyes. Once again she had more questions than answers. If she could have found her voice, she might have asked what was going on between them.

Behind them, Mrs. R. cleared her throat. Max blinked and the moment vanished.

"I guess we're finished here."

Lilli nodded. Max said goodbye to the ladies, then walked out with the toolbox in his hand. Mrs. R. and Jewel moved to stand on either side of Lilli.

"I don't think he was very happy," Jewel said.

"It's his job to be upset when we don't follow security protocols."

"I don't know what I would have done if the collection had disappeared." Mrs. R. swiped at her eyes. "I should let your mother know what's going on."

Lilli stopped her. She did not want to have to explain this to Celeste. "Nothing bad happened, so let's not worry my mother. We'll be more vigilant from this point on."

Mrs. R. nodded and returned to her desk.

Lilli and Jewel returned to the area where they'd been working.

"Max probably thinks I'm incompetent. Why didn't I ask for the pass code sooner?"

"I doubt it. He's doing a job—simple as that."

"I know. It's just..."

"You seriously like Max."

Lilli nodded, her cheeks going pink.

Jewel's voice gentled. "Maybe you need to take a chance with him. Put yourself out there. You've been so busy with work you've cut yourself off from a lot of guys who would like to date you. Give Max the benefit of the doubt. You're going to Tie the Knot together."

"Not like a real date."

"But it could be."

"And then what would I do?"

Jewel grinned. "From the way he looks at you, girlfriend, I don't think it'll be long before you find out."

"His business comes first. I can't compete with that."

"So make yourself unforgettable."

Lilli groaned. "I've already done that. And not in a good way."

"Then it should be easier from here on out."

If only.

"Why don't we get back to the task at hand."

Lilli glanced at her watch. They still had a good fifteen minutes before they had to get back to the office. "What else did you want to show me?"

Jewel grabbed a notepad she'd been using. "About the wedding favors. I have an idea."

"That's why we're here. Shoot."

"Okay." Jewel showed Lilli a drawing. "How about a twist on the traditional wedding invitation. We take fancy card stock, emboss the front with the historical society logo. On the inside, on delicate paper, we print the fundraiser particulars as if they were a wedding announcement. Only it's information about the recipients of the benefit."

"Clever."

"We can punch a hole in the corner and add a blue ribbon for a finishing touch."

"Perfect. See, I told Mary you'd have great ideas. She's relieved to let you run with them."

"I love it," Jewel said as she gathered up her tote bag to return to work. "And I'm glad to be a part of it."

"Me, too. Listen, tell Jim I'll be there shortly. While I'm out I want to swing past the car dealership and see what Mr. Danielson has decided."

"Okay. See you later."

Jewel left while Mrs. R. chattered on the

phone again. Trying to suppress the restlessness that came from dealing with Max, Lilli wandered over to the display gowns. She hadn't taken time to truly admire them.

After she'd flown out of here on Saturday, she'd realized she needed to let go of what had happened at her wedding rehearsal. Yes, she'd been dumped. Yes, it hurt. But she'd moved on. She wanted to open her heart to new possibilities, not close it off forever out of fear.

As she looked back, Lilli saw that she'd wanted to marry Rob because it had seemed like the next logical step in their relationship. It was what everyone had expected. She'd lost track of the girl who'd stepped out of her comfort zone one summer night to be free.

Spending time with Max reminded her of that all-too-brief time in her life when she'd been willing to put aside what her parents and society expected in order to follow her heart. Maybe it wasn't too late to revive those dreams.

What if she'd been engaged to a man who respected her decisions and goals? A man she could partner with, not against? A man like Max? He certainly didn't mind that she enjoyed her job. Treated her as a professional equal. He asked her opinions. But could there be more between them as Jewel suggested?

Changing her line of concentration, she admired a silk Chanel wedding dress. As she read the placard, she discovered the short dress worn just below the knee with a court train was from the twenties. A cloche cap with a long veil finished the look.

Next, a slim sheath gown of white lamé with fitted sleeves and a court train cascading from the shoulders to gather delicately on the floor. A tiara held a sweeping tulle veil.

The next dress form in the row showcased an ankle-length trainless gown of white organdy over a crinoline, paired with a short bouffant veil—clearly a style from the fifties. An off-white lace minidress with a long tulle veil made Lilli laugh. The groovy style of the sixties was not her thing, but she could appreciate the workmanship that had gone into the handmade lace.

Her heart stopped when she came to the next creation. Modeled in the spirit of romance, and clearly inspired by Princess Diana, the white taffeta with seed pearls, sequins and antique lace spoke of traditional pomp and circumstance, with a bit of nobility thrown in.

Finally, an exquisite, strapless Vera Wang of ivory satin graced its dress form. Any modern bride would love to walk down the aisle in this number.

After her in-depth research about all things

bridal, the gowns took on more meaning. Each decade had a new look, updating the years before as well as including new inspiration.

One thing remained the same. All the tulle, lace, satin and silk only added to the joy of a bride joining her groom on their wedding day. Hopefully, that one fact never changed.

She fingered the lace on the dress, memories of her own wedding gown filling her mind. She remembered that she and Celeste had gone shopping at an exclusive boutique, having a girls' day out. Now that she reflected on it, though, she realized that her mother had chosen the dress. Lilli had loved the style, but there hadn't been any real emotion behind the choice.

Frowning, she glanced down at the lace in her hand. What had happened to her gown, anyway? Her mother had taken care of it, just as she had everything else related to the doomed wedding festivities at the time. Lilli dropped the material. That part of her life had ended.

She closed her eyes, thankful she hadn't married Rob. What a disaster it would have been. He hadn't been honest with her about his feelings prior to the rehearsal dinner. If they'd gone through with the wedding it would have been worse.

The image of Max standing before the town, defending himself, popped into her mind. Honesty. Max Sanders had it in spades. She now realized more than ever how much that quality mattered. At some point, her admiration for Max had subtly shifted and her heart had become engaged. Could her feelings for him get any more complicated?

With a shake of her head, she collected her purse, ready to get on with the business of the day. At least with her job, she knew where she stood and had a measure of control.

CHAPTER ELEVEN

Max walked into his office late the next morning after a successful appointment.

Blanche stopped typing and looked up. "Good morning, boss." A huge smile filled her elfin face.

"Make that an excellent morning."

"Tell me."

"I'm pretty confident I nailed the Rawlings job. He needs to talk to his board."

"Did you get more details?"

Max crossed the room to the coffee station and poured a mug. "Since Rawlings headquarters are based here, Sanders Security will continue to operate from Cypress Pointe. I'll travel to all his warehouse locations and evaluate security. This is going to take a while. After that, we'll implement and maintain security, and if Rawlings acquires new locations, we'll go in there, as well."

"So, where does that leave Bart and me?"

"I'm planning on hiring extra help to keep

things going in Cypress Pointe when I'm away. I told you I wouldn't let you go."

Blanche fiddled with the mouse beside her keyboard. "It's not me I'm worried about."

Max raised a brow. "Then who?"

"You."

"What? Why?"

"You're starting to fit in Cypress Pointe. If you're gone all the time, you'll miss out on lots of things."

"Like?"

When Blanche didn't respond he eyed her cautiously. "What's up?"

She nodded toward his office. "Special delivery."

"I didn't order anything." He strode through the outer office into his domain, stopping short when he spied the tux hanging from his door, covered by a clear plastic garment bag with the name Buxby's Formals printed on it. On closer inspection, he realized there were three suits.

"What the…?"

"Forget to tell me something?" Blanche teased as she handed him an envelope.

Max took it into his office, tossing it on his desk. "According to you, my life is an open book."

Blanche followed, standing sentinel in the doorway, her hands planted on her hips as she regarded him with an amused tilt of her lips. "See, this is what I'm talking about. Working with Lilli. If you leave, you won't have another chance."

Yeah, he'd considered that. He and Lilli had a spark, no doubt, but he still wasn't sure he could invest his heart only to watch her walk away. Granted, Lilli wasn't anything like his mother, but who knew what women wanted?

"I'm doing this all for Sanders Security. You know that."

"Bottom line, you committed to the benefit. To Lilli."

"I did. And after that, I can commit to another job."

Blanche frowned. "Are you mad Lilli got to you, convinced you to attend the benefit?"

"Who says she got to me?"

"It was your tone."

Okay, there was that. "Lilli catches me off guard. You know I don't like when that happens."

"It's not an off-guard tone. It's an interested tone."

"You can tell interest by a tone?"

"It's my job to read people. That's one of the reasons you hired me, remember?"

He didn't want to go there. "Yeah, well, she won't one-up me again."

Blanche pointed to the tux bag. "I think she did."

"I'm closing my door now."

Her knowing grin said it all as she moved out of the way so he could remove the suits. Nearly tripping over a shoe box, he kicked the door shut. Then he tipped the lid of the box up with the toe of his boot, cringing at the highly polished black leather dress shoes inside.

"Miss Barclay called a few minutes ago," Blanche sang out from the other side of the door. "I left her number on your desk."

He stood there holding the bag, deciding this had to be his worst nightmare. He'd never enjoyed dressing up, not for any reason. But he'd agreed to volunteer, so he had to go along with the dress code. Lilli knew that.

So, here came the sticky dilemma. Should he be ticked that she sent him tuxes to choose from, as though he was so fashion challenged he couldn't pick one out on his own? Or should he be flattered she wanted him to look his best?

He remembered how knock-out gorgeous she'd looked at the forum and decided she probably thought he didn't have a clue how to dress.

He tossed the garment bag on the chair in front of his desk and snatched up the envelope, ripping it open to read the neat writing. *Any of*

these tuxedos would look wonderful with your
build. Pick one and send the others back. Lilli.

Smiling, he searched for Lilli's number on
his cell and dialed. "The tuxes are here," he
told her.

"And?"

"Thanks."

He didn't want to admit it, but her shopping
in his place had him made his life a whole lot
easier.

"And I wanted to thank you for Sunday," she
said. "Taking me to talk to your grandmother
helped me iron out a couple of rough spots for
the event."

"Glad I could help." Okay, deep waters here.
How much more did he want to be involved
with her, besides the whole charity event? He
couldn't deny the attraction, but to pursue
her? He'd gone to the forum to network, nothing more. She had a schedule filled up with
work and the fund-raiser. If they did get together, would they be too busy to make time
for each other? What would she expect from
him? Would she want him to change, to fit in
with the country club set that seemed so much
a part of her life? He glanced at the garment
bag. Any woman who could pick out a tux at
a moment's notice probably wouldn't be inter-

ested in a man who lived in T-shirts and jeans anyway.

"While I have you on the phone," he continued. "I wanted to let you know I stopped by the historical society office this morning. Everything looks okay."

"Good to know"

"All part of the service."

"Great," Lilli said in a less-than-perky tone. "I need to get back to work. Big account. You know how that goes."

What had he said wrong? "Right. Again, thanks for the tux options."

She hung up after a soft goodbye, leaving Max to shake his head. He had to get her off his mind. He had a business to run, a tux to choose and Bart waiting for his first assignment. He turned to the window framing the pale green Gulf water sparkling in the morning sun. As much as he'd love to be out on a boat skimming the waves, his life was nothing if not demanding.

With one last longing glance at the water, he moved away from the window before he chucked all common sense and took off for the day.

By the time he made some phone calls and reviewed a couple of promising cases, the clock hit noon. He needed a breather. He stepped from his office as Blanche hung up the office phone.

"Did you pick out a tux?"

"Blanche, I have a business to run. This isn't a modeling agency."

"You have to make a decision."

On so many things in his life. "Right now I'm deciding to eat lunch."

"I'll look forward to a fashion show this afternoon." She shot him a wide grin.

Max scowled and jogged down the stairs, stepping out of the doorway onto the sidewalk in front of his office. Heaven save him from women. All women. From smart-alecky secretaries to persuasive society babes.

LILLI GAVE UP her free Wednesday night for an emergency meeting at the club with the historical society charity committee. If she hadn't known better, she would have thought Marisa had staged a coup. Each woman expressed concern over some plans or failure to carry out other plans. It had taken two hours to sort through the mess. Anyone else would have thrown her hands up walked away, but Lilli's sense of responsibility kept her from doing just that.

Finally, after nine o'clock, all she wanted to do was go home and down a few aspirin.

"Mom, where are you?" she wondered out loud in the now empty room.

Celeste still hadn't come home. Ever the dutiful daughter, Lilli had checked in with her, keeping Celeste up to date. When Lilli asked when she'd be home, Celeste continued with vague answers. It was unusual for her mother to stay out of the action this long. Lilli had even called her father, but the call had gone to voice mail. Weird, because her father usually picked up when she called. What was up with her parents?

With a sigh, she stuffed her tote bag. The lists, which had been getting smaller, had suddenly doubled in size, and she still had material to review for a possible new account at work. She needed to focus on work more and the benefit less.

With work on her mind, she shouldered her bag, turned off the lights and stopped by the front desk to let the assistant manager, Tom, know the meeting had ended. He asked about planning, chatted about the bridal dress collection, wondering when the dresses would be brought to the club from the historical society office and assuring her the collection would be safe. His concern seemed overboard, and Max had security under control, but she appreciated his attention to detail.

After saying goodbye, she headed to the nearly empty parking lot, more than ready to get home. The meeting had sapped what little energy she had left after a full day at work. Unlocking the driver's side car door, she tossed her bag onto the passenger seat before sliding inside. Something felt off.

She got out of the car and inspected the exterior, finding her front left tire flat. "What on earth…?" she muttered, already pulling out her cell phone. She scrolled through her numbers, trying to decide who she should call for help. She tried AAA, but the line was busy. She didn't relish the idea of waiting alone in the parking lot at night. She supposed the attempted break-in at the historical society office still had her a little on edge.

She found a phone number for a local automotive garage, but got an after-hours message for an emergency number. She called that number, only to hear another recording stating someone would call her back.

Frustrated, she scrolled through the contact list again in hopes of finding another alternative when she came across Max's office number. Should she bother him? He did tell her to call if she needed anything. A flat tire constituted need. She pressed the Send button, not expecting him to answer but secretly hoping he would.

He picked up on the third ring. "Sanders."

"Max, it's Lilli. Got a minute?"

He hesitated a beat. "Sure. What's up?"

"I'm standing in the country club parking lot and I have a problem with my car."

His voice went from personally bothered to professionally alert. "What kind of problem?"

"Flat tire."

Silence. Then, "Are you alone?"

"Yes."

"I'll be right there."

He clicked off, not sounding thrilled at her request. She shouldn't have bothered him. Should have waited on the line for AAA instead. Or she should have learned how to change a tire sometime in her life. It would have saved her the humiliation of a disgruntled Max Sanders showing up to save the day.

About five minutes passed until Max pulled up in his truck. He jumped out, walking straight to her.

"You okay?"

"Yes."

He searched her face, as if looking for some hidden answer. Apparently satisfied, he nodded before turning to check out the damage. "I take it your car wasn't in this condition when you left it?"

"No. I had an emergency meeting tonight. When I got in the car to leave, I noticed something wrong."

"So you decided to call me?"

In the overhead light, she saw the cocky rise of his eyebrow.

"I couldn't get through to AAA or the garage in town. Are you unhappy that I called you?"

"Of course not," he bit out. "Pop the trunk so I can get the spare."

Could he be any more underwhelmed? Lilli suddenly felt foolish for even thinking the spark of interest she'd sensed between them meant anything. Clearly, he didn't want to be here. But he changed the tire, the muscles under his shirt flexing as he made short work of the task at hand. She couldn't turn away.

"What?" Max asked as he stood to put away the flat tire and tools.

"Nothing. Look, I'm sorry I bothered you."

"Lilli…"

She held up her hand. "I get it. You only came out here because you work for the historical society. You don't have to be a friend. Don't worry, unless it's about the event, you won't hear from me again."

"I didn't mind."

At his calm tone and the concerned expression on his face, Lilli sighed. "My mother's project is taking up too much of my time and I'm not even active in the society. A flat tire is icing on the cake."

"You aren't part of the historical society?"

"No." She shook her head. "Technically, yes. My name is on the roster." She let out a frustrated breath. "It's a long story."

"I have time."

Surprised by his response, since a few minutes ago he'd seemed put out, she hesitated, not sure what to do. Should she confide in him? She wanted to. And she didn't want to.

What a mess. "It's my problem and I've bothered you enough for one night."

"I'm happy to listen."

"Maybe another time."

Max shrugged tight shoulders. "Whatever you want. I'll follow you home."

Much as she hated the ingrained response, her back went up. "There's no need."

"Humor me."

The overhead light caught the steely resolve reflected in his eyes. Okay, so maybe she wasn't used to having someone concerned about her welfare. "Okay, you win."

She got into her car and headed in the direction of her apartment, Max's headlights steady behind her. She let out a sigh. Much as she would never admit it, knowing he followed brought her comfort. Only a stand-up guy would bother seeing to her safety.

Minutes later they arrived at her apartment complex. He joined her as she locked her car. "You gonna be okay?"

"Yes, thanks." She glanced up at him. Took a chance. "Want to come in for some iced tea?"

"You sure?"

"It's the least I can do since you came to my rescue."

"Let me get something out of the truck first."

She waited. When he joined her, he thrust a large envelope into her hands. "Photos from Gram. She wants you to pick your favorites for the benefit."

Lilli hugged the envelope to her chest. "Thanks."

They stood under the moonlight for a long moment. The sweet aroma of orange blossoms scented the air. Lilli risked a glance in his direction to find Max's intense focus directed at her. She couldn't decipher the look in his eyes, but the heat that emanated from him sent a delicious shiver over her skin.

"Um, we should go up."

They climbed the stairs in silence and entered her apartment. Max stood in her living room while she hurried about turning on lights.

Strange, having this larger-than-life male standing in her very feminine apartment, blatantly checking out her digs.

Sure, friends like Jewel spent plenty of time here, but having Max filling the space felt new and a little nerve-racking.

"I'm not normally a damsel in distress," she blurted. Even to her own ears she sounded needy and hated it.

A grin tipped his lips, as if Max knew how she felt and sympathized with her.

"What can I get you? Coffee? Iced tea?"

"Tea is good."

"Have a seat, and I'll be with you in a minute."

She poured two glasses then joined him on the couch.

Max leaned forward and picked up one of the bridal pictures Lilli had left spread out on the coffee table. "Pretty dress. Ever think about wearing one?"

"Almost did, once."

His brow rose. "And?"

"He ended it at the rehearsal dinner. At the country club."

"Ouch."

"Exactly." She pushed her glass around, unsure if she should give details or leave it at that.

"So, a fund-raiser with a wedding theme."

He glanced over at her, his gaze dark and steady. "Think your Mom planned it on purpose?"

"On purpose?"

"Since your wedding never took place, maybe she's trying to tell you something."

"I wouldn't put it past her, but not for the reasons you think."

"You'd be surprised what I think."

She supposed she would. "My mother wants me to consider the possibility of marriage, especially after the breakup. I don't think she planned this on purpose. She's not an intentionally mean person, but she really gets immersed in her projects. She would never come right out and tell me to get back into the dating world, but I'm sure that's what she wants."

"Seems extreme. Why not sit down and talk it out?"

"In my family, that's not so easy." She took a sip of her tea then asked, "How about you? Do you talk things through with the people in your life?"

"Not usually." Max took a sip of the tea then said, "I guess Gram is right."

"About what?"

"I'm not very good at opening up to people."

"Old habit?"

"Guess you could say so."

"Hmm. We have that in common."

They sat in silence.

"Maybe your mother has a point. Life goes on."

Her shoulders sagged. "I know."

"It's just…you've got a lot going for you. Don't let some jerk get you down."

She glanced pointedly at him.

"Me included."

Lilli laughed. "I hardly think you fall into that category."

"Darlin', your mother would never consider me marriage material. She'd have blown a gasket if I came around."

"And you know this how?"

"No mother in her right mind would let her daughter near me. And for good reason. You name it, I probably did it. Can't believe Gram put up with me."

"I think that's what parents do—wish for the best and pray a lot."

"That's Gram."

"So why did you give her a hard time?"

"Young and stubborn. I guess it's safe to say you aren't the only one with mother issues."

Lilli offered him a look she hoped would encourage him to continue.

"Like I told you, my dad died when I was

young and my mom couldn't handle me. It was Gram or the foster system."

"Oh, Max, I'm sorry."

He shrugged. "It was a long time ago. Anyway, things didn't go well between Mom and me so she took off."

"Just left you behind?"

"Dumped me at Gram's is more like it. Yep. Gram was the only family I had, so she took me in."

"Wow. I thought my parents were tough."

"I had a major chip on my shoulder. I don't think I really came to terms with how I felt about my mom leaving until I went into the navy. Honestly, if it hadn't been for Gram's tough love and the chief's interference, I probably would have ended up a career criminal."

Max sifted through a few more pictures. Lilli would have loved to know what went on in his mind. He didn't seem in a hurry to leave so she searched for any topic not wedding related. Anything to discover the secrets under his tough exterior.

"Anyway, I straightened up."

"You did a good job." She laughed. "You're an upstanding business owner now, but you were definitely *not* the kind of guy my parents would have let me hang out with back then."

"I think we've already established that fact.

I'm not sure others see how much I've changed, though. Your mother hired me for a job. I don't think she anticipated anything more."

She glanced at him. He still had an air of danger about him, one that spoke of stolen kisses on moonlit nights. "Still, it would have been fun. Doing the exact opposite of what people expected."

"I wouldn't go glamorizing it. I was trouble, pure and simple, and didn't care who I hurt. Not exactly a sterling quality."

Lilli noted the pensive light in his eyes that might have spelled trouble a long time ago, but now he was driven to prove himself trustworthy. To right the wrongs of his past by behaving maturely. Responsibly. "You're a good man, Max. Every person in this town will come to realize what you've done to turn your life around."

He leaned toward her. Her ears began to buzz and her heart raced. His gaze moved to her lips and she went a little lightheaded.

"I like you, Max. Granted, we got off on the wrong foot, starting at the beach that summer night and now with Tie the Knot, but I've discovered you're good at what you do. You care about your grandmother. About Bart. Any woman would be lucky to have you."

"What if I don't care what other women think? Only you."

She swallowed hard. "Then I would tell you the more I've come to know you, the more you've grown on me. Sure, you're controlling and single-minded about your business, but I can overlook that."

"Just like I can overlook you being bossy, not to mention prim and proper."

"Bossy?" Is that how he saw her? "Try I'm good at my job. Or, jobs, I should say."

"Point taken. But you're nice, too. I was ready to read Mrs. R. the riot act and you handled her much more gently."

"Maybe we even each other out."

"Right." Max sat back. "It's probably best we focus on the fund-raiser."

Great. She'd blown the intimate moment by mentioning work. "Why? Is there something else to focus on?"

His gaze moved to her lips again. Heat shot through her. She realized his intention. Tonight they'd moved into new, uncharted territory in their relationship. Not like the night on the beach when a stolen kiss had caught her off guard. That was kid's stuff. By the current look in his eyes, they'd graduated to grown-up awareness.

Max's eyes moved back to meet hers. He

didn't say a word, but he had her complete attention. She swallowed hard, waiting. For him to make the first move? For him to say how he felt? Anything.

When that didn't happen, she tried to downplay the anticipation between them by asking, "So, um, are you going to the fish fry on Saturday?"

He hesitated. "Not sure."

Oops. Had she stepped over the line? "Listen, you don't have to tell me anything."

"It's not that." He looked uneasy. "I kind of have previous plans."

Lilli's stomach dropped. Did he have a date on Saturday? With one of the women she'd seen listed on his calendar? Heat flushed her face. Here they sat, caught in this tug of attraction, and he might have a date? She eased away from him.

"It's not a big deal."

They fell into silence again, turning into a long drawn-out moment.

Abruptly, he rose. "I think I should call it a night."

She followed him to the door, torn between wanting to ask if she was the only woman in his life and wondering if she should just let it go. The small foyer left little room between them. Shadows enveloped them in the dim light. She stared up at him, her heart beating rapidly. He reached for the knob, then dropped his hand and angled toward her. With a frown wrinkling his forehead, he leaned down and pressed his lips against hers.

Her heart nearly stopped beating. She rested her palms on his chest and sank into the kiss, determined to make this moment last. The kiss went a little deeper and she fell for Max a little harder. Just as she slid her hands to his shoulders he pulled away.

"Not a good idea," he said, his voice low, clipped. "I gotta go before I do something stupid."

"Like kiss me again?"

He closed his eyes. "I'm not the right guy for you. You need promises. A future. I'm not that guy."

"You could be."

He stepped back. "I need to go." He opened the door and slipped away before she could think of any way to stop him.

She pressed her forehead against the cool door, eyes closed. Did he regret coming here tonight? Kissing her? Did he want more between them, as she did? Or would it always just be about work?

She wished she could go back to that electric kiss and ignore the world around them.

She wished she didn't care if he was interested in her beyond the job. If he wanted to try for more. Considering his past, maybe Max didn't want to take a chance. She'd felt the same way not long ago. Now…something in her had shifted, and she suspected it was because of the man who'd just walked out her door.

MAX TOOK A SIP of the too-hot coffee and grimaced. He'd stopped at Cuppa Joe for his morning fix, looking for caffeine and absolution. Last night's kiss with Lilli had left him replaying and overanalyzing the moment until he finally fell into a restless sleep.

Yeah, he meant to keep Lilli at a distance, if only to cover his own reaction to their kiss. It had rocked his universe, right down to his toes.

No way he'd fit into her future. Right now the only thing they had in common was the historical society. After the benefit, they'd both move on to new work projects. He was working long hours already, and if he got the Rawlings account, it would mean being gone frequently over the next few months, maybe longer. They couldn't build a relationship that way.

"Max, are you listening to me?"

He snapped out of his mental grousing, turning his attention to the owner of the coffee shop, Dorinda Hobart, one of his grandmother's friends. Since returning to Cypress Pointe, he'd made it a habit to stop into Cuppa Joe every morning. Not only to shoot the breeze with the older lady, but to check in on her. She kept him busy with all kinds of handyman jobs around the shop. Along with Gram's other ladies, he had a lengthy to-do list and a full calendar.

"Sorry, Ms. Hobart. You were saying?"

"The back door is sticking. I tried calling last night, but got your voice mail."

"By the time I got home last night, it was too late to return your call."

Dorinda waved her hand. "Neither here nor there. You'll take a look? The Merchants Association is after me all the time to fix this, update that. They're never happy with what I do, especially since they've revitalized downtown. It seems I have a notice for improvements taped on my door at least once a week. I'm getting too old for this."

"I'm on it."

He made his way to the back room, checking out her complaint. Yep, it was sticking. Nothing a wood plane couldn't smooth out.

If only he could fix his personal life so easily.

He headed back to the front of the store. "I

can take care of it for you. I'll bring the tools tomorrow morning."

"You're a good man, Max."

"If I were a few years older, watch out," he quipped.

She laughed. "My Joe was the only man for me."

"The world's loss."

"And you're too handsome to still be single."

He shrugged. "Haven't found the right woman yet."

"I find that hard to believe."

"Believe it." Did he say that for her benefit or his?

Not only did Dorinda brew a rich cup of coffee, she had a big heart, always seeing the best in people. That's why some folks stopped by for coffee and advice, and some because they just wanted to hang around. Gram said the coffee shop was Dorinda's living room. Max didn't know about that, but he knew the woman was well liked.

Dorinda's eyes twinkled. "The right woman will come into your life."

He tried not to visualize Lilli, her cheeks flushed after his kiss, and failed.

"How do you know when it's right?"

"Your life changes. You think about that person all the time. Stop to consider their needs.

See something funny and want to share it with that special someone. There are lots of ways, Max, but you just know."

Did he know? Lilli got to him, in ways no other woman had. She was ambitious, but not cutthroat. She hadn't wanted to head up the fund-raiser, but helped her mother anyway. She volunteered at the animal shelter. He supposed if he put his mind to it, the list could go on and on. He was definitely attracted and, bottom line, he liked her. Liked being with her. But was that love?

To get his mind off Lilli and his clumsy attempt at romance last night, he nodded to one of many pictures on the wall behind the counter featuring a familiar woman posing with different Hollywood stars. She looked familiar. "Who's that?"

Dorinda beamed. "That's my engaged granddaughter, Nealy."

"Wow. She sure grew up." Frowning, Max looked closer. "Is she with George Clooney?"

"Yes, I think that's what she told me."

"She's engaged to Clooney?"

"No, a different man. She works with many celebrities. George happens to be one of them."

"Huh."

"So, young man, no changing the subject.

Your grandmother and I would like to see you settled. What do you say?"

"Did I mention you make great coffee?"

"Your grandmother says you always put off talking about the future." Dorinda scrutinized him sagely. "Love is going to happen, Max."

"I promise to tell you when it does," he replied with lack of conviction. He needed to figure out this attraction to Lilli. "But right now I'm working on building my business contacts. There's a good chance I'll land a nationwide security job. It'll involve travel."

"Travel? Oh, dear, your grandmother just got you back home."

"It's a good move for the business."

"But not for settling down."

"I'm not ready."

She shook her head. "You are stubborn."

"What can I say? It runs in the family."

"Then remember this. You can't escape love. Your grandparents had an abiding love. Even your mother and father, before he passed. I know you can't see it because of the way your mother left. She was heartbroken, Max. I don't agree with how she handled the situation, but I can understand why. The memories were too much for her to bear."

Just like his memories of his mother not loving him enough.

"I have no doubt you'll fall in love one day. Just keep your heart open." Dorinda patted his cheek and went to wait on customers.

He considered the older woman's words. His father's passing away became too much for his mother to handle? He'd never stopped to consider that. Was seeing her son daily a reminder of what she'd lost? That still didn't justify her actions, but he could almost understand. Loving another person was not for the faint of heart. It took dedication. Commitment. Qualities Max possessed, but he didn't know if he could risk sharing them with a woman.

He finished off the last of his coffee and waved goodbye to Dorinda as he exited the coffee shop. A lot to take in, this ah-ha moment. He headed down to the beach to walk by the water where he did his best thinking. City workmen were busy assembling booths for the fish fry. Saturday would be another celebration in Cypress Pointe.

Security jobs, an intern and a fancy benefit were about all he had to celebrate right now. He wasn't about to complain. This was what he wanted. Because, while he may wish for more with Lilli, he wouldn't expose his heart only to be trampled again by an important woman in his life.

CHAPTER TWELVE

TIRED AND OVERHEATED, Lilli exhaled a relieved sigh when her shift helping out the animal shelter at the Merchants Association Annual Fish Fry ended. Jewel, who had been working beside her, whipped off her apron and grabbed her purse.

"You're really going to leave me?" Lilli asked as she handed out her final cold soda.

"Sorry."

Lilli grinned. "No, you're not. You're up to no good."

"Why would you say that?"

"Because of the mysterious grin you've had all afternoon. And the fact that you keep looking out into the crowd like you're searching for someone."

"You got me." Jewel grinned unrepentantly. "I'm meeting Bart."

"Really? When did this start?"

"Today. Officially." She tried to shrug it off, but couldn't downplay her giddiness. "We've been talking since that day we met him on the sidewalk and Max tried to take Bart to the police station."

"So how long has this crush been going on?" Lilli asked.

"Awhile." Jewel's eyes lit up when she spoke. "A few months ago I ran into him at Cuppa Joe. We caught up and…I don't know, things clicked. For me, anyway."

"I'd say for him, too."

"What have you got planned for tonight?" Jewel asked.

"I'll head home to my quiet apartment," Lilli said, fighting off impending gloom.

"Sounds boring. If you want you can meet us for dinner."

"You're a wonderful friend to offer, but three's a crowd. I'll be fine by myself."

"You're sure?"

"I'm sure." She gestured toward the beach. "Now go. Have fun."

Jewel grinned and hurried off.

Her shift now over, Lilli realized she didn't want to go back to her apartment for another Saturday night alone. Puffing out a heavy sigh, she brushed off her pink tank and denim shorts. Even though she'd been protected by a canopy, she still felt hot and grimy after hours spent doling out sodas under the hot sun. She ran a hand over the damp strands falling from her ponytail and tucked them into place, hoping for the best.

Instead of going straight to her car, Lilli decided to walk off her restlessness. Dodging families and couples enjoying a festive day out, she inhaled the salty air, finally relaxed and headed toward the pier. The late-afternoon sun angled over the beach, elongating shadows as it slowly began its descent.

What a romantic scene. Her thoughts strayed to Max and his mysterious plans. She had to face the fact that she liked the guy way too much. Even though he'd kissed her senseless the other night, he hadn't been in touch since. Maybe he just wasn't into her.

On that depressing note, she trudged through the sand, squinting against the sun to make out the shapes of adults and kids splashing in the water. When she reached the pier, she strolled the entire length of the wood structure to the far end. Water lapped against the pylons and a stray gull swooped by her. In the distance she heard voices and laughter, the aroma of fried food lingering in the air. A breeze swept over her cheeks. For a moment she forgot about the hustle and bustle her life had become and enjoyed the reprieve from it all. She'd take ten minutes to recharge her batteries before heading home. With only a week to go before the event, the pressure was on.

Worry about it later.

She stepped from the railed section down a few steps to an open platform used for public fishing. All the fishermen were enjoying the town revelry, leaving this popular fishing spot deserted. And Lilli all alone. It shouldn't bother her; she'd been alone all her life. Her parents, always so busy, had forgotten about her a vast majority of the time. Looking around at the happy families enjoying the fish fry, she regretted what she'd never had.

Thinking about family made Lilli reflect on Max's grandmother, Laverne. She'd viewed the photos Max had delivered, one part envious and the other touched by the way the couple looked at each other, with a wealth of love Lilli had never experienced in her life. The shining eyes said it all, the hopes and dreams of the young couple. Just talking to Laverne, Lilli knew the older woman still treasured the memories of her husband. Lilli wanted that. Sure, she loved her job and the satisfaction that came with it, but realized she also wanted a husband who loved her, a man to be her partner and friend. Someone to be there for her.

An image of Max popped into her mind. Instead of brushing it away as she normally would, she allowed herself a small smile, indulging in the luxury of a fantasy where they were a loving couple.

She laughed out loud. Even though Max had kissed her like there was no tomorrow, he didn't seem inclined to move their relationship forward. Maybe it was better this way.

Lowering herself to sit on the scratchy wood platform, she dangled her feet over the water and closed her eyes. Images of weddings and handsome grooms filled her mind, and for once she let them. Yes, her heart still ached a little, but not nearly as much as it had just a few weeks ago.

The minutes stretched out until Lilli lost track of time. For the first times in months she felt rested and ready to take on the world. She opened her eyes, glimpsing the cobalt sky streaked with orange and pink as the sun dropped lower to the horizon.

In the distance she heard the heavy thump of footsteps headed her way, causing her to tuck her sweet dreams away for another time. She'd been fortunate up till now that no one from the festivities had come here to watch the beautiful sunset, allowing her to indulge in wishful thinking. With her solitude over, she stood. A fish jumped and a gull swept by again, startling her.

As she came upright, her foot slipped on the end of the platform and she wavered toward the water. Suddenly a strong arm looped around her waist, yanking her back against a solid body.

"W-what in the world?" she stammered.

"Didn't want you to end up in the water." The deep voice in her ear sent shivers up and down her spine.

She twisted around as he loosened his hold. "Max? What're you doing here?"

He shrugged, not letting her move away from him. Not that she planned on going anywhere.

"I didn't think you'd be here today," she said.

"I recall saying maybe."

"Oh, well, then I guess I need to thank you for saving me. Again."

He grinned crookedly, and her stomach flipped. What was it about this guy that got to her? A man with a calendar filled with other women's names. A man who gave cryptic answers about having other plans. A man who kissed her, only to apologize after. How he made her heart race even while he offered her no promises. And why did she like it?

He settled his hands on her hips. "By all means. Don't let me stop you. You can thank me for my heroic deeds anytime."

If she didn't know any better, she'd believe he liked saving her. "Thanks."

"You're welcome."

They stood close, staring at each other. Lilli knew she should do something, say something, but all reason flew from her mind as she stared into his smoky eyes.

Max cleared his voice. "I was thinking about heading back and getting something to eat. Care to join me?"

Should she? She had all sorts of tasks to get home to, but not one of them seemed as important as staying here with Max. She'd be crazy to turn him down.

"I could eat something."

He smiled but didn't move. His hands flexed on her hips. "Then let me escort you."

"Hmm. You can look at this as a practice run for your volunteer groom duties. Minus the tuxedo." She meant to be teasing, but when Max frowned, she realized she's made a mistake.

"Sorry, Lilli. I cancelled my subscription to GQ. Besides, it's a fish fry. Who dresses up for that?"

"Look, I didn't mean to offend you."

"Of course you didn't." He quirked a brow. "Just like you don't trust me to pick out a tux?"

"You didn't sound like you had much experience with tuxedos and I only wanted to help."

"Yeah, well, I've been dressing myself for a long time. I think I could have handled it."

Covering up her embarrassment, she pointedly looked him up and down, as though she questioned the wisdom of that. "Fine. I won't help anymore. Pick out your own tux and forget any pointers on being a gentlemanly groom."

"Hey, I can be as gentlemanly as the next guy. Besides, it's not about the shopping, it's about your—"

Lilli silenced him by grabbing a fistful of shirt and pulling him to her for a kiss. It took only seconds for Max to become fully invested, his hands tightening on her hips. She shivered in the warm air as he pressed his firm lips over hers. Running her hands up his chest to his shoulders, she tilted her head for better access, forgetting time and place as she lost herself in the moment. She twined her fingers behind his neck, brushing them through his hair. All that mattered was keeping Max close. So close that he would never forget her or how she affected him. And the heat of his kiss told her he was more than affected.

Max finally broke the moment. "What the…?"

"After you left my apartment so abruptly the other night, I wondered if it was because

I didn't do it for you." She smirked. "Apparently I do."

Satisfied by making her point and enjoying his kiss at the same time, she turned from Max, intending to march down the pier, her head held high. Just then, the marauding gull from earlier streaked toward them.

Lilli screeched and jumped out of the way, tugging Max with her. She took a step back and realized she'd stepped into thin air. With her mouth gaping, she teetered over the water before dropping straight into the Gulf.

As soon as she went under, she quickly kicked upward. She broke the surface to catch her breath, but a splash coming from Max's direction hit her in the face. Salt water filled her mouth and she spit it out, coughing. Within seconds he surfaced beside her as she trod water, still trying to breathe.

"Lilli," he gasped.

"I'm fine. I can swim," she called out.

Rivulets of water rolled from his dark hair over his face, his strong arms sweeping through the water as he stayed upright. "Let's get to the shore."

They only had to swim a few yards before the water grew shallow. Before long she could touch the bottom, and they were slogging onto the beach.

"What happened?" Max asked as he rubbed water from his face.

"That kamikaze bird startled me again."

They reached dry sand and fell. Lilli took one look at Max's disgruntled face and started to giggle. Reluctantly, he joined in, until they both were on their backs, laughing loudly.

Once the merriment subsided, he turned his head to study her. "Sure you're okay?" he asked.

She nodded.

"I figured I'd have to haul you out of the water."

She sat up. "Hey, I know how to swim. Those years of lessons paid off." Hiding a grin, she wrung out the hem of her shirt. "I thought maybe I'd have to save *you* for a change."

Max also sat, brushing sand from his jeans. "Fat chance."

She arched a brow at him, brushing her hair off her face. "Oh?"

"Navy, sweetheart."

That's right. She'd forgotten.

"Cypress Pointe Country Club swimming instructor," she said, trying to one-up him.

His eyes narrowed.

"Okay, not the same thing. But I get points for trying."

In the waning light she could make out the

lingering concern in his eyes. "What you do to me—"

He suddenly stopped speaking, his eyes going dark. He leaned toward her—to kiss her again, she hoped—when the sound of voices cut him off.

With a frustrated groan, Max rolled away while Lilli looked over his shoulder. Jewel and Bart approached, arm in arm.

"Oh, this is classic," Jewel announced.

"Did you push her in?" Bart asked Max with all seriousness.

"It had occurred to me," Max said as he rose, offering his hand to haul Lilli up.

"Oh, please," she said, reluctantly taking his hand.

"Let me take you home."

"Thanks, but I drove here." She ran her hands over her wet clothing. "I need to get changed."

Before leaving, Lilli glanced at Max, catching a quick flash of heat in his eyes. Then he nodded, reverting to his even gaze, covering any feeling. But she'd seen it.

Oh, yeah, she affected Max Sanders whether he liked it or not.

SHORTLY AFTER NOON, Lilli walked into her apartment following her usual Sunday afternoon grocery shopping. She'd started to put away the groceries when her phone rang. She frowned at the caller ID. The security company.

"Please come to the historical society office. The alarm has been set off."

Grabbing her purse and tossing her cell phone inside, Lilli rushed to her car, still dressed in a T-shirt, shorts and flip-flops. Concern washed over her. What on earth could have happened? Something to do with the gowns on loan from Renata Ogilvy? Maybe someone had succeeded in breaking the door down.

She parked and exited the car, nearly turning her ankle in her haste. Dragging her purse over her shoulder, Lilli raced to the office. Mrs. Rumpold opened the door, pulling Lilli inside. She took a quick look around, noticing Max checking the back door. Of course he'd beat her here.

"I can't make them leave," the older woman stage-whispered.

"What?" Lilli dragged her attention back to Mrs. Rumpold.

"I got a call from the company monitoring the security system telling me that the alarm went off. I hurried over, only to find those two standing outside the wide-open door."

Lilli turned the other way to find Marisa and Sissy Vandermere in the office. "The door was open?"

"Yes. Sissy has a key, but not the code to the alarm. When the alarm went off they had the good sense to stay outside until I could get here and key in the code."

"Was anything taken?"

"No. Max arrived when I did and walked through the office. The Vandermeres set off the alarm. No burglars."

Lilli put a hand over her rapidly beating heart. "Thank goodness it wasn't anything more serious."

Mrs. R. patted her own chest. "They just about gave me a coronary."

Lilli blew out a sigh of relief. Although the poor woman appeared frazzled, she seemed otherwise fine.

Max joined them, sporting a frown. "The alarm went off because of the Vandermeres. The doors and windows are untouched. I'm going to walk around the building, but I don't expect to find anything out of the norm. I'll also let the chief know what's going on." He smiled at Mrs. R. and Lilli swore the woman almost swooned. "Good job remembering to set the alarm."

"After all the fuss the other day, I make sure I set it every time I leave."

"About that, I'm sorry I came down so hard on you."

Mrs. R. patted his arm. "You did the right thing."

Lilli watched them, fighting back a grin. Big bad Max, apologizing.

He nodded at Lilli. "I'll be back." He turned on his heel and headed outside. Mrs. R. started muttering. Lilli glanced at her, then followed Mrs. R.'s pointing finger. Marisa and her mother Sissy fussed over what looked like a wedding gown.

"That's not one of the loaners," Lilli said. The trendy gown the women surrounded did not look vintage in the least.

"No. It's worse." Mrs. R. replied, her eyes round. "Marisa's first gown. From the first wedding. You know, one of the two that never took place."

Oh, boy. This is going to get tricky.

Lilli dropped her purse on the desk and tentatively made her way to the mother-daughter tag team. "Good afternoon, ladies. What's going on?"

Marisa turned on her expensive heel, her mother peering over her shoulder.

"Just my little contribution to the cause."

Lilli stepped around the women, her eyes

on the wedding gown. Exquisite, of course.
Marisa wouldn't own anything but an expensive designer original. The fitted bodice, covered with little seed pearls, stopped at the waist and flared out in layer over layer of lovely silk. Talk about a Cinderella fantasy.

"Why, exactly, are you contributing?"

Marisa placed her hands on her hips and sighed, regarding Lilli like she was a child. "We both know I won't use this dress. That wedding never took place, but it is beautiful and should be seen."

Lilli couldn't argue its beauty, but it didn't add to the vintage theme of the benefit, unlike the gown Marisa was scheduled to model. How many unused wedding dresses could one woman own? Lilli was standing there, contemplating what to do, when Sissy piped up.

"We think you should move those older outfits off to the side, and put Marisa's dress front and center."

Mrs. Rumpold gasped. "Those gowns are works of art."

"They're in the way." That said, Sissy curled her arm around the dress form with the Princess Diana-style gown, lifting it from the floor. As she did, the heavy bottom bumped the dress form holding the Chanel, toppling it to the ground.

Wincing, Lilli ran over, hoping to catch the dress and prevent any damage. She managed to grab the Chanel just as it hit the ground but her stomach sank when she noticed seed pearls scattered on the carpet from the Diana style dress.

"Look what you've done," Mrs. R. scolded, her voice steely as she gently removed the dress from Sissy's grasp. "You shouldn't have touched anything."

"I only wanted Marisa's dress to be seen."

Heart racing, Lilli pulled her hair back from her face as she tried to calm down. "I think it would be best if you took Marisa's dress home."

"Home?" Sissy glared at her. "But we just got here."

Lilli barely held on to her temper. "I think you ladies should leave."

Marisa had the sense to realize the gravity of the situation even if her mother did not. They argued between themselves as Marisa stuffed the gown back into the garment back and ushered her mother out the door. Once they left, Lilli and Mrs. R. inspected the damaged dress.

"It's not too bad," Mrs. R. commented. "Only one section of pearls came loose."

"I'm going to have to call Gabrielle."

Mrs. R. held up the pearls she'd rescued from

the floor in her hand. "Do you think the gown can be repaired?"

"Gab would know. This is her area of expertise."

Lilli went quiet for a moment, the ramifications of Sissy's actions running through her mind. "You know, once I call Gab, the display might be cancelled."

"Sissy would love that, making your mother look bad."

While Lilli hated that her mother might look bad, her friend, not Celeste's, had arranged the loaners.

Not one to procrastinate, Lilli called Gabrielle and explained the situation. Gab went mute at first, probably stunned, but rallied to the moment. "Lilli, we expect some wear and tear on the garments as they age."

"This is a little more than normal aging."

"Are there many pearls missing?"

"None. We collected them all."

"Tell you what. I'll come by tomorrow and evaluate the damage. If possible, I may be able to sew the pearls back on."

"Gab, I don't want you to do anything that'll get you in trouble."

"I'm not making any promises, but Renata is out of town, so as curator, this is my call."

"If you're sure," Lilli said.

"I am. Try not to worry. I'll see you tomorrow."

"Thanks, Gab."

Max walked in the door just as Lilli hung up. "Took care of the police. I saw Marisa and her mother leaving. Problem?"

Lilli exchanged a glance with Mrs. R. "You could say that."

Concern eclipsed Max's expression. "What happened?"

Lilli told him what Sissy had done. He walked to the row of dresses. "It's just the one?"

"One is enough," she said, trying to keep the despair from her voice.

He turned back to Lilli. "Need me to call the owner of the collection?"

"I already called the curator." She relayed their conversation.

"Nothing like this has ever happened before." Mrs. R. dropped the seed pearls into an envelope. "Are you sure there's nothing we can do?"

"Not until tomorrow."

"Let's close up the office," Max suggested. "No point in worrying about something you can't fix."

Lilli collected her purse and followed Max to the door. She and Mrs. R. waited on the sidewalk while Max activated the alarm. When he joined them, Mrs. R. locked the door and walked to her car.

Lilli stood there, not sure what to do. Her stomach still churned. She'd only pace and worry if she went home.

"How about a walk on the beach," Max suggested. "I go there when I have a lot on my mind."

"Does it help?"

"Sometimes."

She shrugged. "Why not."

"Oh, before I forget, Gram sent over the first draft of the wedding thing. Want to read it?"

"Wedding thing?"

"You know what I mean."

Yeah, she did. "Sure."

"Let me get the envelope out of the truck, then we'll go down to the beach."

Before long, they'd walked the block to the beach. Lilli removed her flip-flops when they got there, sinking her feet in the cool sand. "My life is a disaster."

"You've got some problems, but hardly dire."

"Why on earth did those women have to go to the office? Couldn't they leave well enough alone?"

"From what I've seen, probably not."

"I hope my friend Gab doesn't get in trouble over this."

"What about you?"

"I'm in charge, Max. I'll take what's coming."

"Yeah, I know you will."

His acknowledgement of her willingness to take responsibility should make her feel better, but didn't change a thing unless Gab could repair the dress. Someone's head would roll and it most likely would be hers.

"Not the best way to spend a Sunday," Max ventured as they neared the shoreline.

"I had planned on making a list of volunteer groom's duties just for you. Mostly because you didn't want my help."

"That's because we seem to rub each other the wrong way."

"Funny how that happens."

"Hilarious."

Max intently stared at her for a brief moment. "I've never met a woman who knocks me off balance the way you do."

"Is that a good thing?"

"Oh, yeah."

To be honest, he did the same thing to her. From the day she'd arrived in his office, asking him to volunteer and getting his unexpected "No." Who thought she'd look at him now and see so much more than his stubbornness and drive? The man could be hard at times and focused on the job, traits she didn't actually mind, but when his gentle side showed up, well, that's when she knew she'd lost her heart.

"You make me crazy" he said. "But at the same time, I look forward to seeing you. I never know what to expect."

"Makes life interesting."

He grinned. "I never took you for a dog lover, but there you were, working at the animal shelter and not one bit upset about getting muddy."

"I'm really not that superficial."

"I know that now. You're still bossy, but I understand you like things done a certain way. Nothing wrong with that."

"I could say the same about you. Thanks for being gentle with Mrs. R. today."

He shrugged. "There was nothing to get riled up about. She set the alarm. The other women created the problem."

"Don't remind me." She appreciated his getting her mind off the Vandermeres. The walk had worked—she'd calmed down some. To keep that calm, they needed to stay on less stressful topics. "Mrs. R. has a crush on you, you know."

He raised an eyebrow.

"It's cute that you didn't notice."

"I don't even know how to respond to that."

Despite her gloomy mood, Lilli laughed.

"Or you, sometimes."

"And if I admitted to having a crush on you?"

He grinned, slow and wolfish. "Now, that I wouldn't mind seeing."

Max's eyes went dark and she hoped he'd kiss her again. Long, drawn-out seconds passed. She waited, sure nothing would happen, until he finally brushed his lips over hers, light and easy.

"Nope, I wouldn't mind at all," he whispered against her lips.

She sighed softly when he kissed her again, but was disappointed when he broke the kiss and put some space between them.

"Listen, Lilli, whatever happens, I'll be there for you. If you need me to talk to the curator, whatever, call me. I'll be available until after the benefit."

"You're going somewhere?"

"If I sign on this new client, I'll be working out of town."

Out of town? Great. First the Vandermeres ruin a beautiful dress and then she finds out Max might be leaving.

"I'm still working for the historical society," he said.

He might be, but once the benefit was over she wouldn't be involved with the society any further. "Thanks."

"Even though today was a false alarm, I was glad to see you on top of things. You arrived quickly."

"After the alarm company called, I hurried over. I hated to think that someone successfully broke in this time." She shook her head. "Imagine. My worst nightmare taking place without the help of a thief."

"Don't go there. Your friend said she may be able to fix the dress."

"I know, I know. I shouldn't tempt fate." She kicked a clump of seaweed. "How about I take a look at what your grandmother put together? After today, Laverne's involvement may be the only hope of keeping the benefit afloat."

CHAPTER THIRTEEN

LIFTING THE FLAP of the envelope Max handed her, Lilli slid the folded papers out. In neat handwriting, Laverne recounted the story of her engagement, the days prior to the wedding and the wedding itself. One passage in particular caught her attention:

Not a man of many words, Clifford's love for me was always strong, always sure. After the ceremony, as the guests walked to the fellowship hall for the reception, he pulled me aside. "I have loved you since the moment I first laid eyes on you," he said. "I made a vow right then and there that if you agreed to marry me, I would be the best husband I could be. It's so much more than promising to love in sickness and health like the vows state. Those things are important. But in order to be a good husband I have to be a man of my word. And I promise you, Laverne, I will be a husband who puts you

first. That's the vow I make to you. You
can trust me on that.

Vows. Trust. A man who put his love first.
The folks attending the benefit would adore it.
Lilli finished reading and replaced the pages
inside the envelope.

"So?" Max asked.

"Better than I could have hoped," she answered in a husky voice. He'd never know the
letter made her heart squeeze with longing. She
wanted those things, too.

"Hey, you okay?"

"Yeah, don't mind me." She brushed her hair
out of her eyes. "I'm touched."

"Then she did a good job."

Lilli studied his profile. Max Sanders. Confident. Kind. Handsome. Could he be the type
of man his grandfather had been? Trustworthy?
There were men like Clifford in the world, and
if he'd just stop fighting it, Lilli believed Max
could be the same kind of man. The marry-
ing kind.

"Maybe I should read what Gram wrote," he
said in a quiet tone after a few moments.

"I think you should." She handed him the
envelope. "I'll go down by the water."

He lowered himself to the sand to read. Lilli
wandered into the surf, gentle waves caress-

ing her ankles, her busy mind coming up with damage control. She hoped Gabrielle would be able to repair the garment. If Renata decided they could no longer display the collection, the benefit would still go on, even if folks wondered what happened. She was thankful she had recruited Laverne.

Max finally joined her, squinting as he looked out over the water. She shuffled to his side.

"I never knew my grandfather but heard plenty of stories about him. I remember thinking I'd never measure up to a guy like him. Or my dad." He paused. "Losing both of them was a blow to our family."

"I can't imagine."

"Before my mom left, she said some pretty cruel things. I get that she was hurting after my dad died, so she lashed out at me. I understand she wasn't cut out to be a single mom so she bolted, but it doesn't change the fact that she left me behind."

"She was wrong."

He shrugged.

"Do you ever hear from her?"

"From time to time. She talks to Gram mostly. At first, I refused to talk to her. She left me, so I had nothing to say. Now I try to make small talk if she calls. I still don't feel like I measure up."

"Max, look what you've done with your life. How you took a troubled childhood and turned it around. You're going to make Sanders Security a success, I'm sure of it."

"I'm trying my best."

"That's all anyone can do."

"That's what my grandfather did. Loved my grandmother and made a good life for them." He paused. "So did my dad. That's why Mom left. She missed him too much. And I was hurting, too, so I didn't understand."

Lilli placed her hand on his arm. "The good thing about life is it's never static. You can continue the family line of upstanding men if you want to. It's your decision."

"And if I screw up?"

"It's not a question of if. It's a matter of when. Nobody's perfect, Max."

"What if I can't be the Sanders man Gram expects me to be?"

"Then be who you want to be. On your terms."

He looked at her with troubled eyes. "Speaking from experience?"

"Some. It was hard growing up with parents who didn't get along and eventually divorced. Growing up with kids who only put up with me because of who my parents were. I never fit in anywhere. So I focused all my energy on my education, then my career." She grinned. "I'm a little task-oriented."

"No kidding."

"But it works for me. I'm trying to earn a promotion, so KLC keeps me busy."

"How's that going since you've been busy with the fund-raiser?"

"I've had to manage my time to get all my work done, but so far, so good. I have pretty stiff competition, but I've been after the client, making sure he doesn't forget I want his business."

"You're nothing if not tenacious."

"Is that good or bad?"

"You got me to volunteer to be a groom, right? What more can I say?"

They stood a little longer in silence. The shadows began to deepen as the sun dipped into the horizon. The water turned chilly.

"It's late," Lilli said. "We should head home."

When they reached the sidewalk, Max took hold of her hand. "I meant what I said, Lilli. Let me know what I can do."

"I will." She assured him as she slipped her flip-flops on. "I only have a week left, and I can see the light at the end of the tunnel. After this weekend, no more wedding talk."

Walking to their vehicles, Max asked, "So, women really go for mushy displays of affection, huh?"

"We live for it," she drawled.

He chuckled. "Was your fiancé like that?"

Had Rob been romantic? "At first. He'd have flowers delivered to the office or take me for a romantic dinner. After we got engaged, I began to plan and make my lists. Rob kept busy moving up the ladder at the law firm." She gazed at the horizon. "It's sad to say, but I guess I figured I landed the guy, so I could plan a memorable wedding by myself."

"If he cared that much about you, he'd have made sure to stay connected."

"Maybe. I guess I didn't expect his help."

"You should have."

She glanced sideways at Max. "But that's who I am. A list maker. A planner. That's what I do."

"And he should have known that."

Dusk had fallen by the time they returned to the city parking lot where she'd left her car. Max lingered beside the driver's door.

"I enjoyed spending time with you," he said. "Look, not one argument. That's a record for us."

"True, but there's always tomorrow."

A lazy smile tugged his lips. "We should try to get along since we're working together."

"Think that's possible?"

"If we work on it."

Cars drove by. A dog barked in the distance. Finally Lilli said, "Well, I guess I should get going."

Max stepped away, but before she could unlock the door, he took her hand, lifting it to his lips. She couldn't ignore the jolt, somewhere between pleasure and surprise.

"You should expect more," he repeated.

"Excuse me?"

"From a guy in your life. You're special, Lilli. You deserve to be courted. With all the bells and whistles."

"Thanks. I haven't given up hope he's out there somewhere." *Maybe standing right in front of me.*

Long electric moments passed. He lowered his head and brushed his lips over hers. This could be habit-forming, she thought. She leaned into him, to his heat, inhaling his fresh, tangy scent. As the kiss went deeper, her heart pounded. Because this was not just any guy. This was Max, the guy she couldn't stop falling for.

The guy she shouldn't *be* falling for. The timing couldn't be worse, with the fund-raiser, her promotion and a new client that might take Max out of town. The list went on. She may not know what the future held, but right now, she wouldn't worry about it. She wanted this.

He broke the kiss and ran a hand through his hair. "You get to me, Lilli."

"Same here." She ran shaky hands over her shorts. "So what happens now?"

He shrugged. By the look in his eyes she readied herself for another toe-curling kiss. Before Max had a chance to make his move, a bright light caught them in its beam. A disembodied voice sounded over a speaker. "Step away from the car."

"Can't a guy catch a break around here?" Max muttered under his breath.

He held up his hand to keep the blinding light from Lilli's eyes. Seconds later, darkness returned. Bright circles danced before her eyes and she heard an engine stop. Squinting, she made out a burly shape exiting the car.

"The chief."

"What is he doing here?" Lilli sputtered.

The older man approached them. "Is this man giving you any problems, Miss Barclay?"

"Um, no."

"Cause he's a wily one."

"Thanks for the vote of confidence," Max groused.

The chief burst out laughing. "Sorry. I saw you kids out here and couldn't resist."

"Yeah, you're a real comedian." Disgusted, Max glanced at Lilli, concerned she might be embarrassed. He'd gotten used to the chief over the years, but Lilli might not appreciate the man's sense of humor. "I was making sure Lilli got into her car without any problems."

"Didn't look that way to me."

Max ground his teeth together.

The chief pointed the flashlight he still held in his hand toward her car and back to them.

"Okay, well, thanks," she told Max before climbing into her sedan.

Max watched her drive off before turning on the chief. "You're kidding me, right?"

"I take it you don't think I'm funny."

"Not hardly."

"Max, you were kissing the young lady right out here in public. What did you expect me to do?"

"Drive by. Like any normal person would do."

"It's my job to keep the streets of Cypress Pointe safe for citizens," the chief joked, laughing again.

"Yeah, yeah."

The chief headed back to his car. "Say hey to your grandmother for me."

"Sure."

Max stood there long after the lawman left, thinking about the night, the kiss. What did he want out of this relationship with Lilli? He hadn't come to town to get involved with a woman. Building his business and taking care of Gram were supposed to fill his life. How had he let himself get in so deep? How had Lilli managed to sneak into his heart and stay there until he couldn't think about much else?

Too keyed up to head home, Max considered calling his buddy Dane, but decided against it. He didn't need any more advice. Not on women and certainly not on their expectations. Talking about his mother had brought back old regrets. Usually he kept that information to himself, but he didn't mind sharing with Lilli. It felt good to have someone who listened and didn't judge. Instead, she encouraged him. Their relationship may have started out rough, but he realized that he had a friend in Lilli. Probably more if he pursued it.

Of all the things they'd talked about, Lilli had one thing right. The troubled kid who needed excitement to fill the emptiness inside had become a man. A Sanders man. He needed to start acting like one.

BY THE TIME Max arrived at his office Monday morning, he'd almost completely put the unlikely romance out of his head. The lengthy run he'd taken this morning with Jake Riley at his side had gone a long way to getting him back to business.

Blanche already sat at her desk, holding out a sheet of paper to him.

"What's this?"

"Volunteer-groom duties."

"Huh?"

"Read it and weep."

He took the paper and started to read.

Couldn't sleep last night so I made a list of your duties. Enjoy!

1. Groom should arrive an hour before ceremonies begin, even if he has a business to run.

2. Dress code to include formal tuxedo and dress shoes. (No boots. No T-shirts. Definitely no denim of any kind.)

3. Smile as you escort your "bride" down the runway.

4. Please remain with "bride" until the finale.

5. Repeat number three—the groom must smile at all times. (Even if you want to run.)

She'd added the last in her precise handwriting. A reluctant grin pulled at his lips.

"Figured you'd be ticked," Blanche said.

"You'd think."

He imagined Lilli's flushed cheeks as she sent the list. He had to admit, he did get a kick out of her sense of humor. He loved when she got all flustered, especially when he caused the reaction. She couldn't hide her emotions if she wanted to, but he wouldn't reveal that piece of news. More fun this way.

"So you're going along with this?" Blanche asked.

"It's for a good cause." He heard a snicker, but when he looked at his secretary, she stared at the monitor, straight-faced.

"You're loving this, aren't you?"

She finally raised her head. Her eyes crinkled in amusement. "I really am."

He sighed. "How did I get myself into this?"

"Maybe you want a certain benefit coordinator to notice you?"

"Oh, Lilli notices me, all right. Every time I make a boneheaded move."

"It's endearing."

"It's embarrassing."

Blanche chuckled again. "Yeah, that move with the wallet was classic."

"And so good for Sanders Security's image," came his wry reply.

"I think you'd make a cute couple."

"She's so out of my league."

"Don't put yourself down."

He ran a hand through his hair.

"Falling in love is never easy," Blanche went on.

"Okay, but what has that got to do with—"

"Once you get there, it's heaven."

"That's nice, Blanche."

"Look, my point is, if you and Lilli do fall in love, she would never look down on you and you won't ever have to look up. Loving each other puts you on even ground."

If they fell in love. The more time he spent with her, the more he found himself wondering what it would be like to have a permanent relationship. He'd convinced himself that he never wanted one. Until he'd found Lilli again, a woman who exasperated him and totally captured his attention at the same time.

"Thanks for the insight."

"That's what I'm here for."

"And all this time I thought you were here to work. For me."

"That I am." She held out a pink message slip to him. "Klaus called. The courier company bringing the jewelry for the benefit confirmed delivery to the country club today. He needs you and Lilli to come by at one this afternoon."

"Great." He couldn't talk to Lilli just yet. Bad enough he'd have to see her in a few hours and fight all his conflicting feelings. Right now he needed to concentrate on something constructive, like work. "Would you mind calling Lilli to let her know the time?"

Blanche's eyebrows rose.

"Please."

"No problem, boss."

"Thanks." He took the paper and headed to his office. When he got to the threshold he stopped and looked back. "Really, thanks."

Her attention back at the computer, Blanche waved him off.

LILLI STOPPED AT Cuppa Joe. She'd gotten up early this morning, wanting to hit the coffee shop before she met Gabrielle at the historical society office. She had ulterior motives; she was hoping she'd run into Max. Disappointed when he wasn't there, she made up for it by ordering a killer cup of coffee.

"It's been a while since I came by," Lilli told Dorinda after her first sip of the rich roast. Usually she stopped by another shop more convenient to work. "I forgot what I was missing."

"My special blend. Best-kept secret in town." The older woman sighed and glanced around the store. "This place could use some sprucing up. I wish my granddaughter were here. She has a knack for these things."

Lilli had noticed photos on the wall when she came in. "Is your granddaughter Nealy Grainger?"

"Yes. Do you know her?'

"We went to the same school and hung out for a while. Lost track of each other over the years."

"I miss her." Dorinda's eyes misted. "We always had a special bond. Even though she left town years ago, it feels like yesterday."

Lilli didn't know what to say. She'd never felt that kind of bond with anyone.

Dorinda waved off her mood. "Enough of that. I hear Max did some work at the historical society office."

"Work?"

"Mrs. R. said something about having a lock changed?"

"Oh, yes. Last week."

"It was the Merchants Association, wasn't it?"

"Pardon?"

"They're always after me to fix this or that.

Picky people. Whenever I need something done, I call Max and he takes care of me."

That explained the toolbox he carried in his truck.

"The Merchants Association didn't have a problem with the office. Just needed a new lock." Lilli didn't want the older woman to know someone might have tried to break in. Since Lilli didn't know for sure, and nothing had happened since then, she hoped their conclusions had been wrong. Besides, no need worrying Mrs. Hobart about people trying to break in.

"He's very dependable."

"Max?"

"And cute." She winked at Lilli.

Lilli nearly spit out her coffee. What was it with these women and their crushes on Max?

"I may be in my twilight years, but I can appreciate a good-looking man."

Lilli felt her face warm. "He is that."

Dorinda motioned them to an empty table. "My regulars won't be in for a bit. Let's chat."

"Okay." Lilli joined her.

"So, you're coordinating Tie the Knot. I understand you asked my friend Laverne to share her love story with you."

"Yes. And in return, I reserved a table for her."

"I know." Dorinda's eyes twinkled. "I'm attending."

Lilli smiled. "Tell me about Laverne and her husband. It's obvious they were crazy about each other."

"I knew them well. They had a wonderful life together."

"That's something to strive for."

"Do you have a man in your life?"

A man? Max fit into that category, since he was a man and in her life, but Lilli suspected Dorinda meant in a romantic context. "No one serious. Still looking."

"Hmm. You young women today. So busy with your careers."

"Guilty. But not for lack of interest."

"Haven't found the right man?"

"After I got dumped last year, marriage is currently way down on my wish list."

Dorinda put a gentle hand over hers. "I'm sorry."

Lilli shrugged. "I'm over it." And to her surprise, she found she meant it.

"Marriage is a wonderful institution."

Lilli pictured her parents. "Are you sure?"

"You're not?"

"I guess I haven't had real good role models."

The older woman raised an eyebrow.

"My parents. Their relationship wasn't very awe-inspiring. I grew up as the go-between during their arguments."

"Not easy for a child to deal with."

"Tell me about it."

"Doesn't mean every marriage is that way."

"I realize that. But my folks' example, then Rob breaking up with me, has made me a little gun-shy."

"All it takes is the right man. The man who is your match in every area of life."

"That's the thing I was missing with Rob. We weren't in tune with each other. I think I was in love with the idea of being in love. I won't let it happen again." She sighed. "In the long run, I'm glad it didn't work out."

"Connection is important, especially during hard times. Marriage is a lifetime of work, a joy in sharing the good times and bad. When you work together as a couple, love sees you through."

"Sounds like you're speaking from experience."

"We were married a long time before my husband passed away. He'd always dreamed of opening this coffee shop. In honor of him, I've kept it open." Dorinda's smile faded. "I wish Joe could be here. We complemented each other. Saw life very much alike. Not that we were boring, mind you. We just…fit."

"That's why I'm waiting for the right man."

Dorinda chuckled. "My Joe used to quote Henry Ford who said the key to a successful marriage was to 'Stick to one model.' That's what Joe and I did."

Before Lilli could respond, her cell phone rang. When she saw Sanders Security on caller ID, her heartbeat picked up. "I should take this call."

"Go ahead, dear." Dorinda rose and walked behind the coffee counter.

"Lilli Barclay."

"Lilli, it's Blanche. I wanted to let you know that the courier is delivering the Wingate jewelry today. Klaus wants you and Max at the country club at one o'clock."

"Okay," she said, hiding her disappointment. She'd hoped Max would call her personally, not treat her like just another client. "Thanks for letting me know."

"Max would have called but he's busy."

"That's fine. I can talk to him later."

"Really, he is busy."

Why was Blanche harping on what Max was doing? "Thanks for the call."

She disconnected and picked up her to-go

cup to discard on the way out. "I should get to work."

"Our visit flew by so quickly," Dorinda said. "Please come back anytime."

"I will. And please say hi to Nealy for me when you speak to her."

Lilli took one last look around the room, watching as Dorinda greeted her regulars, before hurrying off to the historical society. She needed to start her day, knowing she'd be especially swamped with the one-o'clock appointment added to her schedule.

When she walked into the historical society office, both Gab and Mrs. R. had smiles on their faces.

"I hope this means good news."

Gab help up a needle and thread. "Nothing a few stitches couldn't take care of. Good as new."

Lilli placed a hand over her heart. "You don't know how happy I am to hear that."

Her friend packed her sewing tools away. "I'm relieved, too. I couldn't sleep last night, worried the dress might be permanently damaged."

"So we're okay continuing the display?"

"I don't see why not. Renata is in Italy for a month. I'll tell her when she gets back."

"Gab, I'll understand if you have to take the collection back."

"Don't worry, Lilli. I'll handle it."

With a sigh of relief, Lilli smiled. "Thanks."

Gab grinned back. "My pleasure. Please, be careful from here on out."

"You have my word that nothing will happen."

"Then I'll see you Saturday morning when we move the collection to the country club."

Thirty minutes later, Lilli sat down at her desk at KLC. Mondays were hectic enough and she only had three days to get everything in order for her real job, so when she took two days off later in the week for her volunteer job, her boss wouldn't be all over her. With Tie the Knot this weekend, she had tons of coordinating to do.

She opened a file on her computer as Jim ambled out of his office.

"So guess who I just got off the phone with?"

At his satisfied smile, her heart raced. "Mr. Danielson?"

"With all the wooing and face time you put in by calling and stopping by the dealership, Mr. Danielson decided he wants you to work on his account."

Lilli whooped.

"You really went for it, and you got the job done."

"Wow, I can't believe it. I guess it'll take a while to sink in."

"Especially since you're bogged down with the fund-raiser."

"Thankfully it'll be over this weekend. After that I can completely throw myself into the Danielson account."

"That's another thing I want to talk about." He leaned his hip against her desk, crossed his arms over his chest. "Since you're on a roll, I have another account I'd like you to work with. I had a request come in a few minutes ago from Reardon and Company. They requested you draw up a presentation. I told them yes."

"Starting when?"

"Tomorrow."

She bolted upright. "Jim! I just landed the Danielson account. As of Thursday I'm off. I won't have time to work on a presentation before then."

He held his hands up. "Hear me out. I have a good reason."

"This better be good."

"Mr. Reardon heard about the charity benefit you're coordinating. I kind of bragged about you, hoping to clinch the account. He was so impressed with the last-minute presentation you did for his company last month he offered to make a donation to the historical society as long as you head up a full marketing campaign."

"How can I possibly meet him this week?"

"You can meet him at Tie the Knot. He's hoping to score tickets."

She glowered at him. "You realize there are no tickets left."

He reached inside his suit jacket and pulled out the two tickets Lilli had given him to smooth over her time away from the office. "I'll donate my pair."

Lilli knew her boss's generous spirit only meant one thing. He wanted another way into the event. "In exchange for?"

"Let me be one of the volunteer grooms."

"Jim, the event is Saturday. Everyone is paired off."

"I know, but it occurred to me that not only could I make nice with a client by giving up my tickets, KLC could get even more exposure if I'm in the show."

Lilli rubbed her throbbing temples.

"So, what do you say?"

"How about I put you on standby. I can't promise you'll be in the show for sure, at this late date."

"I can live with that." Jim beamed at her.

"I'm a smart man for hiring you. And to show you what a magnanimous boss I am, you can leave Wednesday afternoon to get ready for the fund-raiser. What do you say?"

"Wow. A whole half day."

"Yep. I bet you're far from finished organizing."

No, she was never finished, and today she would have to spend her lunch hour at the country club. "Anything else?"

Jim pushed away from the desk. "That's it. You're a good employee, you know that?"

Lilli thought about her workload and Jim's expectations and decided to go for broke. "So do I get a title now? Account Executive?"

Jim stopped in his tracks. She could imagine the wheels turning in his head. "After pulling in two accounts this week, I'd say you earned it."

She grinned, mentally giving herself a high five. Oh, yeah, she'd nailed the promotion. Now all she had to do was get through the fund-raiser with as much success and she'd be one happy woman.

CHAPTER FOURTEEN

LILLI BARELY MADE IT to the appointment with Max and Klaus in time, still giddy about landing the Danielson account. She careened into the parking lot with minutes to spare, jumped out and zigzagged between cars as she hurried to the front door, noticing Max's truck out of the corner of her eye.

She smoothed her purple, pink and white skirt, straightened her pink tank top and fluffed her hair one last time. Her sandals sparkled in the bright noon sun. Jewel had put her stamp of approval on the outfit, which pleased Lilli… especially since it had been so long since she worried about her choice of clothing.

She refused to acknowledge that lately she'd taken time to dress to impress. Max didn't need impressing. He needed a keeper. One to keep his mind on the job at hand, not on her lips.

Pathetic, her inner voice scoffed. She hadn't been able to get Max or his kisses off her mind. She rushed inside to find Max waiting. "I'm here," she announced as she breezed into the lobby, her gaze tangling with Max's.

He studied her face for a moment. "What's up?"

When had he come to read her so well? "I got the promotion and Gabrielle repaired the loaner gown."

"Congrats on both counts." His wide smile added to her excitement. "Let's get started."

They walked to Klaus's office, passing the courier on the way. They entered the office. Lilli tried to ignore the heat in her cheeks brought on by Max's smile. She concentrated on the large box in the middle of Klaus's desk, not Max standing next to her. Klaus crossed the room and locked the door. "Precaution," he assured them.

The three gathered around the desk as Max slowly unlocked the box to reveal the magnificent gems nestled in white velvet.

"Oh, my," she whispered.

"Yeah," Max replied.

Her mother's description of the jewelry didn't compare to seeing the pieces up close. Deep blue sapphires and bright diamonds glittered in the overhead light. A shiver ran over her skin. She peered at Max out of the corner of her eye. His brow was wrinkled. Was he worried?

"Rest assured, Miss Barclay," Klaus told her in a serious tone. "The club safe is state-of-the-art. We've never experienced a problem with the system. Mr. Sanders has reviewed club protocol for keeping valuables on the premises, as well as going over the security system with a fine-tooth comb. He has already updated our current system. On the night of the event we will have extra staff available to make sure all is secure. My assistant, Tom, and the entire staff have all been brought up to speed. The jewelry is in good hands."

One less thing to worry about, since she'd promised to keep a better eye on the dresses.

"I'll leave you to discuss details. Call me when you're ready to put the box in the safe." Klaus crossed the room. "Please lock the door behind me."

Max made sure he checked the door. "What do you think?"

"That you have your work cut out for you."

"I can do this."

"Trying to convince me or yourself?"

"You, of course. The client."

She grimaced. The client. Not the woman he'd kissed last night. Pushing that aside, she reached out and brushed her fingers over the exquisite necklace.

"Now that you've seen the collection, what do you think?"

"Magnificent."

She felt the weight of his gaze on her and couldn't help but look at him.

She felt as if the heat in the room had risen ten degrees. Finally cutting the electric connection between them, Lilli turned away, reaching into her purse to remove the drawings she'd done the night before. She hadn't been able to sleep—with visions of Max kissing her clear in her mind—so she'd done some work. With shaky fingers she passed the pad to Max, her hand brushing his. A current of heat snaked up her arm.

"I'm hoping to lay the collection on satin," she said. "But wasn't sure what color until I saw the gems in person. I'm thinking a robin's-egg blue, like a Tiffany's gift box, which is kind of appropriate and it matches the theme."

Max continued to stare at her.

"Tiffany's? You know, the signature box color for the expensive jewelry store?"

He gave her a vacant look.

He was such a guy. "Last week Klaus showed me the display case we're going to use and the way the lights are placed. It will bring out the luster of the gems."

"I've seen the case, as well. Shatterproof glass and the locks are all working properly."

"Good. Then things are under control?"

"So far."

A few minutes later, Klaus returned with his assistant, Tom. They took the box to be safely stored, and before she knew it, Lilli was headed for the lobby with Max at her side. She'd almost made it out the door when Marisa came waltzing in with Chandler in tow. She was wearing a trendy, tightly fitted tennis tank and skirt, swinging her racket beside her as she walked. Lilli wondered how she played in the restricting outfit, then remembered that Marisa planned everything she did with image in mind. The slinkier the outfit, the more eyes were on her. Including Max's.

"Lilli." Marisa smiled, all teeth and no substance, as if the incident the day before with the wedding dresses had never happened. Her eyes lit up when she glimpsed Max. "And Max Sanders. What are you doing here? Together?"

As if her being with Max couldn't happen? "Benefit business," Lilli informed her. Okay, she wished they were together because they were…together, but she wouldn't let Marisa see that. She moved a fraction closer to Max, refusing to look at him to see if he'd caught on to her pathetic ploy.

"Did you happen to stop by the event room? Maybe you could take a walk down memory lane while you're here."

Lilli tensed immediately, angry that Marisa knew which buttons to push. She was way over Rob. Marisa's obvious attempt to hurt her bothered her more.

Chandler placed his palm under her elbow. "Let's go, babe."

She held up a finger. "One moment."

A brief frown crossed Chandler's brow and his eyes momentarily flashed. From across the room, Tom waved to him. "I'll be right back," he told Marisa, his attention focused elsewhere.

"I don't know how you can go in there." Marisa shuddered as if she really cared what Lilli felt. "After the humiliation."

The words hung in the air between them. It took a few seconds before she noticed Max's body heat as he leaned close and placed his hand at the small of her back. "If you'll excuse us, we need to get going."

"By all means." Marisa stepped out of the way. "I guess you two have to get back to work."

"And you have the silent auction details to get to me."

The other woman frowned. "I'll have it."

"The benefit is this weekend."

"That gives me a couple more days."

She turned on her heel and headed toward Chandler. He abruptly stopped his conversation with Tom when she approached, a look of annoyance on his handsome face.

Lilli held on to her temper as Max led her out the door and into the warm afternoon.

"You okay?"

"She's just trying to stir things up."

"How do you put up with her?"

"I try to remember that I'm a bigger person and should be nice to her."

"Tough job."

She laughed. "Sometimes, yes. But it is true, no matter the circumstance."

"You sound like Gram."

"Why? Because she'd tell you the same thing?"

He chuckled. "All the time."

They arrived at her car and Max stood by her as she unlocked the door and tossed her bag inside. When she straightened up, he reached out as though he wanted to touch her cheek, but dropped his hand. All she could think was, he could be leaving.

"So, any news on your potential client?"

"I have the final appointment Thursday night. He'll have an answer then."

Thursday. "Wow. That's soon."

"I know. This opportunity is amazing. If I land the job I'll be able to hire experienced help. I've got a buddy in Atlanta who wants to relocate. He can take care of the local jobs while I travel."

"So you're really going to leave Cypress Pointe?"

"Depends on Mr. Rawlings." He tilted his head. "Does that bother you?"

"I thought you liked it here."

"I do, but this is a huge. I can't pass it up. You understand, right?"

Yes, she did. Wasn't she ecstatic about her own promotion? How could she begrudge him this chance at success? "This way you won't have to look over your shoulder to see if the good folks of Cypress Pointe are watching your every move."

"They're watching. Most of my new clients are Merchants Association members."

"Oh, well, I guess maybe I hoped you'd miss…us."

He frowned. "Lilli, I—"

She held her hand up. "We're working to-gether, right? Nothing more…except for the odd kiss, apparently."

"It's not that."

"Then what is it?"

"I like you…us. But I don't know about marriage. Family."

"Hey, don't get ahead of yourself, Max. I just like spending time with you and want to see where this goes."

"If I get the job, then we'll know."

Yeah. Nowhere. Right back at square one.

They stood together for a drawn-out moment. Lilli was pretty sure she had her answer. She tried to read the emotion in his eyes, but he pulled his sunglasses from his shirt pocket and slipped them on.

"When are you decorating?" he asked.

Grateful for the change of topic, she said, "Thursday and Friday."

He nodded. "I'll bring the rest of Gram's things then."

"Okay."

"I need to catch up on some work, so I'll see you later."

With that, he turned on his heel. Lilli watched him walk to his truck, wondering how she could possibly fall for another man who could so easily walk away from her.

THE WEEK FLEW BY, filled with finishing projects at work and last-minute preparations for the fund-raiser. Despite Jim's offer, she ended up working all day Wednesday and most of

Thursday on the new account, cutting into her benefit scheduling. Late Thursday afternoon, Lilli finally headed up the sidewalk to the club, ready to decorate the event room. She stopped short before entering the building, surprised to find Max lounging by the door and Bart hovering nearby. Her eyebrows rose in a silent question. He tilted his head toward the building. "I thought you might be uncomfortable, you know, with the memories."

His concern touched her. She wanted to lean on him and let him be there for her, but she couldn't help wondering about the days, weeks and months from now when he'd be traveling. He wouldn't be there for her then. The lonely feeling that had subsided since Max had come into her life threatened to rear its ugly head again, but she firmly tamped it down.

"Thank you, Max, but it's just a room. I'll be fine."

He opened the door and she stepped inside, nervously smoothing the well-worn jeans she'd thrown on along with a fitted scarlet cotton shirt and sandals. With everything on her plate today, she'd dressed for comfort to set up the room for the charity event.

"What's up with Bart?" she asked as they crossed the lobby.

"This is his first official on-site assignment

since becoming my intern. I have the meeting with Rawlings tonight, so I've asked Bart to stay with you ladies while you decorate. He'll be working Saturday night, as well, and I want the volunteers to feel comfortable around him."

"You're serious about this internship."

"Turns out he's a natural. He's a pro at installing equipment and he brought in three new customers this week alone."

"Wow. Your business is officially taking off." She tried to smile but didn't think she managed it.

"If tonight goes well." He held up his hand with two crossed fingers. "While I'm gone, don't let Bart get in the way."

"I'll make sure he's put to good use."

"On that note, I'll be leaving shortly."

"Smart man. I'd keep you busy if you were staying."

"I have no doubt."

They reached their destination and Max held the door open for her. Like the other day, when she looked in, she found the event room fairly empty. Max flipped a switch and the chandeliers glowed. He continued to the wall of windows, stopping to take in the view.

Lilli roamed the room and realized memories of the rehearsal dinner didn't dominate her. She could actually breathe, and as she calmed, visions of how the room would be arranged for the benefit took precedence. Celeste had worked hard for years and had gained a stellar reputation in the community. Lilli wouldn't let memories of old disappointments ruin the work her mother had started or the event Lilli had promised to finish. Not even with thoughts of Max's departure on her mind.

She didn't need Max to fill her life. She'd done just fine by herself, so far. If he needed to travel for his job, well, she'd do what she'd always done: keep busy at work. Despite her reservations, she'd enjoyed working with the historical society. Maybe she could volunteer for more organizations. Before long, she wouldn't even notice Max's absence.

Right.

She stopped at the one table in the room, placing her list, along with the room layout, on the surface. Max walked over and stood close behind her as he peered over her shoulder. She tried to move aside to create some space between them, but he leaned in to read.

"You've planned this out."

"You know I'm nothing if not efficient."

He chuckled. His breath tickled her neck. She tried to control a shiver, but failed. Not good. Not good at all. Clearing her throat, she eased past him and walked to the middle of the room. Someone needed to keep this thing between them strictly business because any chance of developing a real relationship was going right out the door if this new client hired Max.

"Klaus had the runway put down this morning. The stage will be set up in front of the windows. I plan to keep the drapes open so the golf course view is the backdrop." She spread her arms, pointing toward the walls. "The dinner tables will be clustered on either side of the runway. Along the back wall is the silent auction table." She glanced at her watch. "Jewel should be here any minute to get started. Seems she's a closet wedding planner. This is her big debut."

"That explains Bart wanting to stay out front." Max scanned the room. "She's got her work cut out for her."

"She's very good."

"So are you."

She shrugged, but enjoyed his praise. She had worked hard and looked forward to the results. "This coordinating gig is a onetime deal. Then I can concentrate on my real job, which my boss will be happy about."

"C'mon, you can't tell me you aren't having fun."

He grinned and stepped closer. Her heart

squeezed tight and she had to admit, "Maybe a little. It's been a definite learning experience. But I'm glad to do this for my mother."

His eyes turned from teasing to serious. Even in this huge room, the walls closed in around them. If he stood any closer she might stand on tiptoes and give him a much-needed kiss. Needed by her.

"I've got to get to my appointment."

The appointment that could take him away from her. "Good luck. Thanks for stopping by." She nodded toward the door where Jewel and Bart came in. "And bringing reinforcements." She glanced back at him, not wanting to say goodbye, not wanting to seem needy.

His eyes grew dark. "Sure you're okay?"

"I'm fine. Go meet your client."

"Gram wants to help with the decorating, so I'll bring her tomorrow night."

"I look forward to it."

For all his talk about a meeting, he didn't move. Could she be as important to him as the new job? Edgy now, she pushed her hair behind her ear. Max's hand joined hers and she froze at his touch. The longing in his eyes mirrored hers.

Her face flamed hot. Could he read her expression? She hoped not. This wasn't the time or place to reveal how she felt. Just as he started to say something, Jewel breezed over to them.

"Okay, the real boss is here." She noticed Lilli's flushed face. "Oops. I can come back."

Max held up his hand. "You have a busy night ahead of you. I'll get out of your way."

Watching Max walk out the door with a final wave, Lilli heard her cell phone ring. Rushing to her tote bag, she pulled it out, barely saying hello before Celeste cried in her overly dramatic tone. "Dreadful news, Lillian! I can't get a flight home in time for the fund-raiser."

"Oh, Mom, this benefit was all your idea. We need you here."

"And I want to be there, but I might have waited a tad too long to book the return flight."

"Can't Dad do anything?"

Celeste's voice sounded funny. "He's renting a car as we speak."

"Dad is still with you?"

Her mother paused. "I have some things to tell you, Lilli. About your father and me."

Celeste sighed, quiet for a moment.

"Mom?"

"I should have reasoned this out better."

"What?"

"Nothing, dear. I just hope I'm not too late."

There was more to what her mother was saying, but Lilli decided not to pressure her. "Is there anything I can do from here?"

"No, dear. You've done a wonderful job. I appreciate you stepping in for me. In the meantime, tell me how things are progressing."

She spent the next ten minutes bringing Celeste up to speed.

"Sounds wonderful. You've made me proud."

Lilli's chest tightened at her mother's words of praise. "Call me when you get into town, Mom."

"Yes, dear."

Lilli closed her cell, wondering what was up with her parents. Celeste had always schemed to get her ex-husband's attention, but this time she sounded different.

"Stop staring into space and get busy," Jewel called out, shaking her reverie.

With Bart's help they dragged the tables and chairs into place. Lillie was thankful the wood flooring for the runway had been laid down so she didn't have to wrestle with it.

Before long, Jewel dug into the big box with all the decorations, pulling out yards of tulle and fabric.

"Now it's time to get serious."

They worked steadily, getting the room set up. The hours passed and the majority of the decorating had been completed. The chairs were draped with tulle and ivory table linens set in place. Candles in Wedgwood blue and pure white adorned each table with the printed schedule of events placed at each setting.

A table was set up to hold the three-tiered wedding cake Celeste had ordered months ago. On the opposite side of the room, tables lined the long wall for all the various silent auction donations and sign-up sheets. The display of designer gowns would be strategically placed nearby. Inside the main door a special table provided information about the Cypress Pointe Historical Society, and another table showcased Laverne's special wedding mementos for the night. Lilli couldn't wait to see what Max's grandmother had in store for them.

The florist would deliver the fresh arrangements of white peonies and blue hydrangea on Saturday morning while the volunteer brides and grooms had the final run-through for the fashion show, all culminating with Tie the Knot festivities Saturday night. Come Sunday morning, Lilli planned on hitting the beach to relax, letting the warm rays of the sun work the kinks out of her body. After that, back to the new accounts and promotion. Her work plans were coming together, even if a relationship with Max was not.

Lilli and Jewel gathered their belongings

and, with Bart in tow, headed to the door. She switched off the lights before leaving and walked with her friends to the club exit.

"You need to rest up," Lilli told Jewel. "Starting tomorrow, things will officially become crazy."

"Are you nervous?" Jewel asked.

"No. Not with all your help." Lilli hugged her friend. She nodded to Bart. "You, too."

He grinned. "Thanks."

As Lilli drove home, Max never left her mind. Who knew where things would go with them after this weekend? Would they run into each other in town, politely greeting each other before hurrying off in different directions? Would he even be in town? Or would they pursue their mutual attraction? And if they didn't? She refused to think that far ahead.

FRIDAY WAS A BLUR of activity and Lilli found herself back at the country club that evening. She placed her purse and tote bag in the corner of the room with the rest of the volunteers' belongings, ready to dive into the final preparations. The committee women were all accounted for, setting out the items for the silent auction.

Excited chatter filled the room and Lilli found herself getting into the spirit. The Vandermere women behaved, but Lilli figured that had more to do with Marisa's fiancé hanging around. The lone male in the room, Chandler stood off to the side, watching the women work. Before long, Lilli lost sight of him.

She hadn't heard from Max all day and her nerves were ragged. How had his appointment gone last night?

At seven, Laverne Sanders walked into the room followed by Max, who carried a large box. All eyes went to him. Mrs. Rumpold dropped what she was doing to scurry over.

"Do you need help?"

Max looked over the shorter woman's head, his amused gaze meeting Lilli's. "No. I'm good."

Mrs. R. sighed. Loudly.

Lilli wanted to run over and grill him about his appointment, but if his good mood was any indicator, he'd landed the job. "Laverne. Max." Lilli waved him to a table covered in cream satin. "Bring that over here."

"Gram's things," he told her, setting the box on the floor.

"Figured." Lilli took Laverne's hand in hers. "I'm so glad you came by tonight. I'd like your input."

Laverne took in the activity in the room.

"Seems like you have everything under control."

"I can always use extra ideas."

"Gram's dress is out in the truck," Max told them. "I'll be back in a minute."

Could the suspense make her any crazier?

While he went outside, Lilli and Laverne unpacked the framed photos. Each photo still tugged at her heart. Next she pulled out the letters and the story Laverne had written, already framed.

"You didn't have to go to all this trouble," Lilli told her.

"I found myself enjoying the process. I want to keep all the letters framed like this as my special keepsake."

Max walked in carrying a dress form draped with a beautiful white lace dress.

"Just set it down there," Lilli instructed. "I'm not sure where that will go, but we'll move it when we're ready."

He nodded and pulled Lilli aside. "I have to meet Klaus for a final walk-through."

She couldn't take it any longer. "So? How did your meeting go?"

"You're looking at the new security firm for Rawlings National. Right after the fashion show, I'm headed to L.A. to get up to speed."

"Wow. After the fashion show."

"Flying out Sunday. Don't worry, I talked to the chief about security for the gowns and jewelry until my friend from Atlanta gets here. I won't leave you stranded."

Oh, but he already had.

"Gotta run."

While her heart sank, he grinned at her before striding out the door.

"Did he have to leave already?" Mrs. Rumpold asked.

"Hmm. What?"

"Is Max leaving?" Mrs. R. repeated.

"I'm afraid so."

"Now?"

"Not tonight. He'll finish up with Tie the Knot first."

Mrs. R. sent her a funny look.

"It's a long story."

Lilli went back to helping Laverne, keeping herself busy so as not to think about Max's good fortune and her loss.

Soon they had the frames displayed at various positions. Once finished, she walked the room, coming to stand before the display case that would house the Wingate collection. She jumped when she felt a strong hand on her shoulder.

"Lilli, I need to talk to you."

She swung around to face Max, noting the

serious expression on his face. "Now? We're still decorating."

He clasped her upper arm and led her out of the room. "It's important."

"What is it? And why are you manhandling me?"

He stopped a few feet away from the main door, his gaze dark and troubled. Her stomach dropped.

"Oh, no. Don't tell me something happened to the dresses after I promised Gabrielle I'd keep a better eye on them."

"It's not the dresses, Lilli. It's the jewelry collection. Some of the pieces are missing."

CHAPTER FIFTEEN

"MISSING?" LILLI SPUTTERED, her heart skipping a beat. But they were in the safe....

He ran a hand through his already disheveled hair. "When I got to Klaus's office he was in a panic. He'd taken the collection from the club safe to temporarily place it in the display case tonight, so we could finalize the security detail. An hour ago he got a call about a club member with a medical emergency. He left the box with Tom to lock in the safe until he came back. Later, when he went to bring the box here, he noticed the ring and bracelet were gone."

Suddenly her world got dark and stars flickered before her eyes. Taking a couple of deep breaths, she tried to pull herself together. "But how could that happen?"

"C'mere." Max led her to an upholstered bench along the wall. She dropped down, just as her knees gave way beneath her.

"Why didn't he call you to look after the collection instead of Tom?"

Max's expression grew dark. "My question exactly."

"Did you call the chief?"

"Not until I've determined the pieces are not on the premises. If I hit a dead end, I'll call him."

The serious expression on Max's face made her realize that as much as the jewelry going missing was a huge scandal for her, it meant a logistical headache for Max.

"Now what?"

"I find Tom and get an explanation."

Lilli jumped up. "Let me go with you."

Using his body, Max blocked her response from the loose-lipped ladies who had come out to the hallway to see why Max had dragged her away. "You can't. I'm hoping to straighten this out as quickly as possible. For now, act normal."

"Normal?"

"Just go back and keep everyone busy."

He strode away, his expression taut. Lilli couldn't help but think he vibrated like a volcano ready to blow. How could this have happened? Trying to cover her concern, Lilli went back to the event room. She encouraged the ladies to keep going and watched them chatting, laughing and working together. What would they think when they heard the news?

She spent the next hour watching the door, praying that Max would come back with good news. The committee had finished now. Jewel placed odds and ends in her box, preparing to leave. Lilli still hadn't heard from Max.

Okay, don't panic. She closed her eyes. She couldn't crumble, although she'd lost any calm she possessed the minute Max had revealed the distressing news. Unless Max returned and told her the whole thing was a mistake, that the entire collection was together, safely locked away once again, she wasn't sure what she'd do.

A mistake. It had to be. Why else would Max be taking so long? When he finally returned, his brows angled over stormy eyes as he shook his head. Her stomach sank.

She closed her eyes. Now what?

She opened her eyes to find Max standing in front of her, his voice low. "We'll figure this out together."

If it hadn't been for this ridiculous situation, she'd have been thrilled to hear him say that they'd do something important together. Anything together. But not now. Part of the collection. Gone. Under her leadership and on Max's watch.

"I've put this place on lockdown. No one leaves until we find the jewelry."

Lilli placed a hand over her sick stomach.

How on earth would she explain this to her mother? She'd trusted Lilli to run this event smoothly.

Max clapped his hands. "Can I get everyone's attention, please?"

The noise in the room lowered as all eyes moved to Max.

"I'm afraid we have a problem. Two pieces of the Wingate collection have gone missing and we'd like everyone to stay put until the police arrive. "

The startled reaction of the women began slowly and quickly picked up speed. Voices grew louder and heads turned toward her.

"Is it true?" Mary Gibbons asked as she hurried to Lilli. "Is there a problem with the Wingate collection?"

So much for holding off panic.

"I'm afraid so."

"Ladies." Max held up his hands to calm the group down, but it was too late.

"I told you this would happen. Didn't I say if I wasn't in charge something bad would happen?" Sissy Vandermere went into full agitator mode. "If I'd been coordinator, I never would have put Lilli in charge or hired Max. He was a delinquent in his youth, you know."

Rapid-fire questions zinged Lilli's way. "I don't have any answers, except to tell you that there is an ongoing search. Let's hope this is all a misunderstanding."

Lilli tried to assure the ladies that things would be fine while Max answered questions. Some of the women brought their purses to Max to show that they didn't have the jewelry. The noise level grew louder as the minutes went by, much like a thumping bass from a teenager's car, giving Lilli a steady headache that grew worse each second.

Trying to appease the women, Lilli and Mrs. R. made the rounds, assuring them that they weren't suspects. Once the police arrived, the situation would be settled and they could all go home.

The women rallied round, making the best of it, but still no sign of the jewelry. Klaus returned. He'd had his trusted employees search the club and still, nothing. Max ran his hand through his hair when the chief strode into the room.

"Got a call about a robbery."

"Part of the Wingate collection." Max explained what had transpired leading up to the current moment.

"I'll get my men on it." He eyed Max. "You, too. Use all your resources."

As the men went to work, Jewel came up beside Lilli. "You and Max make a great team."

Lilli sighed. "Yeah, we managed to lose part of a priceless collection."

"The point is, you're working together."

"I wish," Lilli muttered. Why couldn't she and Max have a normal relationship? From the way things had gone the night they first met and she ended up in a police car until tonight, she couldn't say things between them had gotten much better. She headed for her belongings, knowing she wouldn't get any sleep tonight. On the way, Marisa intercepted her with Chandler, in tow. "Here's the silent auction list."

Lilli took the paper. "Thanks."

"Sorry. I know I should have gotten it to you sooner."

Marisa being nice only made the night even stranger.

Frustrated, she grabbed her tote, stuffing the paper Marisa gave her inside when the canvas strap slipped from her trembling hand. The contents spilled onto the floor beside her. Marisa, still hovering, went down on her knees, along with Chandler, to gather the spilled belongings. When she did, Chandler bumped against Marisa and her purse slipped down her arm to fall beside Lilli's, her belongings now mixed in with Lilli's.

"Really, Chandler," Marisa groused. "Be careful. You nearly knocked me over."

"Sorry, babe." He leaned over the purse contents, taking up all the room as he began to scoop it all together.

"It's okay," Lilli told him. "We can get this."

"Sure. Sorry."

Chandler rested back on his heels to let the ladies straighten out the mess. As Lilli gathered up her paperwork, a shiny object rolled toward her. Marisa gasped and Lilli just stared.

"Oh, my gosh," Marisa exclaimed. "That looks just like the picture of the ring from the Wingate collection."

Lilli stared at the ring. It looked exactly like the ring from the collection. How on earth had it gotten here? And why did it look as if it had fallen from her bag? As the realization hit her, she suddenly felt sucked into a time-warp vacuum worthy of the *Twilight Zone*. Everyone would think she took it. Numb and speechless, she looked up to find accusing eyes directed at her.

As Marisa reached toward the ring, Max stopped her. "Don't touch it."

Marisa backed away. Max kept his eyes focused on the ring. His shoulders grew rigid. She couldn't tell what he might be thinking.

"I have no idea where that came from," Lilli told him, her stomach roiling. The truth, but even she knew it seemed lame in light of the

evidence sitting there on the floor. Max still
didn't respond one way or the other. Did he
believe she'd taken it? Just like that summer
night, she was in a fix with one common de-
nominator. Max. This was all a mix-up, but
would anyone believe her? Except for that one
night with Max, she'd never done anything re-
motely scandalous in her life.

This couldn't be happening, she assured herself. She hoped she was being held hostage in
a horrible dream and in a few minutes she'd
wake up, safe in her apartment, away from
this drama, ready to face a new day without
a priceless ring lying on the floor in front of
her. With all the women circling her. This was
worse than the night before her doomed wedding. Then, people gawked at her in pity. Now,
suspicion loomed in everyone's eyes.

"Lilli, where did the ring come from?"
Mrs. R. asked.

"I don't know."

"I'll tell you where," Marisa said loud
enough for everyone in the room to hear. "It
fell out of your bag."

A chorus of gasps sounded.

"No, it didn't," Lilli said.

Chandler helped Marisa up, patting her arm
and soothing her. "Yes," Marisa told the room.
"You dropped your tote and it fell out."

Oh, Marisa would just love Lilli to get in trouble. "Your purse spilled, too. It could have been in your possession."

Marisa's eyes went wide. "Why would I have it?"

"Why would I?" Lilli grabbed the tote handle and stood. "There's no reason either of us should."

"I don't have access to the collection. You do."

"I haven't seen it since Klaus put it in the safe. I don't have any keys, or passwords or way to get the collection."

Max addressed Marisa. "Did you see the ring in Lilli's bag?"

"Well, no, not exactly."

Lilli lifted her chin and said, "I don't know how it got here."

Max stood beside her, all business and intimidating. When he finally glanced her way, she saw a flash of uncertainty before he covered it.

"Don't worry," he said, but Lilli had no choice but to worry. She looked guilty.

LYING IN BED the next morning, her mind hashing out scenario after scenario, Lilli exhausted every possibility of the theft. She'd spent hours in the police station the night before. Obviously someone had framed her. She didn't have to be a P.I.—oh, wait, security consultant—to figure out that someone had set her up. But why?

Finally, the police had let her go since they couldn't definitively say the ring had been in her bag. She wondered how anyone could think she'd had the time or opportunity to steal the ring, anyway, considering she'd been in plain view of the historical society ladies all evening.

She wished Max would get in touch with her. As much as this all looked bad for her, the jewelry had gone missing on his watch. That had to be killing him. He took his responsibilities seriously. And now not only his business reputation, but his personal integrity, which he'd worked so hard to establish, would be called into question.

Glancing at her alarm clock, she jumped out of the temporary sanctuary of her bed. Max and Bart, along with Gabrielle, were bringing the gowns from the historical society office to the event room. Plus, the first run-through with the volunteer brides was scheduled for this morning and she had to be there. Grabbing a pair of black slacks from the closet, she added a white blouse and slipped into black pumps. After fixing her hair and makeup, she took the garment bag with her gown and shoes in it and left for the country club, trying to ignore the knots tying up her stomach as she made mental lists about what awaited her.

She parked and headed inside, preoccupied with the state of things. She hurried into the event room, flipping on the lights and thinking she'd gotten there first until she noticed a figure standing in front of the empty display case.

"Max?"

He slowly turned, his face expressionless.

She swallowed. "Any word on the bracelet?"

He walked toward her, his fingers jammed into his front pants pockets. His eyes never left hers. "Nothing. Klaus is a wreck. His assistant is nowhere to be found. And the only piece of evidence came from your bag."

She kept her voice calm. "You can't possibly think I took the jewelry."

"No, I don't think you took it. But someone put it in your bag, and I want to know why."

"You and me both."

"Trust me, Lilli. We'll figure this out."

"I hope so." But she wasn't counting on it. Max might offer her comfort now, but what about the fallout after the event? He'd be gone and she'd have to deal with the consequences alone.

She turned on her heel, walking away from the man she'd made the mistake of falling in love with.

ANYONE WHO KNEW Lilli knew she wasn't a thief. His gut clenched when he saw the hurt in her eyes and it had taken all his strength not to grab her and wrap her in his arms. Assure her that things would be all right. Yes, he knew she hadn't taken the ring, would never take a piece from the collection. But he had an investigation going on, with the outcome affecting both their reputations. The evidence against Lilli was circumstantial, but there just the same. In order to help, he had to find out the real culprit.

The local police were searching for Tom, Klaus's missing assistant—the only other person with access to the club safe. The emergency Klaus had been called to was an obvious ruse. Tom had been at the club last night, but after they'd learned about the theft he was nowhere to be found. Neither the police nor Max had been successful in locating him just yet, but at least they were doing something. Klaus had been devastated last night and not much help. Maybe in the light of day he'd remember something.

Max glanced back at the display case. Of all things, to find the stolen ring in Lilli's bag, in this room, in front of all those people, where her fiancé had humiliated her. She'd be humiliated again if they didn't find the bracelet. The least he could do before leaving was prove her innocence and clear her name.

LILLI SMOOTHED HER PANTS before entering the women's dressing room, which had a sitting/ changing area, large mirrors and lockers. Facing a firing squad would probably be less painful, but she had to follow this event through to the end. That meant dealing with Marisa and the other models, knowing they all thought her guilty. Holding her head high, she opened the door and stepped inside. As soon as the ladies saw her, a silence fell over the room.

"We didn't expect you here," Marisa informed her as she sauntered toward Lilli, looking absolutely perfect in her designer wedding gown. "So I took the liberty of getting us ready for the rehearsal."

"I appreciate that." Lilli eyed the women in the room, radiating as much confidence as she could muster. "However, I'm still coordinator of this event, so I'll take over now."

Marisa shrugged and walked away.

Her easy capitulation made Lilli wary. For the hundredth time, she wondered why the police hadn't hauled Marisa to the department. The ring could have fallen from her bag just as easily as Lilli's. But try as she might, Lilli couldn't come up with one reason for Marisa to take the ring. She had money, the fiancé of her dreams and an upcoming wedding. As much as Lilli would have loved Marisa to be the guilty party, it didn't add up.

The rehearsal went off without any problems. Despite her perceived guilt, the ladies took instruction, but she noticed a few women whispering behind raised hands. Flashbacks to her wedding rehearsal pinched her heart, but Lilli ignored them. For the most part the women were more subdued than usual, but worked together despite the circumstances. She rolled her shoulders in relief when rehearsal ended.

Back in the dressing room, Lilli joined the women for final instructions. Then they changed and headed off in different directions before having to return later for the fashion show. Only a few more hours, then Lilli never had to see this place again. All she had to do was stay out of jail until then.

A knock sounded on the door, followed by, "Miss Barclay?"

Lilli opened the door to find a delivery man holding a large garment bag. "May I help you?"

"This is from your mother." He handed her the bag and an envelope. She held it before her, a sneaking suspicion as to the content of the bag. Sighing, she found an empty wall hook, hung the bag and slowly unzipped it. Sure enough, inside she found her mother's wedding gown. "Oh, Mom."

Opening the envelope, she slipped out a note.

Lillian, it would do my heart good to see you wear my wedding dress. You may not be a model tonight, but you are my daughter, and I love you.

And Lilli loved her mom.

She zipped the bag closed as Marisa came breezing into the room, her cell phone pressed to her ear. Once she glimpsed Lilli, her smile faded and she ended the call. "I thought you'd left."

"Just going over some last-minute details."

"Oh, well, I'll just be a moment. I need something from my locker."

Her cell rang again. Marisa answered, her tone terse.

Not wanting to eavesdrop, Lilli crossed the room to leave. As she reached the door, she heard Marisa's high-pitched voice. "Chandler, wait. I told you we'd discuss this later."

Lilli looked over her shoulder to see Marisa staring at the phone in her hand. "He hung up."

Debating on what to do, Lilli decided to see if she could help. She walked back into the room and stopped before Marisa.

"What do you want?" Marisa snapped, her

eyes glimmering with tears. Hmm. Trouble in paradise?

Lilli shrugged. "Just wanted to make sure you're okay."

"Don't I look okay?" She slammed her locker closed. "Please excuse me. I'm joining Chandler for lunch. We have wedding details to finalize."

Lilli moved back as Marisa passed, noticing how shaky the normally put-together Marisa seemed. She must be having as bad a day as Lilli.

MAX INTERVIEWED KLAUS again, this time making progress.

"You're sure you saw Chandler Hayes in the hallway when you left your office?"

"Yes. At the time I didn't think anything of it because Chandler is a member here. But last night, as I tried to remember anything useful, I recall running into Chandler and Tom many times in the past few weeks. Always in deep conversation. Normally the two wouldn't have anything to talk about, but now I have to wonder, especially with Tom missing."

Max pulled out his cell to call Bart.

"Get to the office. Pull up anything you can on Chandler Hayes."

"Got it, boss."

Max turned his attention back to Klaus. "Any place you can think of that Tom might hide out?"

Klaus paced his office. "I know his mother lives down by the water and he has a sister out in the Cypress Cove subdivision."

"I already checked both places, as well as his condo."

"I didn't spend much time talking with him about personal matters, I'm afraid to say. He didn't open up about his life."

Max tamped down his disappointment. His gut screamed at him now, but if he couldn't find Tom, he couldn't prove anything.

"Is he athletic? Does he fish? Have a girl-friend?"

Klaus's forehead wrinkled. "He did mention a young lady once when he left work early for a date. What was her name?" The older man closed his eyes. "I remember. Jenny. He mentioned she works at the Pointe Café."

Max thumped Klaus on the back before heading to the door.

With this fresh lead, he ran out to the truck and headed to Main Street. Pulling into a parking lot, he jumped out and headed into the café, his mind clear even as adrenaline pumped through his veins. He asked for the manager, who pointed Jenny out to him. Then he had the manger call her out back so Max could speak to her.

When she joined him, his heart slammed against his ribs. Her eyes were red-rimmed and she wouldn't look directly at him.

"You know why I'm here."

That's all it took. She started crying and told Max where to find Tom.

When he got back in the truck, his cell rang. It was Bart.

"Any news?"

"Boss, you are one lucky man for hiring me."

"I haven't hired you yet."

"After the news I have, Blanche will be adding me to the payroll."

"Spill it."

"Mr. Hayes is one bad money manager. I found the man's financials, and trust me when I say he doesn't have two dimes to rub together. His clients aren't going to like the fact that he's run through their money, as well as his own."

"Good job. Get it all together for the chief. You did good, Bart."

"Like that was a surprise?"

Max chuckled. "Talk to you later." He signed off and called the police chief with the update. "I'm headed to find Tom now."

"Wait till my officers get there before you do anything."

"Chief, this guy framed Lilli."

"Max, until this is over, think with your head, not your heart."

Max knew that, but all he cared about was proving Lilli's innocence. "I'll scope the place out and give your guys a report."

"We're right behind you."

LILLI THOUGHT THE DAY would drag on, but with all the last-minute checks, the hours flew by. She stood in the event room, taking one final glance over the preparations. The room was more breathtaking than she'd originally envisioned.

She walked the perimeter with a critical eye. Tables set. Check. Loaner gowns safely delivered. Check. Silent auction table fully loaded. Check. Marisa had come through with the donations, even if Lilli had had her doubts. Flowers delivered. Check. Everything in place and ready to go. Tonight would be a success, and Lilli had everything to do with that. She should be proud, but instead, that old sense of loneliness crept over her.

An hour before the event, Lilli went back to the ladies' dressing room to change into her formal attire for the night. She passed her mother's wedding gown, still hanging in the same spot. As much as her mother's request touched her heart, she just couldn't wear it. She retrieved her black strapless dress with the bodice of black sequins and a full skirt in layers of chiffon. When she'd picked it out, she'd been imagining the expression on Max's face when he saw her. Now, she didn't want to think about anything.

She'd just finished the last touches on her makeup when Marisa and Sissy arrived, followed by a few of the other models. Lilli stayed out of their way. She had more important things to worry about than rumors and innuendo.

Packing up her makeup, she heard Marisa gasp. Lilli turned as Marisa fumbled with the locker door while trying to hold on to a cosmetics bag. Marisa glanced her way, her face pale, eyes wide as she hugged the bag to her waist.

"Are you okay?" Lilli asked as she crossed the room, afraid Marisa might be sick.

"I'm nervous about the fashion show."

Marisa never appeared nervous, especially if she was guaranteed a spotlight. She looked down at her bag and with shaking fingers tried to zip it closed.

"Do you need some help?"

"No. I'm fine. I'll be fine."

"Okay." Lilli went back to the mirror to collect her makeup. Concerned, she kept an eye on Marisa.

Marisa scanned the room before turning to open the locker. From her angle, Lilli noticed Marisa shoving a black bag into her tote. A funny feeling swirled in Lilli's stomach. Marisa glanced her way, eyes wide and afraid as she blocked the door from Lilli's view. Marisa never did anything on the sly, always wanting to be the center of attention. Lilli's suspicions went on full alert.

"You're sure you're okay?" Lilli asked again, walking to Marisa's locker.

"I told you. I'm fine."

"Then why are you trying to hide that black bag?"

"I don't know what you're talking about."

Lilli moved into Marisa's space and nudged her away from the locker.

"What are you doing?" Marisa screeched.

"Looking for something." Lilli pulled out Marisa's tote.

"Give me that." Marisa grabbed the handle but Lilli held fast.

"Are you hiding something? A black jeweler's bag, to be precise?"

"Don't be absurd." Marisa's face grew even paler.

"I saw it," Lilli told her. "Give it up."

"It's not mine," Marisa whispered.

By this time, their scene had caught the attention of the other women in the room.

"Marisa, what's going on?" Sissy asked.

"Nothing, Mother. Please, stay away."

"Why, that's silly. I know that—"

Marisa took one final pull and yanked the bag from Lilli, hugging it to her chest. Her wild expression searched the room for a way out, but too many women stood between her and the door.

"We'll figure this out," Lilli assured Marisa, her tone soft and assuring.

Tears glistened in Marisa's eyes and began to trickle down her cheeks. "I don't understand."

A loud knock sounded on the door. Seconds later, Lilli glimpsed Max out of the corner of her eye. She didn't stop to wonder why he'd shown up. Instead she concentrated on Marisa, who came close to losing it.

"Marisa, what's going on?" her mother asked again.

"We know you have the bracelet," Max told her as he made his way through the ladies. "Just hand it over and everything will be okay."

"How can it be okay? I don't know how it got here."

"I do." Max took a few steps toward Marisa. "It was Chandler. He hid it in your bag."

Marisa looked confused. "Chandler? What has he got to do with this?"

"You had lunch with him today?"

"Yes." Her gaze darted to her mother. "We talked about eloping. Leaving town after the benefit."

"What?" Sissy placed her hand over her heart. "What are you saying?"

"Did you leave him alone with your bag anytime during lunch?"

Marisa blinked. "Yes. When I went to the ladies' room."

Max took another step closer. "Marisa, he had possession of the bracelet. He needed your bag to cover his theft."

"But why? This doesn't make sense."

"He's broke," Max told her as gently as possible. "When Chandler discovered Tom was stealing from the club members, he convinced Tom to steal the jewelry in exchange for Chandler's keeping his secret. Chandler planted the ring in Lilli's bag to focus suspicion in the wrong direction. He needed you to get the bracelet out of town."

More tears ran down her face, trailing mascara. As if losing her will, she slid down the locker into a heap on the floor, and the bag slipped from her hands. "I…um…" She turned helpless eyes to her mother. "Get Chandler in here. He'll explain. This is all a mistake."

"Not gonna happen," Max said. "He's having a discussion with the chief right about now."

While Max took control of the situation, Lilli picked up the tote and removed the velvet bag. She turned it over, and sure enough, the bracelet tumbled into her palm, sparkling in the overhead light.

"Chandler?" Marisa asked again.

"Yes. I'm sorry." Max nodded to a uniformed officer hovering nearby. "The chief needs to ask you some questions, but you won't be arrested. Chandler admitted you knew nothing about his plan."

The officers who arrived after Max helped Marisa up and took her by the arms, leading her from the room while she tried to hike up her gown so she wouldn't trip. Her mother hovered nearby, a red splash of anger coloring her face.

"Help me, Mother."

Sissy followed behind hissing, "You've ruined our family name. How could you?"

"It was Chandler. Not me."

Apparently that didn't matter to Sissy.

Soon, their voices faded as they left the room. Lilli's heart went out to Marisa. They'd never be friends, but she couldn't help feel the other woman's pain. All this time Marisa had thought she had the perfect man, would have a perfect wedding. In the end, she'd have nothing but heartache. And by the looks of things, her mother didn't offer much sympathy. At least in Lilli's hour of humiliation, Celeste had been there, her daughter's best interests at heart.

For as long as Lilli could remember she'd been envious of Marisa and the way she floated through life. The current events made her realize that was only an illusion. No one's life was perfect.

"So much for family support," Lilli muttered as she watched the group leave the room. She turned to Max. "How did you know?"

"I found Tom. It didn't take much to get him to tell the truth and rat out his partner. We caught Chandler about to skip town. He also admitted trying to break into the historical society office. Convinced himself he might be able to steal one of the gowns and make some money. You?"

She handed the bag to Max. "Marisa acted strangely when she came in to get ready for the fashion show. Something was off, so I questioned her. Then you walked in."

An awkward silence fell between them as pandemonium reigned in the room and most likely out in the club. But it seemed as if she and Max stood there alone. She couldn't read him, didn't know what to think.

"I should probably do damage control," she said.

"Lilli, wait—"

Before he could say more, Celeste burst into the room. "Lilli. Have you heard?"

Lilli stared straight at Max as she spoke. "Yes. I have. The authorities have the thieves. Max gets to leave on his business trip with his reputation intact."

Oblivious to the tension surrounding Lilli and Max, Celeste hurried over, a huge smile on her face. "I couldn't have paid for better publicity."

She took Lilli's arm and dragged her away, leaving Max to tie up loose ends before he would catch a plane out of town and out of her life.

CHAPTER SIXTEEN

SERVERS SCURRIED ABOUT as they waited on the guests. Any minute now the committee members would take their positions and the fashion show would begin. The wedding gowns were ready, so the volunteer brides could change right before the show. They would wear their own dresses during the hors d'oeuvres hour, model the wedding gowns then change back before dinner. Clipboard in hand, Lilli met with each committee woman as she arrived, making sure they had everything they needed.

"So far, so good," Jewel told her as she sidled up beside Lilli. "The drama about the jewelry has added some extra excitement tonight. You couldn't have planned it better."

"Gee, you think?"

Jewel laughed. "Yeah, getting blamed for something you didn't do stinks, but it all turned out okay in the end."

Maybe, but Lilli didn't feel that way.

"I saw your mother. I'm glad she made it in time."

"Me, too. She's beside herself. Everything that's happened today is better than she could have planned."

"Where's Max? I haven't seen him since they took Marisa away."

Lilli shrugged. "He's needed at the police station."

"He's not going to be a groom?"

"Not now." She didn't want to talk about Max. Lilli wanted tonight to be over so she could go back to life without a troublesome man making her pulse pound and her heart less lonely.

"Who's going to take his place?"

"Jim."

"Our boss?"

"Yes. I've had him on standby."

Jewel blinked. "Wow. You do have everything under control." Jewel's face colored. "Oh, there's Bart. He's the one who found out about Chandler. Basically solved the case. Isn't he wonderful?"

Jewel hugged Lilli before heading off to join Bart. At least they had their happy ending. And again she asked herself how she could let Max get so close to her heart when in the end he'd leave her.

Feeling more than a little melancholy, Lilli circled the event room, waving at the mayor and his wife who were chatting with other guests. After hearing so many oohs and aahs over the display designer gowns, Lilli knew they were a hit. With Tie the Knot officially under way, people mingled and found their tables. The soft strains of the harp mixed with excited voices. Bursts of laughter spoke volumes. It looked like tonight would be a success.

Pasting on her happy smile, Lilli passed from table to table, greeting guests. Her smile drooped when she stopped at Laverne Sanders's table.

"My dear, how are you doing?" Laverne asked as she took Lilli's hand in hers.

"I'll be better when this night is over." She glanced at the ladies at the table, recognizing a few, including Dorinda Hobart.

"We're so glad you reserved a table. The girls and I are having a grand time. Why, Carolyn drove herself here tonight, thanks to Max."

"We all owe him," Carolyn, a blue-haired grandmother remarked.

Lilli frowned and glanced at Laverne.

"Max has helped each one of my friends," Laverne explained. "After Carolyn's husband passed, she was afraid to drive. Max gave her refresher lessons to stop her fear of getting behind the wheel. And there's Terri." Laverne nodded to a frail woman with lovely snow white hair pulled away from her face. "She broke her hip and couldn't leave the house for many weeks. Max went over to play cards."

"And don't forget my gazebo," added another woman with thick glasses.

"Margaret's gazebo needed new steps so Max built them for her."

"And you know he's the handyman at my coffee shop," Dorinda added.

Lilli looked at all the women spouting the virtues of Max when suddenly it dawned on her. These were the names on Max's calendar. He hadn't been out dating a bunch of women. He'd been helping his grandmother's friends.

"My grandson is a good man. But then, I think you already know that."

She did know. Always had. Max was a good man. That's why she loved him.

"Lilli!"

Her mother stood at the main door, waving at her.

"Excuse me, ladies."

She hurried across the room. Once she reached the door, Celeste grabbed hold of her arm.

"Time to change into my gown. With this bandage on my wrist, I need help."

"Okay. I only have a few minutes. The models are lining up to start the fashion show."

Celeste led Lilli into the changing room,

chatting nonstop. "Your father came through for me."

Lilli thought of Max leaving and her throat tightened. *Don't think about him now.*

"He joined me at the spa." She took Lilli's hand in hers. "We had many hours to talk and came to a major decision.

"When I came up with the wedding fashion show idea, I realized I had never gotten over your father. We made a mess of so many things, but I took a chance and called him. We agreed to meet at the spa to reconnect." Celeste squeezed Lilli's hand. "We haven't exactly been the best example of a loving relationship, but we're going to try again. I hope you aren't too disappointed in us."

"Disappointed in you? I thought you both were disappointed in me."

Celeste gasped. "How could you ever say that?"

Lilli opened her mouth to answer, but too many memories filled her mind. She didn't know where to start.

"We love you, Lilli." Celeste's eyes glimmered. "As I said, we haven't been the best role models, but we plan to change that. This time, we're going to make marriage work."

Here they were taking a second chance to build a relationship and Lilli hadn't gotten a first chance with Max. Still, she was happy for her parents. Lilli hugged her mother. "Good for you."

Celeste wiped her eyes and took her dress behind the privacy screen. "I'm glad you understand. I hated to put all the responsibility of the benefit on you, but I was desperate. And I knew you could do this."

"Thanks for believing in me, Mom."

Just then, Sissy Vandermere rushed inside, cheeks flushed. "I cannot believe my daughter did this to me."

Celeste came out from the screen in her silver full-length Valentino, presenting her back to Lilli. "Please finish zipping me." To Sissy, she said, "You can't blame Marisa. She looked forward to her wedding."

"Of course she did. She couldn't afford to lose another fiancé."

"But she didn't know what Chandler had planned."

"That makes it worse. How will she ever find another man to marry her now?"

Lilli figured Marisa had other things on her mind right now. Lilli's heart went out to her. Now they both shared the experience of being publicly humiliated by a fiancé.

"She'll survive," Sissy said. "But she's too

embarrassed to show her face here tonight.
And Chandler's in jail. What a disaster."

Celeste twirled to face Lilli, her eyes wide
with panic. "We don't have a finale couple."

The thought had occurred to her before her
mother stated the obvious.

"Mom, there's no time to fix this."

"Of course we can." Celeste grinned, the
look she got when she came up with an idea
Lilli wouldn't like. "I sent my wedding dress
here."

Lilli glanced at the garment bag still hanging across the room. "How convenient."

"And Max Sanders is a volunteer groom.
You two can pair up."

"No offense, Mom, but I'm not pairing up
with Max for anything."

"Why not?"

"Many reasons. But number one? He's not
here."

"Minor detail." Celeste waved her hand. "I'll
call him and tell him to get over here."

"Mom, he's got too much on his plate right
now. We're fine without him." She'd be fine
without him.

"Do we have stand-ins?"

"Of course we do. I've taken care of everything." Except when it came to Max.

Turning away from her mother, Lilli walked

to the dressing room door to head back to the event room. She had enough models in the show and didn't need a finale couple. It had been Marisa's idea to begin with and since she wasn't here, no one would know the difference.

She'd just made it to the door when Max stepped into her path, dressed in a tuxedo. She blinked twice, sure her eyes were playing tricks on her.

"Max? What are you doing here?"

"I gave you my word I'd be here tonight. That's what Sanders men do, right? If I can't keep my word with you, I have no business working for anyone else."

"But what about after tonight?"

He touched her bare shoulder, his fingers lightly brushing her skin. She barely controlled a shudder of pleasure.

"When I came back to town, the only thing I wanted was to start my business and prove to the town I had changed. Never in a million years did I think I'd run into the girl I met on the beach all those years ago. I fell a little bit in love with you that night, but when I saw you again, got to know the beautiful woman you've grown up to be, I lost my heart again. I'm sorry it took so long for me to tell you. I want you to be first in my life, Lilli, not my business or my reputation. Neither one means anything without you by my side."

"What about the new account? The traveling?"

"We can work our lives around this job. It won't be forever. Maybe you can travel with me sometimes. And once I get a security protocol established at Rawlings, I can hire more people so I'll be home. Sanders Security isn't going away. So what do you say. Can we work this out? Together?"

The uncertainty in her heart melted at his declaration. She'd learned today that no relationship was perfect. But with Max, she wanted years to practice. Joy filled her as she looked into his eyes and saw the truth of his love reflected there. She smiled, reaching up to ease the frown from his brow. She wanted things to work out with this wonderful man. She wanted a future with Max. "I love you."

"I love you, too," he said, voice rough with emotion. "More than I ever thought possible." His fingertips lightly trailed down her arm, leaving chills in its wake as he took her hand. "And I'll spend the rest of our lives proving it."

"I'll take you up on that." Overwhelmed with love, she leaned in close to him. Max, being an intuitive security consultant, realized her intent. He lowered his head, and their lips touched softly, full of promise.

As they reluctantly broke the kiss, Lilli noticed frantic movement out of the corner of her eye. Max, seeing her interest elsewhere, turned. Celeste cleared her throat and pointed to her watch, then Max.

"I see your mother is back in control." He grinned at Lilli. "What's she all worked up about?"

"We're missing a finale couple."

He held out his arm. "What do you say we walk down the runway together?"

"If you're game, so am I. Just let me slip on a wedding gown."

With Celeste's help, Lilli changed into her mother's dress. Once Celeste zipped Lilli in, they both stood before the mirror.

"Thank you for wearing my gown," Celeste whispered.

"You're welcome."

"Go on. You have a groom waiting for you."

Lilli joined Max and eased her hand into the crook of his elbow. Celeste beamed at them before entering the event room where the fashion show had already started.

He nodded toward the stage. Straightened his jacket. "We're the last couple. I want to make you proud."

She slipped her hand from his arm and stepped back, observing him.

A worried frown creased his brow. "Something wrong?"

After a few seconds she reached up to muss his hair and loosen his bow tie. "Much better." She leaned up to give him a quick kiss then took his hand in hers as the doors opened. "Now we're ready to walk down the aisle."

* * * * *